Julie Lancaster lives in Staffordshire and is a part-time library assistant. When not writing she enjoys reading and travel and 70's nostalgia. *Remember Where You've Buried the Bodies* is her second novel.

REMEMBER WHERE YOU'VE BURIED THE BODIES

JULIE LANCASTER

One More Chapter
a division of HarperCollins*Publishers* Ltd
1 London Bridge Street
London SE1 9GF
www.harpercollins.co.uk
HarperCollins*Publishers*
Macken House, 39/40 Mayor Street Upper,
Dublin 1, D01 C9W8
This paperback edition 2025

1

First published in Great Britain in ebook format
by HarperCollins*Publishers* 2025
Copyright © Julie Lancaster 2025
Julie Lancaster asserts the moral right to be identified
as the author of this work

A catalogue record of this book is available from the British Library
ISBN: 978-0-00-860054-9

This novel is entirely a work of fiction. The names, characters and incidents portrayed in it are the work of the author's imagination. Any resemblance to actual persons, living or dead, events or localities is entirely coincidental.

Printed and bound in the UK using 100% Renewable Electricity
by CPI Group (UK) Ltd

All rights reserved. No part of this publication may be reproduced, stored in a retrieval system, or transmitted, in any form or by any means, electronic, mechanical, photocopying, recording or otherwise, without the prior permission of the publishers.

Without limiting the exclusive rights of any author, contributor or the publisher of this publication, any unauthorised use of this publication to train generative artificial intelligence (AI) technologies is expressly prohibited. HarperCollins also exercise their rights under Article 4(3) of the Digital Single Market Directive 2019/790 and expressly reserve this publication from the text and data mining exception.

For Mike, always

Prologue

This isn't how she wants to die.

It's mourning black, church quiet. There's no feather of light, no flicker of life.

Strange shapes spread like ink in the darkness. She imagines the horror of what they might be, what they might mean. Stretching out an arm, she searches for something solid, an ending, and focuses on her breathing, on the way that it sounds inside her chest, wondering if she's already dead, if this is what death looks like, feels like.

Never actually knowing.

She stretches forward until her fingers can go no further, extends her fingertips as she gathers her thoughts, imagining the space as a colour, hoping that it isn't a grave. Her legs ache, having been folded awkwardly beneath her, but it's too dark to trace their outline. Her cheek feels sore. A tooth throbs. Her right hand touches something sticky. The stickiness expands and solidifies. Its presence calms her, the fact that there's something here that can be shaped into something else, that can be two things, that can still exist regardless of circumstance.

She returns to the beginning. How did she get here? By car? On foot? She can't remember. She reaches inside her pocket for her mobile phone, her lifeline, but it isn't there. She searches for a door, but there's no latch, no door handle, no lock for a key. It's a room without a door, a magic trick, an illusion. Someone has dragged her to the ends of the earth and left her to perish in the darkest of spaces. Breathe. She must remember to breathe, to let go of the fear so that there's more room to breathe.

As her lips form the hollow shape of a scream, she wonders if there's someone outside the room, listening, someone who wouldn't appreciate her screams, and she pauses. Perhaps the room is soundproofed and screaming would be nothing more than an indulgence, a release. Until she knows for certain her screams remain silent, trapped inside the brushstrokes of a painting. A tear spills from her left eye. She wipes it away. Unless her tears can form a length of rope that she can abseil away on or coins that she can trade her life for, then they're of no practical use.

Some time later, an arc of light skims her face and illuminates the space for a brief second and that's when she sees the blood. She's never seen so much blood in one place. Is it all hers? She can't see who else might be bleeding. She feels as if she's somewhere between life and death, neither one thing nor the other.

She wonders if they're coming back – whoever *they* are. *Don't try anything*, she vaguely remembers hearing as they were leaving. Their little joke, she suspects. The walls are reinforced with steel panels studded with nails. She's counted each nail. One wall at a time. There are one hundred and forty-two. The floor is concrete, no crevice, no indent, nowhere for a fingertip to squeeze into, nothing for a fingernail to peel back. She would need to be able to walk through walls to escape this room.

It seems ridiculous that you can be locked inside a room without anyone knowing that you're there. There may even be a bedroom to the left or right of her, where her jailer or a neighbour sleep, and the neighbour will have no idea that she's sitting on a filthy mattress a few feet away unless they can hear her fists pounding the walls or her screams when the screams inside her head are no longer silent. She assumes that she's upstairs, but maybe she's mistaking the room for a bedroom or an attic when it's an outbuilding or a barn. Maybe she's underground. That feels worse somehow, being entombed below ground, buried alive, buildings and people piled on top of her.

Suddenly, she can't breathe. There isn't enough air in the room. She feels like a ball of wool unravelling at breakneck speed until it gets smaller and smaller and then becomes nothing at all. She can't feel her legs. She can't feel her arms. She can see herself getting smaller and smaller, fainter and fainter, until she's barely a comma and almost a full-stop and she wants to be more than a punctuation mark, a footnote.

She doesn't want to be forgotten.

She doesn't want to be a full-stop.

This isn't how she wants to die.

Chapter One

THE BATTLESTAR GALACTICA

The residents of Sunset House were canopied beneath rainbow-coloured streamers and bouquets of glossy pink balloons that had escaped frail grips and were now trapped beneath the ceiling cornices. It was Doris Gordon's ninetieth birthday and Marks and Spencer's iced fingers and glasses of warm sherry were being passed around the lounge. Will walked over to the CD player and removed the CD from its case. Doris had requested 'anything by Miles Davis' when Will had asked her what she'd like to listen to and in his self-appointed role as custodian of birthday wishes he'd duly obliged.

Jolene had been pushing Doris's swollen feet into a pair of men's slippers at the time and had brusquely informed him that they weren't there to take requests and she'd listen to Vera Lynn like everybody else. He'd of course disregarded Jolene's insistence that they not pamper the residents ('what's the point, they can't see or hear anything') and had purchased a Miles Davis CD from Cancer Research the following weekend.

He wasn't like the other care home assistants, who ignored and presumed, and had forgotten the residents by the time they'd changed out of their uniforms and switched on Netflix – sometimes even before that. When they were sitting in front of them desperate to go to the toilet. Like Elvis and the Pet Shop Boys, they were always on his mind. Often, he and Elvis (the Pet Shop Boys to a lesser extent) were the only ones who *were* thinking about them, which sometimes felt like too much responsibility. Shouldn't they have been in a relative's thoughts, a spouse's? Shouldn't there be more people missing them?

He glanced at the deep scratch running across the second-hand CD, the length of a scar, and hoped that Miles Davis wasn't planning on jumping and skipping his way through the celebrations (the deepest scratches weren't always the most serious), although the frenetic and chaotic nature of jazz might hopefully mask the poor quality if he did. Vera Lynn might not have been so forgiving.

Doris was sitting in her usual chair by the far wall beneath the watercolour poppies, their red stems dripping down the canvas and onto her scalp like blood. She was wearing a pink synthetic wig and a purple crepe crown from a Christmas cracker. Not wholly appropriate for someone who'd lost two husbands in two wars and who'd once been a grammar school deputy headmistress.

Jolene had apparently found a box of Christmas crackers and a selection of fancy dress items in the storeroom and had placed the wig and the crown on Doris's head as he was inserting the CD into the CD player and crossing his fingers. To complete the humiliation further a pink feather boa had been draped around Doris's shoulders and glittery silver eyeshadow swept across her eyelids while he was searching for paper napkins. She looked like an extra from the Battlestar Galactica.

Treating the residents like five-year-olds wasn't something that Will actively endorsed, although a certain amount of papier-mâché and collage engagement was expected. You can still be the life and soul of the party at ninety, Jolene would remind him. There are no age limits on having fun. They're not here solely for your amusement, Will would respond, disapprovingly, Jolene often the one deciding what was fun. They're not dolls. That's exactly what they are, life-sized dolls, she'd exclaim earnestly, as if he'd hit the nail on the (doll's) head. Jolene always made him feel like a killjoy, made his good intentions appear trite and banal and humourless.

Just as he was about to go over and ask Doris if she'd like him to remove the childish accessories and wipe off her eyeshadow with a tissue, her two daughters arrived with armfuls of gifts. The older daughter, Penny, a chiropodist, visited regularly, while the younger daughter he knew only by name, Veronica, or Ronnie, as Doris affectionately called her. Doris's smile was always a little wider and a shade brighter when she reminisced about Ronnie. But that was usually the case, in Will's experience. There was normally one sibling who lived closer and who by default was expected to visit more often, the primary contact in the event of an emergency, governed by a sense of obligation rather than an inherent desire to check on a parent's welfare. And ironically it was always the one who rarely visited and provided minimal levels of care and attention who was most missed. Living closer didn't necessarily denote being closer.

'Ronnie,' cried Doris, when she saw her.

Penny's lips tightened into a hyphen of thin cotton thread.

There were varying degrees of degeneration and disability in the care home, the residents reaching recognised milestones such as rheumatoid arthritis and vascular dementia at different stages. Doris was highly unusual in that she had perfect vision, excellent hearing and knew which daughter she liked best, her short-term memory mostly intact, unlike many of the other residents, who were repeatedly being asked to count backwards from a hundred in sevens, which frankly most twenty-year-olds would have found challenging.

She was also exceptionally charitable. All the gifts that she was now opening would be in the other residents' rooms by teatime. 'How many watches do I need?' she'd say. 'They'll all tell me the same time.' The advantage of being middle class, Will supposed. You could afford to be generous.

He was reminded of Rosemary Tate, who'd died earlier that week, so few possessions that she'd have been equally at home in one of the Premier Inn hotel rooms on the ring road. She'd been similarly selfless, more so really, because she owned so little. She'd have given you her last of everything, her last custard cream, her last pound coin, the sterling silver cross around her neck that had belonged to her mother. It meant more somehow when it meant everything.

Cora Wainwright, one of the more mobile residents, was standing in the middle of the lounge, swaying from side to side to 'So What', the Miles Davis track that was currently skipping every third or fourth note. She'd been a professional ballroom dancer when she was younger and had won several national dance competitions with her husband, Charles, who'd died of pneumonia five years ago. He and Cora would apparently host dance classes at Sunset House (it was called The Gables then) and even though Charles had by then forgotten who Cora was, he could still remember every dance step that he'd ever learned, but that was before Will's time, before most of the current staff's time.

There was an unusually high staff turnover at Sunset House. No one stayed longer than eighteen months. Will was midway through his eleventh month and he was one of the longer-serving employees. Climbing aboard the Death Express took its toll on everybody eventually, even the ones who could disembark. Including Rosemary, three residents had died already this year and it was only March. Relationships and employment records were fleeting at Sunset House, the sun setting at an alarmingly swift pace.

While Cora was spinning around the lounge in her slippers, her son studied his phone (Will wondered what on earth people had entertained themselves with before mobile phones). His overalls were splattered with red paint. Or maybe it was raspberry jam. There was a half-eaten doughnut on a paper plate on the armrest of his chair. He was always in his work overalls as if he'd just come from work or was just going to work, and he never stayed long, but at least he visited. Some residents never had any visitors, having either outlived their relatives or become estranged from them or, worse, unimportant to them. Placing someone in a care home was akin to locking a door and losing the key.

Gilbert Williams, another resident, was sitting by the muted television, scowling. It didn't necessarily mean that he was annoyed or angry. Scowling was simply his default setting. Will sat down on the empty chair beside him. John Thorley, who normally sat there, had earlier been escorted back to his room. He disliked excessive noise and would become visibly distressed during birthday celebrations or cabaret evenings.

'How are you, Gilbert?' Will asked, not anticipating a response.

Gilbert was mostly uncommunicative, sullen and watchful (or mistrustful) for prolonged periods, with the occasional grunt or one-word response or incomprehensible mumbling, and it was almost impossible to engage him in conversation, but he spoke to John sometimes. Or John spoke to him. Will wasn't sure which. He was on the lower spectrum of the clinical dementia tests, but his lucid moments were getting fewer and there were occasions when he didn't appear to recognise you at all, a haunted faraway look in his eyes that made you wonder where he'd gone. Or whether he'd ever been there to begin with. Will imagined a whole other life being lived in parallel to this mostly mute one.

His son and daughter hadn't visited in a while, but when they did visit they sat in silence. Consequently, Will's interactions with Gilbert were largely functional, the questionnaire that his son, Martin, had completed woefully inadequate, either because he didn't want the care home to know personal information about his father or because *he* didn't know personal information about his father and there was no one else to ask. But however tedious or intrusive those questions might seem, they were important cornerstones of data. If you were planning to leave a relative in the care of strangers then knowing a person's favourite meal or their favourite television programme guaranteed a smoother transition, ensured that the seam between one life and the next couldn't be seen, that the stitches couldn't be unpicked.

It all helped to build a picture that they could continue to look at.

Gilbert suddenly leaned towards him.

'She thinks she's special,' he confided.

Unusually, he stated this slowly and clearly, punctuating it with a customary derisive snarl.

Will wondered if he'd imagined the sound of Gilbert's voice, summoned the words from his imagination.

'Who does?' Will asked when he realised that it actually was Gilbert speaking, assuming that he meant Doris.

Doris's crepe crown was now angled like a beret and salmon-pink lipstick had been smeared across her chapped lips. Were there no limits to the 'fun' that Jolene could inflict?

'Her, over there,' Gilbert gestured irritably, vigorously nodding, 'the one smiling.'

Did he mean Veronica?

'She wasn't smiling then, though, was she?'

Will had no idea who or what he was referring to, but he played along.

'Wasn't smiling when?'

'When I killed her.'

Chapter Two

WHITE SPACE, DARK MATTER

Jolene was in the care home staff toilets purposely ignoring her mother's texts. She normally left her mobile phone in her locker in the staffroom or in her coat pocket so that she wouldn't hear the fearful sound of yet another missed call or a message being received. Just hearing a ping or a ringtone now sent a shiver down her spine, spoiling her enjoyment of several songs that she'd previously considered favourites. She stood staring at the phone (currently masquerading as a bar of soap on the porcelain sink) as if it was a soap-shaped grenade that might explode at any second; afraid even to touch it in case it suddenly started ringing, even though it was currently on silent mode.

She sighed. She'd have to respond to her mother's calls and texts eventually or she'd start making personal visits. She remembered her mother nervously pacing the pavement outside Next last summer where Jolene had been working as a temporary retail assistant, a hand shielding her eyes as she'd squinted through the glass doors. Carol, the manager, had squinted back at her, had threatened to call the police if she didn't leave, convinced that her mother had a knife and was one of those 'unstable types' who were being released back into the community so that they could kill again.

'There's nothing in the till,' Carol had yelled at Jolene's mother through the glass, as if she was a wild animal scavenging for food, 'I've just cashed up.'

Jolene had stood anxiously watching events unfold, no conciliatory words forthcoming, no placatory footsteps intervening, because she was too ashamed and embarrassed, and the situation had escalated so quickly that she didn't know how to stop it, didn't know how not to make it worse. Fortunately, her mother left before the police arrived.

Jolene recalled the cruel things that she'd spat at her mother later that night, how distraught she'd been that she'd humiliated her in front of her work colleagues (it didn't seem to matter that her work colleagues didn't actually know that the woman peering through the glass door had been her mother) and how she'd never *ever* forgive her, emphasis on the *ever*. She didn't think that she *ever* had.

After splashing her cheeks with tap water, Jolene dried her hands on a paper towel and then readjusted her ponytail. She examined her reflection in the mirror and, noting an unacceptable trace of vulnerability, she reapplied her sneering and uncaring Sunset House Face. It took three attempts. She'd often witness Will's appalled expression whenever she ridiculed or belittled a resident and she'd hear herself involuntarily gasp. She'd have to take several deep breaths to stop the mask from slipping. She didn't want to be that lazy, derogatory, insulting colleague that nobody liked, she didn't want to be like Carol, who saw the worst in everyone, but if she wasn't that person, then who would she be? And didn't most people bring a different person to work with them? Will probably wasn't as saintly or as devoted as he appeared. He no doubt lashed out like everybody else when he was hungover or upset.

Even serial killers took their children to the park and smiled in family portraits.

Unfortunately for Jolene, the person whom she introduced into the workplace was formally disciplined more than most. Janette, the care home manager, was always calling her into the office for 'a quiet word', which often turned into a much louder word and always exceeded just the one word once she'd gathered momentum, the list of grievances that she'd written down brandished like a series of slaps. Because there was always a list. An extensive list. Jolene would patiently listen to the complaints, allegedly received from fellow employees and residents' families, along with some particularly imaginative ones that Janette had clearly fabricated herself because Jolene hadn't even been on duty that day, while counting the pens on Janette's desk. If they weren't so short-staffed they'd have doubtless dismissed her months ago.

Jolene neither admitted nor denied responsibility. Let them think her a monster. It was preferable to the alternative, thinking her pitiful and weak, although her real self was now buried so deeply that few people even knew that it existed. Sometimes, even she had to fight her way through carefully constructed defences to locate it, the part of herself that was considerate and compassionate, that actually liked the elderly and infirm because they had nothing left to prove. For better or worse they were always themselves (until they weren't).

Last winter she'd had the sanctuary of her grandmother's bungalow to escape to whenever she couldn't bear to listen to her mother crying; coffee, chocolate digestives and *Countdown*. Now all she had was a toilet cubicle in a care home that smelled of antiseptic and Trebor mints.

The little things. You think that they don't matter, but they're all that matters.

Could nobody tell that it was a matter of survival? Had they never had to smile when they felt like crying?

Did it look like she'd been crying? Her eyes were definitely puffier than they'd been when she first came in, although would anyone even notice? Probably not. Not here. There could be blood pouring from a head wound and no one would ask if you needed a doctor or offer to drive you to the hospital. They'd just tell you not to get blood on the bed linen. She wondered why it was so imperative that she wear a suit of armour when no one but Janette (and a handful of disgruntled employees and family members – *allegedly*) particularly cared about her temperament or disposition. Perhaps it was now as natural to her as breathing, although breathing wasn't always as straightforward as it should have been, mostly too shallow or too fast.

Still, if anyone did ask, she'd say that it was hay fever. Was it too early for hay fever? Allergies, then, she told her reflection. Best to keep up the façade.

Walking back along the corridor towards the lounge Jolene remembered that she'd been on her way to collect Doris's birthday cake and retraced her steps back to the storeroom for the second time that day. The first journey had been to retrieve the party poppers and the paper hats, much to Will's disdain. Will's idea of a party was a few canapés and an orderly queue for the toilets. And he didn't know the residents as well as he thought he did. Doris was partial to a sprinkling of glitter and a feather boa.

The cake was Tesco's Finest (expiry date imminent and heavily discounted) and Janette had decorated it with a plastic nine and a plastic zero and some rose-pink marzipan petals that Jolene wasn't sure were edible. No candles of course because that would have been a fire hazard. Will had apparently been instructed to keep a close eye on Jolene in case she smuggled in candles or a fire eater or organised a lavish pyrotechnics display. She clearly couldn't be trusted to not burn down the care home in Janette's absence.

As soon as Will spotted the birthday cake his arms became batons and he proceeded to orchestrate a tuneless rendition of 'Happy Birthday'. Everyone joined in, everyone except Jolene of course. If it wasn't Jay-Z or David Guetta then she wasn't interested. And she didn't 'sing along' to anything. Ever. But at least it drowned out the sound of that dreadful CD that Will had brought in. She didn't think that she'd ever heard anything so mournful and depressing. Vera Lynn was like Steps compared to this. And even she, who knew absolutely nothing about jazz, could tell that it was scratched and wasn't supposed to sound as disjointed as it did.

While Will was searching for a knife to slice the cake, Jolene replaced the Miles Davis CD with a Katy Perry CD that wasn't scratched and was far more appropriate for a birthday celebration, and nobody except Will even noticed.

As usual, Cora Wainwright was getting under everyone's feet, daintily twirling around the room like a music box ballerina, her twig-like arms and arthritic knuckles jabbing visitors' vertebrae and grazing their scalps as she pirouetted by. Jolene managed to intercept her just as Sheila's walking frame went spinning across the carpet, and escorted her back to her chair before someone (namely Cora, if Gilbert Williams' expression was any indication) got seriously hurt, but not before Cora had gathered her in a chokehold, pulling her along like a riptide. She was surprisingly strong.

Cora's son hadn't even noticed that Jolene was being wrestled into promenade position by his mother. He was staring at his phone. Doris began to slow-clap, which sounded vaguely menacing. Jolene could feel her cheeks burning. She loathed being the centre of attention. She was the faded square of wallpaper behind an oil painting, the ambient music in a city centre restaurant, unless her mother was nearby of course, when her wallflower and supporting-cast-member status was illuminated in flamingo-pink neon. She was the second most important thing in her mother's life because the most important thing, her sister Dolly, had vacated that position. And Jolene didn't want that accolade.

Sometimes, she wished that she was the one who'd disappeared. But then, perhaps part of her had.

When she'd finally managed to extricate herself from Cora's iron grip and found her a footstool she noticed Gilbert Williams exiting the toilet with his trousers undone. It didn't look like he was wearing any underwear. She hurried over to him and quickly zipped him back up. That was one birthday present that Doris could do without. Her, too, quite frankly.

She wondered if he did it on purpose, neglected to zip up zips and button up buttons, so that someone else would do them for him. There was something about Gilbert that unnerved her. He was like a ubiquitous shadow, present and yet not present, and he uttered odd things occasionally, which she mostly ignored. But sometimes she wondered.

Any of these people could have done something terrible and conveniently forgotten all about it. They only knew what they or their family deemed appropriate for them to know – a diluted, heavily filtered version of themselves. A little like her own public persona, she supposed – no one needs to know everything. But when the last lucid memory finally slips away, what remains? Long-buried memories that unexpectedly rise to the surface? Memories that have been fastidiously filed away over the years, layers of other, more commonplace memories filed on top of them? Does your memory betray you in those final months, unintentionally exposing your darkest secrets, your true self? Maybe there's nothing but white space, dark matter. Maybe none of your memories are genuine, but borrowed or stolen from somebody else.

Jolene wasn't sure why she cared and maybe she didn't. Did it matter what these people had done or who they'd been or whether they were now empty vessels, stripped of everything that had made them them? Perhaps some things were better left unsaid, unknown. What good could come from unearthing the past, from excavating forgotten traumas and confessing?

Fortunately, she was working late tonight so her mother would hopefully be asleep when she arrived home. That was something, at least.

Chapter Three

THE MYSTERIOUS CASE OF THE CARE HOME CONFESSION

Will wasn't sure that he'd heard Gilbert correctly and was about to press him further when he abruptly stood up and left the room. Will watched him shuffle unsteadily through the double doors, concluding that he must have been repeating something that he'd heard. Will glanced at the television, the volume muted because several of the residents were now asleep, having found the birthday celebrations exhausting. Subtitles flashed across the screen for those who were still awake. Father Brown and Lady Felicia were enjoying one of Mrs McCarthy's award-winning scones.

Will's attention remained on the scones. They did look delicious. His stomach rumbled appreciatively.

Maybe Gilbert had been reciting a line from a film or an ITV crime drama, although Will had no idea which one. They didn't let the residents watch anything with a high body count unless it was *Poirot* or *Inspector Morse*, where murders were deemed more palatable when they were committed in stylish and elegant surroundings. Will had witnessed litres of blood pool beneath crystal chandeliers, drip from dagger wounds on night trains during blizzards. He'd seen fuchsia skies above Oxford spires turn a deadly driftwood grey, Edwardian London prostitutes with crimson smiles strangled with silk stockings. People were still being shot and poisoned and stabbed to death, but because they were wearing top hats and tiaras, morning coats and cravats, it was somehow more acceptable.

Jolene never adhered to such etiquette of course. She'd slipped *Wolf Creek* into the DVD player last week, insisting that she was the only one watching it, but John Thorley had seemed fascinated by the burnt orange Australian landscape and the shimmering blood.

Will patiently waited for Gilbert to reappear. It was probably nothing. But what if it wasn't? What if it was important? I wish he'd stop speaking gibberish, Jolene would complain, as if gibberish was a recognised language. Apparently, life was too short to be translating other people's nonsensical sentences into English, 'They'll get what they're given' Jolene's standard response. But Jolene wasn't the most tolerant of people. She still hadn't forgiven her mother for naming her Jolene. And no, they're not fucking emerald green, she'd snapped at Will when they were first introduced. So she certainly wasn't going to spend valuable minutes of her shift listening to a roomful of octogenarians asking her the exact same question in a variety of dialects twenty times a day.

'You need to learn to unwind,' she'd told him, when he'd pointed out that *Wolf Creek* wasn't appropriate resident viewing. 'They're over eighteen and it's nothing that they haven't seen before.' He sincerely hoped that that wasn't the case. 'Now, shush,' she'd said. 'It's getting to the gory part.'

Will wondered why she worked there at all. The role clearly infuriated her. When he'd once diplomatically broached the subject, she'd said that he probably never imagined himself getting up close and personal with the genitalia of elderly strangers after finishing his 'A' levels either and yet here they both were. Life didn't always turn out the way you'd hoped, engaged to Liam Hemsworth and living in a Malibu beach house. She was right, of course, he couldn't remember ever mentioning a desire to care for the elderly in any of his career one-to-one discussions but, unlike Jolene, he seemed to have unintentionally stumbled into a profession that he found hugely gratifying. He was genuinely interested in the residents. Some of them had led incredibly interesting and fascinating lives.

Theo Winchester had been in the Royal Navy and Marilyn Andrews had been a stage actress who'd worked with Sir Ralph Richardson ('he never spoke a word off stage') and Sir Laurence Olivier ('a true gentleman. We once had to share a dressing room and he refused to rehearse until a privacy screen had been installed in the room'). There was a glamorous black and white signed headshot of Marilyn in her room, her luminous eyes gazing up at the light cord by her bed. She looked like Vivienne Leigh in *Gone with the Wind*.

Gilbert, however, remained a mystery, a dark hooded figure beneath a solitary streetlight. Will had absolutely no idea what kind of life he'd lived, what kind of person he'd been. Maybe that's why he'd been so surprised by what he'd said. It had seemed out of character, an anomaly, although an ordinary, non-eventful life was of course no less important than a flamboyant one. Everyone had the same health concerns in the end. Nonetheless, it was often the quieter residents who intrigued him most, the ones who didn't advertise their achievements, the ones who kept their accomplishments in sock drawers behind closed doors.

Noticing a glasses case beneath a chair, Will turned his attention to locating the owner of the case. He'd obviously been watching too many *Poirot*s and was now writing his own scripts.

A few minutes later, a humiliated Jolene was guiding a waltzing Cora back towards her son, leaving a trail of chaos in her wake. Sheila's walking frame was rolling unaccompanied into the corridor while Sheila limped after it, Penny was clutching her side, having just been elbowed in the ribs by Cora, John Thorley had returned and was whimpering softly by the window, his palms pressed tightly against his ears, and a half-eaten chocolate éclair had fallen from Enid's plate and was being trampled into the carpet. Collecting a dustpan and brush from the cleaning cupboard, Will wondered if it had been Cora's husband, Charles, sweeping a sequinned and chiffoned Cora across the Blackpool Tower ballroom. If so, he hoped that she'd always have those memories, the happy memories – the 'standing on a podium holding a trophy in the air' memories.

The not-so-happy memories they could all live without, although Jolene claimed that the residents spent far too much time living in the past when they should have been focusing on the present. ('What use are memory boxes and sensory aids when you've forgotten how to use a fork? And that matted piece of fur has had everybody's grubby fingers all over it. It's unhygienic.') Will considered it an inevitable consequence that the more you aged the more nostalgic you became, the past a vast and familiar life raft that you were desperate to cling onto. Sometimes, of course, the past didn't stay in the past. Sometimes it tried to outrun you, hurtling towards you, daring you to remember, questioning what you thought you knew.

When he next saw Gilbert he was making his way towards the kitchenette area at the back of the lounge, shaking his head. Who had he mistaken Veronica for and what did he mean, *When I killed her*? Will sighed. He couldn't seem to let the comment go. It was like an annoying song lyric, an anxious thought that kept you awake at night.

Across the room a recovered Penny was unsteadily angling her phone so that she could capture the special occasion, the feather boa sportingly draped around all three of them. Veronica pressed the tip of the knife blade into a glacé cherry as they arranged their smiles.

Will rushed over and offered to take the photograph for them, waiting while they repositioned themselves.

Say Cheese.

Cheese…

Click…

This was Doris's special day, Will reminded himself.

The revelation of a murder would have to wait.

The First Girl

Naomi

My father was in Amsterdam with Uncle Melvin the night that Owen, my younger brother, was kidnapped. He'd spent the morning at the National Maritime Museum, the afternoon in the botanical gardens and the evening with a prostitute, who wore a leather catsuit like Emma Peel in *The Avengers*, Uncle Melvin told us later. My mother had been asleep in the bed next to Owen, but it was me she blamed, me she yelled and screamed at and cried in front of, me who should have been awake, who should have heard something, anything. My father blamed her and she blamed me. I was five years old.

I didn't understand why it was my fault. I didn't understand why I should have been awake when I was supposed to be asleep. I already hated Owen for being born, for making my mother choose between us. I hated the way that he squirmed like an eel whenever I placed my hand over his mouth to stop him crying. But I hated him even more after that because he must have been really special to have been *wanted twice. There hasn't been a day since then when I haven't wished that it was me who was taken instead of him. It's far worse for the child left behind.*

All the photographs of me were pulled out of their frames and replaced with ones of Owen looking exactly the same, and whenever I asked my mother where my photographs were, which were infinitely more varied, she would leave me to consider this alone while she went into the kitchen to fry onions. She always fried onions whenever she didn't want to speak to me. At other times she'd sit squinting at me hatefully, no doubt wishing that I'd been the one taken, too, even though parents aren't supposed to have favourites. They're supposed to love you equally, no matter what.

One day when my father never came back from the racetrack my mother locked the back door and we left.

A few months later, I remember my mother's car screeching to a halt. She'd seen a boy with blond hair who would have been about the same age as Owen. She was always looking past me, looking for Owen. She cried when she realised that it wasn't him and we drove to a nearby campsite where she warmed a tin of chicken soup on a camp stove and wrapped a tartan blanket around her knees and forgot that I was there. I tried to remember her before, before all of this began, but I couldn't. She didn't smell like soap powder and cake mix anymore. She smelled of smoke and ash, of swirling bonfires.

On Sundays she went to church. Whenever we moved she found another church to attend, looking for all that she'd lost. I was maybe eight by this point, but it was difficult to keep track and it didn't really matter how old I was, I suppose. There was no one to tell. I couldn't ever remember being any age. When I did once ask my mother how old I was she wouldn't tell me, insisting that it wasn't important. People ask too many questions, she cautioned. Resist temptation! Refrain from satisfying an outsider's curiosity. It will lead you down a dark and troubled path and serve no purpose. It sounded like something that she'd heard during a church sermon – Beware of the Devil. He'll trick you with questions. So, no wiser as to how old I might be, I threw my questions on the campfire where they sizzled and popped.

When I prodded the fire with a pitchfork the papery ashes swirled like black snowflakes and a familiar smoky aroma filled the air.

No more remembering, she told me, *let's forget instead.*

'Okay, Mama,' I said.

Whatever you say.

I'm never quite sure why my mother didn't just abandon me, leave me on a train like a piece of lost luggage, but I think she enjoyed having a sparring partner, someone whom she could control and manipulate, and as soon as someone inched a little too close to us or began to pry she'd toss a suitcase into the boot of the car, push me into the passenger seat and we'd be gone, leaving nothing of ourselves behind, as if we were the ones who'd done something wrong, as if we were the fugitives.

I never attended school, a place where people asked questions and had those questions answered, but that didn't mean that I wasn't educated. You can teach yourself pretty much anything, acquire all sorts of knowledge, if you put your mind to it, and my mind was like a beehive. It buzzed and whirred every minute of the day. My mother wasn't fond of educating herself. She liked to live in the past (she refused to practise what she preached), but from a safe distance, where she could keep an eye on it. She would spend most days staring at pristine photographs of my brother that I wasn't allowed to touch. 'Keep your filthy fingers to yourself,' she'd say, when I asked if I *could look at them. My fingers were apparently always 'filthy', even when I'd just rinsed them in river water.*

When she was asleep I'd search for the photographs so that I could touch them as much as I liked with my 'filthy' fingers, maybe even lick them with my 'deceitful' tongue, but she hid them well. She'd bury them beneath moss and silt, slip them inside the dark hollows of tree trunks, and I'd only know where they'd been when we were leaving and she was throwing our things into a suitcase. She cherished those photographs more than anything else, so you can imagine her distress when I finally found them and burned them.

We were staying in an abandoned caravan without wheels that leant lopsidedly against a blackberry hedge on some farmland when I followed her, watched her scrape at the earth with her fingernails and cover the photographs, secured inside Liverpool Echo *headlines, with armfuls of copper-coloured leaves. She placed two twigs in the shape of a kiss on top of the leaves to remind her, like a cross on a treasure map, a scar on her heart. I ran back to the caravan and slipped out later that night with a box of matches and awaited my punishment, but she never mentioned the loss of the photographs, even though she knew that I was the one who'd burned them.*

I didn't know it then but she was starting to become afraid of me. As I got older she couldn't push and pull me around as easily, couldn't order me into the car, raise her hand when I didn't do as I was told. I was taller and stronger than her. I could twist her wrist, tell her to get her fucking hands off me. And I wasn't intimidated by silences anymore, or her changing moods. I could go for days not speaking and it not bothering me, but she seemed anxious about the silence sometimes, wondered what might be behind it. I could play so quietly that it was difficult to know if I was actually playing. Silence can be such a huge thing, so incomprehensible at times, that it's often best when it's broken.

Ultimately, however, I think she realised that burning those photographs was the only sensible solution — she couldn't keep looking back — even if she did leave saucepan lids on the floor where she slept so that she'd hear me coming, a hand curled around the handle of a hunting knife in case I managed to tiptoe around them. I suppose I kept her alive for so long because I grew to like the fear in her eyes. I grew to expect it. I blame my mother for the way that I am. Because of her I was always searching for the fear in people's eyes.

Everyone thinks that it's my brother who's the victim in all of this, but it's me, I'm the victim, the child left behind. Imagine your own mother despising you and wishing that you were the one taken instead. Imagine wondering if the original plan had been for you to be abducted and something went wrong. I told the policeman with the missing teeth that I was asleep that night, but I wasn't. It was too hot to sleep and there was a fly buzzing around my room. I wanted to kill it. I did kill it eventually, rubbing it between my fingers until it was nothing but bluebottle dust. When I opened the bedroom door to let out the heat someone was walking down the stairs carrying my brother. They turned around when they heard me and pressed a gloved finger to their masked lips. I closed the door. I was glad that he'd gone.

Naomi and her father, Derek, arrived in the spring. If I were to guess I'd say that I was about thirteen or fourteen. By then I'd created a makeshift calendar in the back of a notebook that I'd found because it was important that I knew more than my mother. I was a little behind calculating my exact age, I didn't even know when my birthday was anymore, but each morning I crossed off the corresponding day. I checked my calendar. It was Thursday.

By the autumn Naomi was dead. It was a Monday.

We were living in the end cottage of a row of four dilapidated stone cottages in rural Wales, in the shadow of Snowdon. Most of the roof slates were missing and the walled gardens had been vandalised, but there were some allotments behind tiny potting sheds where cabbages and pea vines still grew. Nobody had thought to tell the vegetables that they were leaving.

I called it the Forgotten Village. It was as if the residents had been evacuated unexpectedly and there'd been no time to pack. Metal buckets and plastic watering cans clattered along paths, and armchairs and sofas, green with mould, lay in front gardens waiting for the weather to change. My mother dragged two stained single mattresses into the living room of the cottage that she chose for us. I would have rather slept in the car, but she was insistent that we sleep in the same room. She kept the car keys on a belt around her waist, worried that I might take the car and leave her stranded, I expect, even though I couldn't yet drive. That came later when I befriended a farmer who offered me driving lessons in exchange for letting him take naked photographs of me. I'd already learnt that sometimes I had to do the things that repulsed me in order to acquire the things that didn't.

The eyes of a French woman (Claudette Dubois, according to the inscription on the back of the painting) would follow me around the living room, while the urine-yellow pages of the Good Housekeeping *magazine lining the pantry shelves disintegrated in my hands. Upstairs, a sticky lilac-coloured chenille bath mat had been nailed to one of the windows and there was a three-legged table hanging precariously from a light fitting like a booby trap. I found it far too claustrophobic and when my mother was asleep I slipped into one of the potting sheds – I called it my Plotting Shed – where Claudette's eyes didn't burn into me and I could sleep undisturbed. The jagged floorboards left splinters in my skin and I could feel insects crawling along my arms and legs but at least I could breathe. I'd long ago learnt to live with very little and now couldn't live with so much. But I did enjoy eating the peas and the radishes. I couldn't remember a time when I'd eaten something so flavoursome. They were like drops of summer rain on my tongue.*

There was a tap on the cottage door. My mother was reading some romance novel that she'd found at the side of the road. I was just about to go for a walk. I spent most of my time walking and thinking, wondering how to turn those moving thoughts into non-fiction, shape them into something solid and three-dimensional. My mother placed a finger to her lips and I was reminded of another finger pressed against a ski mask. I so wish that I'd screamed that night. I wanted to go back. I wanted to sleep in my own bed. I wanted soft pillows and warm milk and bedtime stories and goodnight kisses, even if they were duplicitous. I didn't want this. We both tried to quieten our breathing, which only made it seem louder.

The door handle turned and Derek (no surname) walked in. He was a tall, muscular man who looked and smelled like he'd crawled out of a sewer. My mother thought that he'd come to kill us. I thought that his arrival signalled something far worse. I thought that he was planning to take everything from us first.

It was several minutes before he introduced his daughter, Naomi, who was standing in the doorway like a sunlit angel, a halo of light illuminating her honey-gold eyes. On closer inspection, however, she was significantly less angelic, her heavenly presence a deception, an illusion. She looked as if she'd been raised by wolves while Derek had been out foraging; taking what wasn't his to take. Derek squeezed himself into the room until there was no air between us. I couldn't stand the smell of him so I pushed past him towards the light, Naomi blocking my way. It seemed pre-planned – him squeezing himself inside while Naomi guarded the door.

'Don't go far,' my mother said.

I'll go as far as I fucking like, I thought but didn't say.

Naomi, her eyes bruised with tiredness, reluctantly let me pass. She was tall like her father, her skin stretched over her protruding bones like a dirty doily. She was a few years older than me, I estimated, certainly older than she looked. I wasn't yet at the stage when the dirt on your skin begins to form its own creases that can't be washed off with soap and water, the roadmap of your nomadic life inked across your flesh. And you never smell clean no matter how many rivers you bathe in.

While I mostly avoided them, my mother treated them like visiting royalty, showing Derek around the allotments as if she'd grown all the vegetables herself, pointing out the chard and the celery. They moved into the cottage next door and my mother would go round with kitchen utensils that she'd found and teaspoons of sugar and slivers of soap to use in the river. She didn't mind where I slept now, although I rarely slept. I lay awake waiting for The Others to come. I was convinced that there were others, others like them.

In the autumn I told my mother that it was time to leave. We rarely stayed anywhere for longer than seven or eight months. My mother always said that when roots began to wind themselves around your ankles like tentacles you needed to uproot yourself before they took hold. But she wasn't ready to leave. She told me that Derek had plans – Big Plans – and we were going to be part of those plans. I *suspected that those plans included his friends placing a hand on my crotch too. Little did he know that I had some big plans of my own.*

Before I could put those plans in motion, however, my mother gave Naomi a brooch that had belonged to my grandmother. It wasn't the brooch itself that angered me, it wasn't as if I would wear it or that I'd even known my grandmother, although of course I could sell it – it was the fact that she'd given it to someone whom she barely knew when she'd never given anything to me. Nothing. Ever. Everything that I had I'd found or stolen or tricked someone out of.

I left the brooch where it fell, told my mother that Naomi was dead and that The Others would be coming soon, and we left.

Chapter Four
GHOSTLAND

When Jolene unlocked the front door, her mother was shivering on the bottom stair, clutching her mobile phone to her chest as if it was a crying infant. Her skin was ghostly pale, her eyes gleaming like distant planets. She remained like this for several seconds, unable to move, even though Jolene, the source of her distress, had arrived home safely.

'Where've you been? I've been calling and texting all day,' her mother sobbed.

'I've been at work. I told you this morning I was working late. How long have you been sitting here?'

'I don't know. A while. I couldn't sleep. I thought that something terrible had happened to you.'

'Nothing terrible is going to happen to me,' Jolene sighed. 'Try not to worry.'

Jolene looped the strap of her fake Victoria Beckham Half Moon handbag over a coat peg, draped her puffer jacket on top and unlaced her trainers.

'Come on, let's get you upstairs.'

Her mother's fingers were like icicles. She was wearing a sleeveless nylon blouse, cotton pyjama bottoms and no socks or slippers. Heaven knows how long she actually had been sitting there, but it was definitely longer than 'a while'. Her joints clicked mechanically when she stood up.

As she followed her mother upstairs Jolene glanced at the photographs of Dolly that lined the staircase walls. Most photographs she could walk past without noticing them, but the Dolly on the stairs always managed to catch your eye and being on the stairs meant that she did this several times a day. She was an unavoidable road that you had to cross to reach your destination, a row of slippery stepping stones, a bridge connecting the past and the present. Jolene had long ago accepted Dolly's continued presence, even though she wasn't physically present, but it was still infuriating that someone whom she barely remembered could leave such lasting scars and affect her life so negatively. Dolly wasn't even there anymore and yet she stretched into every corner of the house like elastic, burrowed deep inside every open pore.

Her mother would never recover, Jolene realised that. She'd been allowed to mourn for far too long. She didn't even go through the motions of living, most of the time, so intent was she on worrying that the same thing might happen to Jolene, that Jolene would similarly disappear if she didn't keep a close enough eye on her. She really did think that lightning could strike twice, that she might lose two daughters if she didn't check the weather forecast.

Jolene lowered her mother onto the bed and went back downstairs to fill a hot water bottle. She then collected a glass from one of the kitchen cupboards and a sleeping pill from the bathroom cabinet. Her mother was still where she'd left her, staring at her hands as if she'd never seen them before. Jolene passed her the sleeping pill and the glass of water and waited while she swallowed it. The gulp that her mother made was excruciatingly long and loud, the pill seemingly the size of a boulder.

Jolene was reminded how disconcerting it felt to give your mother pills and to then watch her swallow those pills, almost as if it was for her benefit rather than her mother's, which truthfully it probably was, although even with a sleeping pill coursing through her bloodstream her mother rarely slept, repeatedly checking on Jolene during the night, like a door that you couldn't remember locking, an oven ring that you couldn't remember switching off.

'Night, then,' Jolene said, before closing the bedroom door.

Communication between the two of them was currently reasonably civil and had been for several months. It hadn't always been like this, of course. There'd been endless hours of screaming and swearing and loathing and friction over the years. Maybe they were both screamed out. Or maybe the screaming would unexpectedly resume again at some point. Who knew? It certainly didn't feel as if the ground that they were walking on would always be this solid and accommodating.

Jolene deleted her mother's sixteen frantic texts and twenty-six missed calls and brushed her teeth. Tomorrow was an early shift and she really needed her mother to not wake her tonight. She hadn't been able to persuade Janette to change the rota, even though Alison and Jean both loathed late shifts and would have willingly swapped with her. It isn't all about you, Janette had told Jolene, when it clearly *was* all about her.

When she glanced down, she noticed splatters of blood-speckled saliva stippling the sink, the toothbrush bristles stained pink, and she realised that she was still annoyed that Janette had refused to allow her to change shifts and was now inflicting that annoyance on her gums. Although the request had initially been for the sole purpose of avoiding her mother's night-time neuroses, Jolene actually preferred overnight shifts – the echoing silence, the Marmite buttered toast, the absence of Janette, criticising and reprimanding her. It was like inhabiting a different world, a secret world. And the residents were generally in bed by seven o'clock, the sleeping pattern of toddlers, apart from the ones who roamed the corridors throughout the night like the ghosts in *The Haunting of Hill House*.

Jolene would be watching a DVD, helping herself to a Celebration or a shortbread finger, and a tiny figure in a cotton nightgown would come drifting towards her, sometimes wailing. She'd have to blink twice to double-check that it wasn't a ghost because she'd no doubt been watching a horror film, which always made her a little more jittery than normal.

Not that she believed in ghosts. Her grandmother certainly hadn't called in to say hello to convince her otherwise, and if any of the residents *had* been back, it was undoubtedly only to show their friends where they'd spent the last few years or months of their lives. Tell them what a shithole it was. Rather than judgemental spirits (everyone's a critic) drifting through the care home, it was usually Cora or Enid shuffling along the corridor, asking her where they were. In prison, Jolene wanted to tell them. You're all in prison, unable to come and go as you please, unless you know the door code. And even then you'll have forgotten it a second later. Your old life no longer exists. *You'll* soon no longer exist.

But she didn't.

She wrapped them in knitted blankets and blew on their too-hot cocoa and let them watch *Hostel* or *Final Destination* or whichever other horror film she was watching. She treated them like her mother, as if they were made of glass and if you touched them too often or too roughly they might shatter. She was particularly fond of Cora, who reminded her of her grandmother, and she'd listen without interrupting when she reminisced about her husband Charles and the Viennese waltzing and the championship trophies. She'd actually done something with her life, been somebody. That's what Jolene wanted. She wanted to be somebody, to accomplish something. She wanted to be remembered. Not in the way that Dolly was remembered. For all the wrong reasons. But for something illustrious, prestigious, providing that she wasn't centre-stage of course.

She wondered if she should have been spending more time with her mother instead of less, tiring her out like you would a small child or a pet dog. It had been the twentieth anniversary of Dolly's disappearance in December. She'd been fifteen when she disappeared, would always be fifteen, Jolene supposed. Perhaps anniversary wasn't quite the right word. There were no cards or gifts, no congratulations. But it wasn't a memorial either because that would have implied that Dolly was dead, and her mother had never publicly entertained the possibility that Dolly might be dead. *I'd know if she was dead, a mother would know*. It was more of a strategy meeting, an annual Remember Dolly reminder, a day when her mother relived the worst day of her life over and over again in the ice rink car park (the last place that Dolly was seen), where she'd light candles, hand out flyers and pray for Dolly's safe return.

A few regulars would join them – Angelina Merry's mother, Erica (Angelina had disappeared sixteen years ago, but most people believed that she'd left voluntarily to escape the advances of her father so she was never missed in the same way), church wardens Lesley and Philip Hillman, who'd spent years extolling the virtues of a God that her mother would never believe in and who attended most small gatherings regardless of their purpose, Glen Taylor, who lived with his agoraphobic mother and spent hours wandering aimlessly around town, presumably because his mother couldn't, and Marcus Richardson, who owned the ice rink and who liked them to stay in the far right-hand corner beside the British Heart Foundation recycling banks if it was busy, which in December it usually was. Jolene always prayed that Liam Cole, Dolly's ex-boyfriend, wouldn't be there. There was usually at least one broken taillight when he was.

Earlier, she'd texted her father to ask if she could stay with him over the weekend. *I haven't seen you since the New Year*, she'd typed. Truthfully, she'd been getting so many headaches due to her mother's nightly patrols that she was desperate for an uninterrupted five hours' sleep and it was normally as quiet as a graveyard at her father's house. *How about tomorrow?* he'd suggested. *I'll order pizza.*

She texted her friend Laura before locking the front door and switching off the downstairs lights – all those night-time rituals that signalled the end of another long day and were currently her responsibility since she and her mother had seemingly swapped roles and she was now required to be the parent – and told her that she'd finally managed to watch *Hostel III*. Laura replied immediately. *You've got the best job ever!* Not strictly true. But that was because Jolene had never told Laura about the darker side of care homes – the howling and the screaming, the pinches and the punches (residents *and* staff), the loneliness, the sickness, the endless cycles of grief. Jolene hiding in the laundry room (her safe place) when someone whom she'd watched a DVD with or shared a mint Aero with died and she was so overcome with loss that she'd have to build a wall of industrial-sized boxes of washing powder and fabric conditioner around her and remain cocooned within it until she'd stopped crying.

But that was the Jolene that she didn't want anybody else to see. That was caring and sensitive Jolene and there was no place for that Jolene at Sunset House.

When she came downstairs the next morning her mother was sitting at the kitchen table staring at the oven clock. The skin around her eyes was a strange lizard green. Jolene wondered what colour her own eyes were this morning. She hadn't yet summoned up the courage to look in the mirror. But she imagined them to be similarly reptilian and most definitely bloodshot. Her mother must have opened her bedroom door fifteen times during the night, the light from the landing flooding the room with a dizzying amount of watts. But at least it wasn't torchlight, she supposed. Sometimes her mother would stride across the room, peel back her eyelids and shine a torch in her eyes to check that no one had abducted her during the night and left an imposter in her place, a cross between being subjected to an impromptu interrogation and an unscheduled eye examination. It was a miracle that she didn't have retinal damage.

'Have you remembered that I'm staying at Dad's tonight?'

As Jolene had forgotten to tell her mother that she was spending the night at her father's house, it was unlikely. Was she now gaslighting her own mother? Sometimes Jolene despised herself, but sadly interactions with her mother were far easier when it was assumed that information had already been communicated and appropriately digested.

Her mother nodded hesitantly, her eyebrows knitted together in confusion. Jolene pulled the written reminder from the pocket of her jeans and attached it to the fridge door with the 'Greetings from The Lake District' bottle-opener magnet that Dolly had brought back from a school trip. Her mother gazed pensively at the bottle-opener for a few seconds and then slid some foil-wrapped sandwiches towards Jolene. She'd probably give them to Cora later. Cora liked her mother's sandwiches. They reminded her of wartime rationing. Jolene was planning to have a KFC bargain bucket for lunch. She suspected that it was going to be a 'bargain bucket' sort of day.

'I'll call you later, I promise. Please don't worry.'

Her father's house was like Fort Knox – patrolled, alarmed and bolted by nine p.m. Instead of wrapping a leash around people's necks her father deadlocked and double-glazed the properties that they lived in instead. And she was hardly likely to be bludgeoned to death by an eighty-year-old geriatric male with a walking frame while she was at work. She was probably in one of the safest places on earth, somewhere between a smallholding in the Outer Hebrides and the passenger seat of a Volvo XC90, although the building *was* a little eerie sometimes and *Most Haunted* would doubtless find evidence of paranormal activity. They usually did.

Sunset House was located on the crest of a steep hill above a car park, like a cherry on top of a coconut madeleine, although less visually appealing, and had once been a children's home. Occasionally, Jolene would notice a stick man in biro on one of the walls or a tiny *help me* behind a cupboard door, which she assumed one of the children had written, but it could have been one of the care home residents, she supposed. It was a draughty building, especially at night and during a thunderstorm, a Trespass fleece an essential requirement. Windows would rattle in their frames and hinges would creak and sometimes Jolene would feel a warm breath on her neck or sense a shadowy blur to the right of her and suddenly she was in her very own horror film.

She'd have to remind herself that it was just a building and buildings couldn't hurt you, no matter how eerie they might be. Only people did that.

Chapter Five

SILVER LININGS

Will was exhausted by the time he arrived home. After Penny and Veronica had left, Doris had suggested that they play 'Pass the Parcel' so that she could distribute her birthday gifts fairly (a distinctly unfair undertaking sadly, Theo amassing two women's gilets, a gold locket, a red leather purse and a floral bra that he refused to surrender), and then Sheila Warner had had one of her 'funny turns', as she liked to call them, although they were anything but. Her muscles would spasm and her eyes would roll beneath her eyelids and she'd crumple to the floor like dirty laundry, even though she wasn't epileptic, according to Doctor Rush, the visiting doctor, who would form a diagnosis without looking at you and rarely requested further tests, his surname particularly apt.

And you'd think, *This is it*, she's been suffering from an undiagnosed medical condition that's been left untreated and she's going to die on the lounge carpet that has all sorts of grime embedded in it that can't be removed with the vacuum cleaner and there'll be a dead spider in her hair when the paramedics arrive and in her final moments it'll look like she hasn't been cared for at all.

That was one of Will's main concerns – that everyone would suddenly start dying because the care home wasn't clean enough or caring enough and their Care Quality Commission rating would plummet to 'inadequate', forcing them to temporarily close, which was what had happened at their sister premises, Sunrise House, a couple of years earlier, and it had left a shameful, sour taste in everyone's mouth, tarnishing Sunset House's reputation by association.

Fortunately, Jolene, a godsend in a crisis, had swooped in like a Spanish matador and Sheila had been sitting in Enid Cooper's chair twenty minutes later with a cup of sweet tea on her lap as if nothing had happened, having scolded Enid for sitting in her seat, causing Will to wonder if she was merely confused or severely concussed, although it was too late to ask Doctor Rush. He'd already left.

Will's father was sitting on the sofa watching the closing credits of *The Chase*, his prosthetic leg lying on a cushion beside him. It was his fourth artificial limb. Replicating a human limb and persuading the rest of your body to accept it took all the advancements that technology had to offer. It still didn't deter him from removing the leg as soon as he was indoors, however, as if it was a new shoe that had given him blisters and that he was desperate to unlace.

His right leg had been amputated below the knee after he developed sepsis during a routine operation, but if anyone ever asked (and, surprisingly, people often did) he placed the blame on a Gold Coast shark. Or if it was a child asking, a pirate on the Seven Seas, a 'me hearties' and a 'shiver me timbers' in a Cornish accent added for authenticity. Far more exciting and less awkward for everyone, he claimed. But that was his father, always searching for silver linings. Never mourning the thing that he'd lost, but celebrating everything that he still had. *I've still got the other one.*

'That's the second time I've beaten The Governess this month,' his father announced proudly. 'I'm now twelve points ahead of Isaac.'

Isaac lived next door and he and Will's father kept daily tallies of their quiz show scores on an Excel spreadsheet. They also competed in the weekly pub quiz at the White Hart most Thursdays, calling themselves 'Three Legs and a Welshman', and often came home with a bottle of port or an Argos voucher.

'How was the birthday party?' he asked Will.

'It was fine until Sheila had one of her turns and Theo won all of Doris's gifts in five games of "Pass the Parcel". He's been walking around in a woman's fake fur gilet all afternoon. Shall we have fish and chips for tea?'

While waiting in the queue at The Fish Bar, Will was reminded of his mother, and the potato fritter, small carton of mushy peas and two slices of bread and butter that she always ordered. He'd been in Normandy on a school trip when she died. He hadn't even been in the same country. His father had contacted one of the teachers as they were walking around Mont-Saint-Michel in the rain and that same teacher (Miss Yates) had travelled back to the UK with him. *Really, Will, I don't mind at all. François, a head waiter at La Sirene who I've been seeing for the past couple of years, told me last night that he's going back to his wife in Provence. Better weather apparently. I didn't know that he had a wife. I told him that I was going back to England. Worse weather unfortunately. And then I poured a glass of Merlot over his head.*

Will had willed Miss Yates to stop talking. On any other occasion news of the end of Miss Yates' long-distance love affair with a married French waiter would have been worth several rare football stickers, maybe even a twenty-four-hour loan of *Dragon Quest VIII*. But his mother was dead. And he hadn't been there. He'd never wanted to get home quicker and yet part of him hadn't wanted to arrive home at all. He'd wanted to still be on French soil, his life unchanged, no urgent telephone call from his father and no Miss Yates gazing through the coach window with tears in her eyes.

When his father was in hospital Will worried that it would happen again, that he wouldn't be there when he died, that he'd be on another overheated coach in another country not wanting ever to arrive home. He had nightmares about his father disappearing, his limbs being snapped off one by one as if they were made of gingerbread, leaving just his head and his torso, and then his head and his torso would roll away from him, splashing into the ocean, and there'd be nothing left of his father, nothing left to mourn. He often wondered if it was his fault that his father lost his leg, because he'd dreamt it, afraid that if he slept then another limb would inexplicably disappear, snapping like butterscotch.

His phone pinged. It was Sophie, asking if he wanted to do something later. He told her that he couldn't tonight (he was planning to watch the last two episodes of Season Five of *The Sopranos* with his father), how about tomorrow?

I suppose I can reschedule if I must. Frowning Face emoji.

He'd been standing beneath the bus shelter opposite Angelina Merry's house with two vanilla slices (both his) when he first met Sophie. Angelina was in his geography class and a few weeks after his mother's funeral he'd found himself following her home, not intentionally of course, at least not initially, he'd just found himself gravitating in that direction. Angelina hadn't noticed him at all. She'd had headphones in her ears and an open magazine in her hands and had spent the entire forty-minute journey crossing roads without looking, narrowly missing two passing cyclists and a guide dog. He'd imagined himself walking beside her instead of a few steps behind, listening to what she was listening to, reading what she was reading, wondering what it would be like to kiss her, his imaginings destined to remain imaginary when she disappeared a few months later.

It's something that he still does occasionally, not imagine what it's like to kiss someone, although he does do that, but follow people. He doesn't know why. He doesn't consider it stalking – a word that suggests a more sinister motive, which isn't his intention. He's simply walking a few steps behind people, a reassuring presence rather than a menacing one. He doesn't mean them any harm. He's an ally, a confidant. Sometimes he gets to know a person intimately, until they're no longer strangers, even though he's never spoken a word to them, his world so much more fascinating with these people in it.

He'd just taken a bite from the second vanilla slice when a girl suddenly appeared to the right of him.

'Should you be eating that?'

'What business is it of yours?'

'None, I expect, just curious.'

Her hair was two different colours, the top half black, the tips orange, like reverse flames. It was as if she was trying out colours and couldn't decide which colour should take precedence.

'Which bus are you waiting for?' she'd asked him.

'The next one.'

He'd felt self-conscious licking custard from his fingers and wished that she'd leave.

'That's funny 'coz you've already let two go past.'

'Are you keeping count?'

'Like I say, just curious. She's got a boyfriend, you know.'

'Who's got a boyfriend?'

'The girl whose house you're watching.'

The name 'Andy' had been carved into the bus shelter glass above a cigarette-singed penis. He looked away.

'A boyfriend?'

'Yep, comes round three or four times a week.'

'Right.'

He suddenly felt sick, the second vanilla slice far sweeter than it should have been.

'Still, it might not be serious. It could just be for sex or something.'

The last of the vanilla slice was wedged somewhere

between his larynx and his ribcage, steadfastly refusing to move. He couldn't seem to shift it.

And he couldn't erase the image that had now been planted in his mind of Angelina Merry having sex with someone who wasn't him.

'Hey, just thought you should know.'

He'd nodded, as he'd repeatedly thumped his chest.

Reverse-flame girl had looked at him as if it was no more than he deserved. What did he expect? He'd just devoured two vanilla slices as if his life depended on it.

Why wouldn't she leave? Did she want to watch him choke to death?

She'd continued to stare at him.

'I'm Sophie, by the way.'

'Will,' he'd spluttered.

She'd nodded, as if the name suited him.

'Where there's a Will…'

'What bus are you waiting for?' he'd interrupted, hoping that it was the bus that was at that moment rolling over the brow of the hill.

'I don't do buses.'

'What does that mean?'

'It means … I … don't … do … buses…duh. I'd rather walk. Anyway, I've come to talk to you. I thought you might like some company while you're watching, I mean, waiting.'

He'd frowned at her.

'I don't suppose you've seen my mum on your travels, have you, at the infirmary maybe, or the police station? What about outside the Bell Jar? This big, two black eyes and a mad ginger perm that she never brushes. She never came home last night.'

'I don't think so.'

She'd glanced at her watch.

'I expect she's probably dead in a ditch somewhere. Fingers crossed.'

As she'd swung her backpack onto her shoulder, Will had noticed the cigarette burns on her right wrist.

'Perhaps see you again sometime if you're still stalking her.'

'I'm not stalking her.'

'Whatever you say.'

A woman wearing a hairnet and a diamante stud in her nose slapped a white carrier bag onto the counter and glared at him. He'd been hoping to see Alana, the owner's daughter. She always gave him extra chips. And she didn't slam and snatch and snarl. She took her time, asked about your day. Will hurriedly reached for the carrier bag and turned to leave.

As he was leaving he noticed Gilbert Williams's son, Martin, in the queue. He must live nearby, thought Will, although he'd never seen him in The Fish Bar before. A coincidence? Or was Will now the one being followed? Will smiled politely and Martin Williams reluctantly nodded. It was always a little embarrassing when you saw a resident's relatives in public. Being overly familiar with the family genitalia redefined the rules of engagement.

Will hadn't followed anyone in a while and he was curious

to know where Martin Williams lived, but his fish and chips were getting cold and *The Sopranos* were waiting. A new target had definitely presented itself though, Will determined, as he unscrewed the lid on the tomato ketchup, particularly in light of Martin's father Gilbert's revelation. Will had uncovered a circus of secrets and lies following people in the past. There was no reason why following Martin Williams shouldn't prove similarly productive.

Chapter Six

MINIATURE WORKS OF ART

Jolene had asked Will four times if he'd given Sheila her medication and he still hadn't answered. She wasn't usually so conscientious; a missed pill here and there was hardly life-threatening (the amount of pills that some of the residents were prescribed, sometimes as many as twelve a day, meant that they were virtually pill bottles anyway, so they had plenty of reserves), but she didn't want a repeat performance of yesterday's fiasco, Sheila flailing around on the carpet like a rainbow trout and Will drawing up a chair as if she was the afternoon entertainment.

It was Jolene who'd had to quickly turn Sheila onto her side and check her airways. Will was fine with the listening and the empathy and the applause when you'd won first prize in a raffle, but if you needed a fishbone removing or a fight breaking up then that was Jolene's department. She was left to deal with the more unpleasant and practical issues.

She waved the medication folder at Will until he finally responded. *No, he hadn't.*

'If you didn't keep chatting to them, we'd be done by ten.'
'What's the rush?'
'*Loose Women*, that's the rush. I missed it yesterday.'

Last week, during one of her 'quiet words', Janette had spent fifteen minutes praising Will's courteous nature and work ethic. There should be more Wills in the world, she'd declared, passing Jolene a letter from human resources confirming the date of her upcoming disciplinary hearing. Jolene hadn't responded. If there were any more Wills in the world the UK economy would grind to a halt and they'd be trapped inside an inflatable plastic bubble of nostalgia with no first-aid skills. Jolene was no doubt an example of how not to behave in the workplace, a cautionary tale. *If only there were fewer Jolenes in the world.*

Janette didn't know that Will followed people. Jolene hadn't known until a few months ago when she'd seen him in the precinct outside Card Factory watching a dark-haired woman pushing a pram and when the woman had turned left towards the train station he'd started following her.

Not that it was any of her business (unless he followed people into their homes and it became a police matter). She didn't care what other people did in their spare time. Live and let live and don't cry in public. That was her motto. And she liked Will. She just wished that Janette was aware of the stalking and then she might not feel it necessary to continually blame Jolene for mankind no longer being kind. And she might also want to look in a mirror, thought Jolene, before casting aspersions elsewhere.

When she next glanced over at Will he was talking to Gilbert Williams. Or was Gilbert Williams talking to him?

He looked unusually animated. Normally, Gilbert sat with his arms tightly crossed and a spiteful look on his face, mumbling incoherently to himself, but today there was a fiery glint in his rheumy eyes, as he whispered something in Will's ear. Probably 'Fuck off!' His language was appalling sometimes. Jolene didn't shock easily but even she didn't want to repeat some of the disgusting things that he said.

When Will saw her staring he came over.

'You two are getting very cliquey these days,' she told him.

He didn't answer. Gilbert's son, Martin, had just arrived and was obviously infinitely more fascinating.

She hoped that she wasn't going to have to repeat herself four times and shake a folder in Will's face *every* time she asked him something.

'Hello, Earth calling Will,' she yelled in his ear.

Finally, he acknowledged her.

'Has Gilbert said anything strange to you recently?'

'No more than usual. Why? What's he said?'

She tried to sound interested. It didn't come naturally.

'Something about killing someone. And today he mentioned a Naomi and how they'd never find her.'

Jolene glanced over at Gilbert. He certainly looked like he wanted to kill someone. And that someone was currently Cora, quietly nibbling the edges of her mother's ham sandwiches like a field mouse while she gazed blankly out of the lounge window. He appeared to want to strangle her. Listening to people chew and slurp in close proximity was sometimes all that it took to raise a person's blood pressure. Or breathing too loudly. In fact most things were frowned upon in here; even minding your own business could make a person livid.

But that's what happened when you forced people together like lab rats.

Perhaps he had killed someone, intentionally or accidentally. Perhaps he'd been in prison, changed his name so that no one would ever know. The residents could have had a thousand secrets between them, decade-old mysteries that they were keeping to themselves. Still, it was best not to admit that to Will. He spent enough time trying to extract slivers of personal information from them.

'I'm sure it's nothing. Naomi was probably the name of a childhood friend or a pet rabbit. Maybe he's got a crush on Naomi Campbell. You shouldn't take everything that they say so seriously. Most of it wouldn't stand up in court.'

'You're probably right.'

'I'm definitely right. Look at him. He couldn't kill anyone with those arthritic knuckles.'

'He was young once, you know,' Will reminded her.

It was difficult to imagine any of them ever being young.

And she'd tried. She really had.

'Anyway, enough snooping for one day, duty calls. Enid and Marilyn are due a toilet visit. Heads or Tails?'

Towards the end of her shift Jolene texted her mother to remind her that she was spending the night at her father's house. Her mother had only texted her twice so far today, the first time to ask her if she'd eaten the sandwiches, the second time to tell her that there was a black cat in the back garden, both of which she'd replied to (*Just eating them now* and *It's probably Mungo)*. Initially, the lack of contact was a welcome relief, but then Jolene would start to wonder why there weren't more texts. Her mother couldn't win really. Jolene worried when she texted her excessively and she worried when she didn't. No news always felt like bad news.

Her mother didn't text back until she was pulling into her father's driveway. *It wasn't Mungo,* she'd typed.

Dawn, her father's girlfriend, owned a nail parlour (unimaginatively called Dawn's Nails) on Victoria Road next to the doctor's surgery and always offered to paint Jolene's nails, which Jolene was immensely appreciative of because it always looked like she'd spent the day digging her way out of a shallow grave, and she liked having manicured nails. The last time she'd stayed, Dawn had painted decorative flowers on her nails that had looked like miniature works of art, although Laura said that they looked like the flowers in a Mapplethorpe book on photography that she'd seen in the library where the lilies resembled vaginas. Not quite the reaction that Jolene had been hoping for, prompting her to remove the flowers with nail varnish remover a few hours later. Nobody wanted vaginas on their fingernails, no matter how decorative they were.

Her boisterous and excitable two-year-old half-brother, Nicholas, could similarly also be relied upon to lift her sour mood. Whenever he galloped towards her, his eyes sparkling like dinner plates, there was no time for wallowing and catastrophising. It was 'buckle up and grab a crayon' time, your hopes and dreams still possibilities, the future unwritten, although Dawn might disagree. She said that as endearing as such unbridled innocence might seem, he ran her ragged most days.

While Jolene and her mother lived in a small terraced property behind the railway station, her father's house was practically palatial. You didn't step onto the pavement when you opened the front door, confronted by pedestrians and exhaust fumes, no breathing space between you and passersby. You drove along a private driveway towards a six-bedroom, three-bathroom Georgian mansion overlooking the park, where the afternoon sun bathed a south-facing conservatory in flaxen sunlight and the acre and a half of landscaped lawns, ornamental fountains and a trellis-panelled gazebo transported you to the Tuscan countryside.

But, more importantly, there was no one opening the bedroom door every five minutes checking that you were still there, and no photographs of Dolly adorning the walls, her frozen smile forever taunting you – *I'm not even there and I'm still loved more than you*.

If Jolene had known about the proposed living arrangements earlier and had been given the choice then she'd of course have chosen to live with her father. Who wouldn't want to live where there was topiary and summer barbecues? But she couldn't possibly do that now. She couldn't abandon her mother. It was too late. She'd seen too much. She knew too much. And, besides, her father had another family now – a family untouched by grief.

For him, moving out and moving on had been a natural next step (*and* a more lucrative one – Dawn's father owned several multinational companies), although it hadn't been without its setbacks. Jolene had heard her father crying when he thought that no one was listening and it was far more upsetting than hearing her mother cry because he never cried.

He didn't have permanent tears in his eyes that had given him an unfocused liquid gaze. He didn't have mucus continually dripping down his chin. His grief was less visible, more litigious, her father forced to hire a lawyer and say nothing further when suspicion had fallen on him because it had nowhere else to fall.

These things left a mark, a stubborn stain that was almost impossible to erase, although the dimmer switches and the walk-in closets inside Sunny Hollow no doubt helped eliminate some of those stains.

It had been twenty years since Dolly disappeared and most people believed that she was dead, suspected her own father of killing her. But what if she wasn't dead, if her mother's intuition was correct? What if she'd knowingly caused all of this turmoil, forced Jolene to live in a house that shuddered when trains roared past?

Jolene didn't think that she'd ever forgive her if she had.

Chapter Seven
QUICKSAND

Gilbert had been in his room all morning watching horse racing – Will could hear the frantic commentary every time he walked past – and it was after eleven when he finally entered the lounge. Will was serving tea and coffee and Alison and Jolene were clearing away shoeboxes. Pam, from the local mobility shop, had brought in a selection of non-slip, extra-wide-fitting shoes for residents to purchase. And Amy, the kitchen assistant, had been in earlier with her Yorkshire Terrier, Bruno.

There were always collective *ooh*s and *ahh*s, accompanied by a string of Cora's shrill sneezes, when Bruno appeared (Cora was allergic to dogs, but refused to stay in her room). You could almost see Bruno rolling his eyes as he made his surprise entrance, but he managed to keep up the pretence of not minding being patted and ruffled and pawed for the next few hours.

A magician had been booked for Easter to give Bruno a few days' respite – 'The Great Supremo', a sales assistant from

B & Q who'd once auditioned for *Britain's Got Talent*, but failed to make the live shows. It was all magicians that year, he'd told them. Will remembered the last magician that they'd booked, 'Jay Presto', who'd been entertaining them with chipped gambling chips and a malnourished guinea pig in a blood-stained top hat when Janette had suddenly excused herself mid-conversation and pulled him to one side. Will had watched in horror as she'd relieved the magician of Theo's pocket watch, Doris's pearl bracelet and a twenty-pound note that he swore was his, but which she took anyway ('compensation for the emotional distress caused'). She also retrieved the guinea pig from inside the top hat and told him that she'd be contacting the RSPCA.

'Let's hope we have more luck with The Great Supremo,' Janette had sighed.

Will glanced over at Gilbert. There was a scab on his chin, he was wearing odd socks and his hair hadn't been combed. Will wondered if Jolene had dressed him this morning. She tended to do the bare minimum and sometimes not even that. 'It's not as if they've got anywhere to be,' she'd argue.

He'd decided to ignore Gilbert's comments. He definitely hadn't killed anyone, well, not definitely, that was perhaps a little overly confident, considering he barely knew him, but he was reasonably certain that he hadn't.

And for now that was enough.

'Tea, Gilbert?'

Gilbert stared at him blankly, his eyes cloudy and watery, all types of weather trapped inside them.

'They'll never find her,' he said.

'Never find who?'

'Naomi.'

'Naomi?'

Will would obviously need to reassess his earlier evaluation.

Just as it seemed as if Gilbert was about to reveal more, his eyes refocused and he said, 'Yes, please. Two and a half sugars.'

It was like a cliffhanger at the end of a *Line of Duty* episode.

Will poured his tea, adding the two and a half spoonfuls of sugar requested. Gilbert had specific sugar requirements.

'Who's Naomi, Gilbert?' Will asked, eager to resume the next episode.

'I've no idea. Is she new?' Gilbert replied, glancing over Will's shoulder.

When Will turned round to see what he was looking at, he saw Martin Williams striding towards them. He hadn't visited in months and now Will had seen him twice in two days.

Another coincidence?

He hoped so.

'All right,' Martin Williams said.

Will didn't think that it was an 'all right' that required a response and he wasn't sure that it was directed at him anyway so he didn't respond. Gilbert didn't respond either, noisily slurping his tea.

Noticing Jolene watching them, Will politely excused himself. She yawned loudly as he approached.

He asked her if Gilbert had said anything strange to her recently, while simultaneously trying to lip read what Martin Williams was saying to Gilbert. He regretted not attending the free lipreading course in Durham that he'd cancelled because

Janette had told him that she'd be attending too and that they'd need to stay overnight.

But Jolene didn't seem at all concerned that they could have been serving tea and coffee to serial killers and paedophiles. She'd have merely recommended not leaving minors unsupervised and child-proofing the cutlery drawer.

All afternoon Gilbert's words raced around Will's head like Ferraris on a racetrack and he couldn't seem to silence them, no matter how busy he kept himself. He repaired a couple of chair legs, which seemed to irritate Jolene further (perhaps she'd been hoping that someone would sit on one of the chairs, fracturing an ankle, and she'd win two hundred and fifty pounds on *You've Been Framed!*). And then he hammered eight nails into one of the lounge walls to display a series of photographs that Janette had had enlarged and framed of the residents wearing Santa hats and tinsel garlands while singing along to local tribute act Sing Crosby, the residents frighteningly life-size and a little grotesque, courtesy of Jean, who'd been in charge of wardrobe and make-up. They were like deleted scenes from the horror film *What Ever Happened to Baby Jane?*

On his way back from the storeroom he noticed that Janette wasn't in her office and, remembering that she kept a collection of notebooks in the stationery cupboard, he wondered whether to formally document Gilbert's comments in writing. Last autumn he'd broached the possibility of becoming Sunset House's official in-house biographer and immortalising the residents' lives on tape. There may even be publisher interest, he'd told Janette excitedly, it might become a bestselling anthology, a percentage of the royalties donated to

Sunset House, but Janette had told him that you couldn't just tape people saying things. There were all sorts of data protection issues and confidentiality clauses and permissions to consider, *although it's an excellent idea, as always, Will. Keep up the good work!*

His first investigative task would be to check online for any Naomis who'd been reported missing or found deceased, to corroborate Gilbert's claims, although there were no doubt several missing or deceased Naomis. There were probably very few girls' names that weren't connected to unsolved murders or disappearances.

'Need something, Will?'

While he'd been receiving a commendation from the mayor for his key role in solving the disappearance of one of Gilbert Williams' victims (he was receptive to the notion that there might be multiple victims), Janette had walked into the office.

A lined A5 notebook was in his hand.

'I wondered if I'd be able to have a notebook. I'm thinking about doing an NVQ in Health and Social Care and wanted to make a few notes,' he lied.

He wasn't a particularly accomplished liar. Telltale damp patches were already developing beneath his armpits. He was, however, impressed with his quicker than usual quick thinking.

'That's very admirable, Will. I wish that there were more people like you, people eager to update their workplace skills, people with career aspirations. Unlike Jolene, who looks like she's just rolled out of bed most days.'

Will wished that she wouldn't be so derogatory about Jolene. It was unprofessional and unnecessary. Jolene's detached approach should have been applauded. Nothing scared her. Nothing fazed her. She'd sprinted across the room and attended to Sheila as if she was a qualified paramedic.

Janette meanwhile appeared to be conveniently ignoring the fact that she'd just caught Will taking something from the stationery cupboard without permission and although Will found Janette's flagrant displays of bias and discrimination reprehensible, he didn't yet feel confident enough to publicly express those opinions.

He turned to leave – he was finding it difficult to breathe – but Janette immediately blocked his way. When he moved to the right of her, she mirrored him. When he moved to the left of her, she mirrored him again. It was like a bizarre children's game. His heart was thudding like a train. He felt as if he was walking through quicksand, sinking lower and lower into the beige office carpet.

'If you ever need a chat ... about anything ... you know where I am,' Janette told him.

His collar felt too tight. He could feel beads of sweat on his forehead. He'd been foolish to enter Janette's office alone.

Suddenly, the fire exit door alarm sliced through the silence, startling them both.

'Fuck,' cursed Janette.

She glanced at Will's horrified expression.

'Sorry, Will. Slip of the tongue.'

Presumably, it was Theo. He regularly activated fire door alarms, believing himself assigned the task of guaranteeing the safe release of 'hostages'.

He'd have to remember to give him an extra helping of sticky toffee pudding as a thank you.

Later that evening, Will and Sophie were in Symphony, a local nightclub, Sophie seemingly dancing without actually moving, Will nursing an empty pint glass and staring longingly at the exit sign. Nightclubs made Will uneasy. Men didn't electric slide onto dance floors, moonwalk beneath disco balls. They didn't shimmy at the drop of a hat.

Sophie returned to his side briefly to steal a handful of salted peanuts before disappearing inside a soup of swivelling feet, hallelujah arms and abandoned clutch bags. He should ask the nightclub manager to make a courtesy Tannoy announcement, warning everyone not to leave their personal belongings unattended.

When he first met Sophie she'd spend hours in Sid's Diner sipping Pepsi and stealing the occasional wallet. She only took the cash though, she'd told him, virtuously, never cards. It's a ball-ache, having to cancel debit and credit cards. Although people don't actually carry that much cash around these days, she'd lamented, so it barely covers my morning Pepsi and my afternoon flapjack. *Poor you*, Will had commiserated.

When Sid's Diner was closed she'd sit in the park reading magazines that she'd stolen from the Co-op and checking beneath park benches for dropped wallets. She had to do that more often after Sid caught her rifling through someone's handbag while they were in the toilet. He told her that he wouldn't contact the police if she gave him a blowjob, so she followed him into the back office and kneed him in the groin. As she was weaving past the diner customers towards the door he yelled that he was going to fucking kill her if he ever saw her again. Since then, she swears that her criminal past is behind her, although she doesn't appear to have passed the news onto her fingers.

Finally, fifteen excruciating minutes later, Sophie was ready to leave. *Now!* Will didn't need telling twice.

He heard a commotion behind them as they were leaving.

'Someone tried to grope me so I kneed him in the bollocks,' Sophie told him, matter-of-factly.

This appeared to be her go-to method of retaliation when confronted by male assailants. Will was enraged at the thought of somebody sexually molesting her in public, remembering how uncomfortable Janette had made him feel earlier. He asked her if she wanted him to have a word. She laughed and shook her head and then sprinted out of the nightclub.

Will jogged after her.

'I'll find you, you fucking bitch,' a voice yelled after them. 'You won't get far.'

'That was fun,' Sophie said when Will finally caught up with her.

She was slipping banknotes into the pocket of her jeans.

'Thanks for coming. I know nightclubs aren't really your thing.'

They strolled along the path beside the river, although they couldn't actually see the river in the dark; just hear the odd gurgle every now and then, reminding them that it was still there. Or maybe that was Will's stomach. He just didn't feel full enough. It was like there was a yawning cavernous hollow inside him that could never be completely filled. They sat on a wall for a while, Will gazing up at the stars, speculating on the likelihood of a parallel universe where he ate smaller portions and Sophie wasn't a kleptomaniac, while Sophie deftly removed a SIM card from an iPhone that she'd obviously just stolen.

On the way home Sophie offered to keep him company if he felt like some Peeping Tom practice, as if he was some unstoppable stalking machine who needed to be indulged. He'd told her numerous times over the years that he didn't do that anymore, had never done that in fact, which of course wasn't true. Sophie still pickpocketed and shoplifted and he still followed people. Nothing had changed.

Except that Angelina Merry didn't live opposite the bus shelter anymore. She hadn't lived there in a long time.

And he should know. He'd been the last person to see her.

Chapter Eight

SALAMANDERS AND BUBBLEGUM-PINK DINERS

Jolene had volunteered to escort eight of the residents on a daytrip to a garden centre followed by a three-course lunch at the Lakeside Country Hotel, primarily to avoid Janette, who'd been in a vile mood since Theo Winchester's thirteenth escape attempt (Janette had been keeping count), but also because Luke Trent, a janitor at the care home, was driving the minibus. Luke worked on a casual basis, responsible for non-electrical repairs, garden maintenance and chauffeuring duties – something that was more suited to a retiree, but apparently the extra money funded record company demos and replacement guitar strings for his band The Lost and Found. Jolene had tried to look nonplussed and unimpressed when he'd told her that he was in a band. She wasn't sure that she'd been entirely successful. She'd never met anyone who'd met Jason Orange.

Yesterday, when Will had suddenly taken it upon himself to repair some loose chair legs and hang up some framed photographs of the residents looking like Yuletide clowns,

Jolene had been furious. She'd been just about to page Luke. And when Will had said, 'Ta da, all done', she'd wanted to smash the chair that he was holding over his head, partly because she was so angry with him and partly because she'd then have a legitimate excuse to contact Luke so that he could repair the chair (*again!*). When she'd seen Will unwrapping the picture frames, she'd had the foresight to hide the spirit level in Enid's wardrobe but, annoyingly, Will hadn't been deterred, and none of the photographs that he'd hung up were straight, which was even more infuriating. When she finally retrieved the spirit level, Luke had already left.

She wasn't sure if Luke was single or not, but probably not. Who didn't like boys in bands, even drummers? She'd seen Janette, the target demographic for a Magic Mike Live show, undo two extra buttons on her blouse whenever Luke was on duty.

Janette had recently taken an unhealthy interest in Will and Jolene had wondered whether to anonymously report Janette for sexual harassment – it would certainly deflect the spotlight from her – but had ultimately decided that Will was more than capable of looking after himself. She shouldn't be expected to complain on Will's behalf. She wasn't Head of Human Resources or his union rep.

Jolene had tried to establish Luke's relationship status a couple of weeks ago when he'd been trimming the rhododendron bushes in the courtyard, bribing him with four chocolate Hobnobs and a Yorkshire tea, but he'd been extremely evasive and she'd felt as if she was interrogating him in a windowless room under harsh lighting.

And Jolene Edwards interrogated no one. She let events

unfold from a safe distance, which was why she'd checked the drivers' roster before volunteering for today's daytrip. Sometimes, surprises required pre-planning. And Luke had excellent taste in music, unlike Tom, the other minibus driver, who would terrorise her with Nat King Cole and Andy Williams.

Currently, they were listening to the Doors' 'Riders on the Storm', which was hugely atmospheric. It transformed a mundane retail-park-garden-centre excursion into a panoramic, canyon-fringed American road trip soundtrack.

By the time they'd reached the motorway, she and Luke were the two romantic leads in a Nora Ephron or Richard Curtis screenplay, driving along a 'dark desert highway' ('Hotel California' by The Eagles, another seventies classic) in a black-beetle Cadillac.

Maybe in the next scene they'd eat marinated ribs with sticky fingers at Chuck's Diner as a blood-red sun sank into scorching prairie sand and salamanders ran across a black and white James Dean and a flame-haired Rita Hayworth Blu-tacked to a bubblegum-pink diner wall. And in the third scene they'd ring the reception bell of a roadside motel with a flickering neon vacancy sign and views of violet mountain peaks and moonlit velvet skies, where a motel manager with rotting teeth and a scratch across his left cheek would reach for a room key.

Jolene's compulsive horror film consumption inevitably seasoned everything with an undercurrent of darkness, even in her imagination, and regardless of setting.

Just as they were about to have their first scripted kiss, Luke slammed on the brakes, and Jolene was no longer on

Route 66, cool wind in her hair, but had been deposited somewhere north of Leicester where Sheila was being sick in her hand. Jolene rushed over and cleaned her up as best she could. She always carried wet wipes and packs of tissues and Polo Mints in her handbag. She liked to be prepared. Something that she'd learned from her mother, who was never without plasters and safety pins and spare buttons for fabric emergencies and minor abrasions (losing a daughter had seemingly turned her into an unhinged Girl Guide).

The look of admiration on Luke's face made Jolene's heart flutter. He seemed captivated by this Jolene, the Jolene who sprang into action without hesitation, the Jolene who knew exactly what to do.

Let's hope that he never gets to see the other Jolene, she thought, the Jolene who shudders when a phone rings, the Jolene who cries when an animal dies on *Animal Hospital*, the Jolene who sometimes tells people that her mother died in a house fire when she was a child. She'd kidnapped Bruno yesterday, threatened to confiscate him if they didn't stop telling him what a good boy he was, and then she'd taken him into the activities room so that she could bury her face in his fur for twenty minutes while he wriggled and squirmed, and forget that her father was emigrating to Canada.

'But you can't,' she'd whined. 'It's too far. Please don't leave me' ('with her' the unspoken end of the sentence). 'You can visit whenever you like,' he'd promised. 'I'll pay for your air ticket. And we can Skype and email. It'll be like I'm still here.' 'Hardly,' she'd sighed. 'You'll be thousands of miles away forgetting that you've got a daughter.' She'd glanced across at Dawn for support, but Dawn had suddenly found something more interesting to look at on the carpet, which was cream and spotless, but which Jolene supposed was a blank canvas upon which anything could be summoned into existence.

'Who'll do my nails?'

She was starting to sound pathetic. Nicholas saved her in the end.

'Come and see my dinosaur, Jo-Jo. It's purple and green.'

She so envied her father. If he wanted to do something, he could just do it. Her mother wasn't his responsibility anymore. He didn't have to endure the silent tears and the frenzied note-taking when she was watching a television documentary about another missing person, searching for tenuous links and similar victim profiles. He didn't have to explain to the police that he wasn't missing, her mother insisting on the completion of yet another missing person report because she'd forgotten where she was.

The police officer whom her mother had been dealing with for the past few months, the latest in a long line of police officers who'd lived their lives and retired in the years that Dolly had been missing, was often on 'annual leave' or 'away from his desk', when her mother called. Dolly wasn't his child. He didn't care in the same way. It wasn't even an active case anymore, but her mother wouldn't let them file Dolly away on a shelf and forget about her.

During the initial stages of the investigation, increasingly disillusioned with the police handling of the case, her mother acquired the services of a private investigator, loaning money from finance companies for the luxury hotel rooms, first-class travel and other extortionate expenses invoiced. The relationship quickly became sexual, according to her grandmother. He was known to prey on vulnerable, distraught mothers of missing children, and sex was often all that they had left to offer.

After everyone had purchased a houseplant from the garden centre – Jolene had asked the garden centre assistant for plant recommendations for the elderly and he'd suggested cacti because they required minimal care, although an African violet and a peace lily had also somehow found their way into the trolley without her noticing – they drove to the Lakeside Country Hotel for lunch. Jolene hadn't visited this hotel before. The one that they usually went to was being refurbished, which was unfortunate because that one had a spa and treatment room that Jolene might have managed to escape to for thirty minutes during dessert. There were only so many varicose vein and liver spot dilemmas that she could tolerate in one sitting.

There were no other diners in the hotel restaurant and it was funereally quiet. When the waitress appeared, Jolene asked her if there was a radio that she could switch on so that it didn't feel as if they were at a wake. Beside her Luke was making coins disappear and doing John Wayne and Michael Caine impressions. Jolene, having discovered a twenty-pound note that she didn't know that she had in her purse, ordered a bottle of wine, which regrettably Luke wouldn't be able to have a glass of because he was driving. She thought that he might have been a little more candid after a glass of red wine.

When the wine arrived, she splashed a little into everyone else's glass while they were deciding between the beef and the pork.

'Cheers, everyone,' she toasted.

They all raised their glasses.

'I've really enjoyed today,' Marilyn Andrews said. 'Thank you, Jolene.'

Jolene felt like she'd won a BAFTA (or whatever the care home equivalent of an outstanding achievement award was), two BAFTAs in fact (Best Daytrip and Best Care Worker) when Luke leaned across and asked her if she'd like to go for a drink on Saturday.

And for a brief moment, Canada and her mother blurred into soft focus, as distant as a harvest moon.

Chapter Nine

BLUE JASPER

Although Gilbert's comments were now gathering momentum, and Will had already filled the first three pages of his notebook, the untangling and assembling of those comments into some kind of chronological order was not. They certainly didn't follow the normal narrative of a confession – the Who, the How and the Why? They were far more ambiguous. 'She never saw me coming' (*Who* never saw you coming?), 'It was easier then' (*What* was easier then?), 'Girls hitchhiked all the time' (*And*?).

And now another potential victim had been introduced – Joanne – but Will had no idea if she was before or after Naomi. Or entirely unrelated. He'd tirelessly persevere, hoping to extract a surname, a year, a location, perhaps even a season – was he wearing a coat? – but then Gilbert would fall silent, exhausted, as if that was all that he could remember or they were the only lines that he'd learned. Maybe in a few months' time Will would have a piecemeal account of these things, maybe even a theory. He might even be in possession of a confirmed sequence of events along with a signed confession.

Or he'd have a notebook of random ramblings and little else.

And he might not have the luxury of a few months. Gilbert could die imminently, taking his secrets with him. Certainly, his memory would deteriorate further over time.

Keen to learn more about him, Will had asked Evelyn, the part-time finance and administration assistant, if he could access Gilbert's personal details. Evelyn was sixty-four, but looked much older. She was often mistaken for a resident by visitors and asked if she needed assistance. And the closer she edged towards retirement the less conscientious she became, never questioning a request, no matter how unusual that request might be. If you needed petty cash for an undisclosed purpose she simply handed you the cashbox key. She wasn't interested in specifics.

There was no mention of a Naomi *or* a Joanne on Gilbert's admittance and assessment forms, no social worker who'd interviewed him, no doctor he'd seen. No relative or friend. His wife's name was Ruth, no middle name, and she was deceased. Will copied down Gilbert's last known address, his date of birth and his employment history – he'd had a range of jobs, including warehouse operative, delivery driver and hospital porter – and then he'd returned the file to the cabinet, leaving Evelyn furiously jabbing at the buttons on a calculator. On his way home he'd drive past the address that he'd noted down, see how large the garden was, establish its potential as a possible burial site.

On his afternoon break he sat in the car with a Twix and a

packet of cheese and onion crisps and conducted some preliminary online research on his phone, but he could find no missing Naomis, although the disappearance might have occurred decades earlier and not been widely reported, if it had indeed happened. He'd need to consult archived material held at the public library. There were, however, several Joannes who'd been reported missing. His initial search located five, one of them having disappeared in January and potentially unconnected. Gilbert had been a resident at Sunset House for nearly two years and Will didn't think that he'd be physically capable of abducting or killing someone without assistance.

He circled his son Martin's name in his notebook with an additional reminder to cross-reference the date of the January disappearance with the visitors' book to check if Gilbert was absent from the home that day.

He then searched for information on Ruth Williams, Gilbert's wife. Maybe she'd provide an alternative pathway into his life.

While he was waiting for the web pages to load, wishing that he had an identifiable middle name to narrow down his searches, he noticed Jolene talking to Luke Trent. Her cheeks were flushed and she was smiling. Jolene rarely smiled, but when she did, she looked like a completely different person, an approachable person. Luke's headphones were draped around his neck. He often wore headphones, his head nodding to an inaudible rhythm, the headphone wires flapping like bird's wings against his chest. Thrash metal guitar riffs and indie drumbeats, Will imagined, something loud that affected his hearing (interest). He certainly knew how to wash a vehicle though. The minibus gleamed like blue jasper when he'd finished.

Will remembered the white earbuds in Angelina's ears, the music that he'd never heard and would now never hear, until his phone alarm beeped, signalling the end of his break. He cast a quick glance at the Google search results.

Gilbert's wife had apparently committed suicide when she was forty-three. According to a newspaper article she'd been found hanging from an oak tree in nearby woodland by a dog walker. Will wondered how strong or athletic a woman would need to be to hang herself from an oak tree. She'd have had to climb the tree, securely knot the ligature and then tighten it firmly around her neck. It seemed a strenuous enough task for a man. But a woman? Unless she'd been a body builder or a rock climber it didn't seem plausible. Someone else must have been involved. He circled Gilbert's name, and then, a few seconds later, he circled his son's name again.

When he closed his notebook, Jolene was laughing. Will had never heard her laugh before and wondered what her laugh sounded like. Was it high-pitched, sarcastic, infectious, or was it deeper, quieter, more forced? Sides to Jolene that he'd never witnessed before seemed to be emerging in Luke's presence. He hoped that Luke wasn't like the men whom Sophie slept with, who after making you laugh then made you cry when they never called again.

Five hours later Will was parked outside the address that he'd written down. He'd been unable to verify who currently owned the property, so was going to have to do it the old-fashioned way, by waiting for the owner to emerge. And if that didn't work he'd canvas the neighbourhood or consult the electoral register when he had more time.

The semi-detached house was what an author might call 'rambling', a child 'spooky' and an estate agent 'a renovation project'. The wooden shutters framing the windows were warped and weatherworn and twisting vines of ivy spiralled around the brickwork like gluttonous green flames. The house was on a corner plot, a neglected, crescent-shaped garden arcing around it like an open bracket. Behind the property was the wood where Ruth Williams had allegedly hung herself, casting its long shadow. The house was in darkness. There didn't appear to be anyone home.

Sophie texted him while he was watching the house. *I'm meeting someone who I've been chatting with online in three hours and I haven't straightened my hair yet*, she told him. *Surely it doesn't take three hours to straighten your hair*, Will texted back. *Of course not, but I haven't put on a face mask, whitened my teeth or decided what to wear yet either. What should I wear?* Will wasn't someone you solicited for fashion advice. His off-duty uniform was jeans and a T-shirt. She was obviously panicking. And what did it matter what she wore? She'd be devastated in a few days when they never contacted her again.

Where are you meeting? The Skylark. The Lost and Found are playing. It'll be packed. Will wondered if Jolene would be there. *Do you want me to pick you up afterwards? No, I'll be fine. Stop worrying. Be careful*, he warned her, sounding like the father that she didn't have. *Always am. Always not. And don't steal anything. I told you, my stealing days are over, unless it's someone's heart.*

He replied with a Face Vomiting Emoji.

Placing his phone on the passenger seat of the car Will checked the glove box for something to eat, annoyed that he hadn't remembered to purchase snacks, a necessity when on a surveillance mission. Mercifully, a Terry's chocolate orange glistened back at him in its orange foil. He smashed it against the dashboard and, carefully unpeeling it, began to separate the segments, treating it as if it was one of his five a day. Or was it ten a day now? He'd barely swallowed four segments when there was a firm tap on the driver's window. He was so startled that the remaining segments flew from his hands and scattered like crows in a cornfield as his head hit the roof of the car.

Martin Williams was motioning for him to wind the window down. It was like a menacing game of charades. Will really didn't want to wind the window down, but compromised by winding it down by approximately a fifth, hopefully not enough to accommodate a fist.

'If I didn't know better, I'd think that you were following me,' Martin Williams said, not entirely pleasantly.

If only you knew, Will thought, although he hadn't officially started following him yet. It was purely coincidental that Martin Williams happened to be there, frowning at him through his car window. Will hadn't considered the possibility that one of Gilbert's children might now be living in the house.

'I'm waiting for someone,' Will replied, hoping that he wouldn't be asked who he was waiting for and where they lived.

'Dad says you like asking questions.'

Just then, Will's phone beeped.

The second time that he'd been rescued this week. It must have been some sort of record.

It was Sophie.

'It looks like my passenger awaits.'

Martin Williams reluctantly stepped away from the car.

Will closed the car window and started the engine, his chocolate-smeared trembling palms sliding around the steering wheel as if it was made of banana skins. He didn't have time to retrieve the errant chocolate orange segments. When he glanced in the rear-view mirror Martin Williams was squinting at him like Clint Eastwood in *Dirty Harry*.

As soon as he was a safe distance away Will parked in a side street, threw his head back onto the head rest and exhaled loudly.

Martin Williams had scared him and he wasn't sure if it had been intentional.

Chapter Ten

THE DOLLY YEARS

It was Saturday afternoon and Jolene still hadn't told her mother that she was meeting Luke later. Each time she tried to tell her she just couldn't seem to find the right tone, the right words, didn't want to be inundated with questions – an actual typed list of Twenty Questions: emergency contact details, intended destination, estimated time of arrival and departure, mode of transport, etc., that required accurate and comprehensive answers. If her mother could have stitched a tracker into her clothing without her knowledge then she would have.

Only last week she'd asked Jolene to share her location on her phone so that she could trace her whereabouts on Google Maps. 'Everyone's doing it.' 'Everyone isn't doing it,' Jolene had snapped. She wasn't a recently paroled prisoner or a six-year-old child. It was an infringement of her civil liberties, she'd told her mother, and she'd be obtaining legal advice if this continued. She needed to live her life. She needed to be able to meet people for a drink once in a while.

Jolene peeled back the layers of her vegetable lasagne with a fork, searching for a sliver of resolve among the peppers and courgettes.

'I've made your favourite,' her mother had informed her earlier, when she was texting Luke to confirm when and where they were meeting so that she'd at least be able to answer the first two questions – nine p.m., Wetherspoons.

It wasn't Jolene's favourite – the lasagne, not the Wetherspoons. It was Dolly's. So often, Jolene wanted to scream that she wasn't Dolly. She was Jolene. Jolene! It was a miracle that she had any sense of self at all. It didn't help that the inspiration for their names had originated from the same person but, as currently only one of them was actually in situ, there really was no excuse. Her mother even called her Dolly sometimes and she never apologised. She might as well have been christened Dolly, too. Or, perhaps more accurately, Dolly2.

At Sunset House's compulsory dementia training last month, the trainer had reminded them never to correct what a person with dementia was saying. Agree with them, let them believe that what they're saying is true. You're there to listen, to make them feel safe wherever they are, wherever their memories have taken them. Don't tell them that someone's dead if they don't know that they're dead. They're then experiencing a traumatic event twice. And that's how she treated her mother. She rarely corrected her or disagreed with her, never told her that Dolly was almost certainly dead or that her name was Jolene, not Dolly, but under no circumstances would she agree to an electronic tag or a phone tracker.

She wondered if it would be a blessing if her mother were

to suffer early-onset dementia so that the Dolly years could be erased. But she suspected that it didn't work like that. You couldn't pick and choose what you wanted to forget.

She took a deep breath.

'I'm going out later with someone from work.'

Her mother went very still. She didn't appear to be breathing.

'Anyone I know?' she eventually asked.

The question was brimming with underlying tension.

There was no point lying.

'His name's Luke. He works at the care home.'

'Where are you meeting him?'

'Outside Wetherspoons at nine. I'll text you when I arrive and again when I'm leaving. There's no need to worry. He's perfectly normal and I'm always sensible.'

Jolene had no idea if Luke was perfectly normal, she barely knew him, and as for always being sensible, there were countless times when she hadn't been – when she'd let strangers buy her drinks, when she'd taken shortcuts home.

A taut silence stretched between them. Why did her mother always have to make her feel so guilty and ashamed? It was like being summoned into Janette's office.

'I'll get the list.'

'I'm not working tomorrow. Maybe we could visit that National Trust property that you like, the one with the boating lake and the farm shop that sells homemade lemon curd.'

If her mother had something to look forward to it calmed her a little and Jolene was hardly going to disappear if they were planning to walk around the Japanese gardens on Sunday, maybe follow the sculpture trail up to the viewpoint (that was the hope anyway). Jolene was highly unusual among her friends in that she preferred hiking to shopping. In her imagination she was often scaling Welsh mountains in Regatta waterproofs and Berghaus walking boots, free to go wherever she pleased with no human interaction whatsoever.

The Twenty Questions answered in some shape or form, Jolene went upstairs to change. When she came back down her mother was sitting at the dining table sifting through jigsaw pieces. Her bottom lip was bleeding where she'd bitten it and Rome lay in ruins beneath her.

Jolene had decided to drive instead of booking a taxi – she was only planning to have a couple of J2Os – but there were no free parking spaces in the town centre car park so she had to drive to the multistorey car park, a fifteen-minute walk away, instead. She'd have to omit that revised update when she gave her mother a summary of the evening's events later. Her mother didn't like her parking in the multistorey car park at night.

Fifty-five minutes later Luke still hadn't arrived. She'd spent the first fifteen minutes shivering outside in the cold, the following thirty minutes huddled in the doorway along with the smokers – Glen Taylor had strolled past twice, his hands in his pockets, his glasses slipping down his nose – and the remaining ten minutes locked inside a toilet cubicle listening to teenage girls vomiting. She'd repeatedly checked her phone for messages and missed calls, texted Luke twice but received no reply and, unwilling to wait any longer, she'd texted her mother to tell her that she was leaving.

Was there another Wetherspoons that she was unaware of? Had he never intended to turn up? She was furious. It had all been for nothing. She couldn't even find room in her heart for the possibility that he might have had an accident, that it might not have even been his fault.

The town hall clock struck ten as she was crossing the square. The dimly lit multistorey car park loomed ahead of her and the expanse of wasteland to the right of her murmured and whispered. She thought that she saw a flash of something in the darkness. A fox? An owl? Her eyes playing tricks on her? An ideal place to bury a body, she remembered thinking, a ghostland, like the corridors of Sunset House. And then it suddenly became eerily quiet. Her footsteps echoed on the pavement.

She recalled a police visit on personal safety at college – *don't walk in secluded areas alone, always be aware of your surroundings, improvise, house keys, body spray, a stiletto heel, aim for the eyes, the windpipe, the genitals and always carry a personal alarm.*

Often, all Jolene had was an Adidas trainer and her car key.

She now wished that she'd attended the self-defence class that Laura had recommended. But she didn't want to have her mother's fears confirmed. She didn't want to live in a world where you needed self-defence skills, where you could be abducted and killed while running errands, while out jogging. That was her mother's world. A world where predators frequented every street corner and good things never happened.

Hearing a second set of footsteps behind her she quickened her pace, glancing briefly over her shoulder, but there was no one there. One of the streetlights wasn't working and she was momentarily thrust into a blacker black, a liquorice sea of nothing and everything all at once. Was it Will? She'd seen him following people. Or maybe it was Glen Taylor. He walked so much that he was bound to be behind you at some point. Perhaps it was Luke. The thought that it might have been Luke made her shudder. An icy chill ran down her spine.

When she reached the car park entrance the security booth was empty. She quickly paid the parking fee at the ticket machine and then sprinted up the stairs. She didn't want someone slipping into the lift behind her. On the third level stairwell she heard the footsteps again, slow and measured. Her heart was pounding. When she opened the door she was relieved to see her car parked exactly where she'd left it, opposite a red Opel Corsa. She pulled her keys out of her handbag and then, parodying all clichéd horror movies, she dropped both her weapon and her means of escape in her rush to reach the car. The footsteps were getting closer. Stay calm, she told herself. There's no one following you. This isn't a film.

A car door slammed shut, startling her, and, disregarding her own advice, she frantically scooped up the keys and ran towards the car, checking that there was no one on the backseat before she climbed in. She was shaking. Her mother's constant paranoia didn't help – all those warnings and forebodings dripping into her ears like evangelical propaganda, Chinese water torture. They were bound to affect her negatively at some point. Hopefully, there wouldn't be anyone lying in the road on the journey home, feigning an injury to entice her out of the car, another dreadful horror movie cliché. Everyone, it seemed, was conspiring against her, determined to ruin her horror film viewing by blurring the distinction between fantasy and reality.

'You're home early,' her mother remarked when she walked into the living room.

'I felt like an early night.'

'Did you have a nice time?'

Apart from Luke not turning up and thinking that there was a multistorey car park serial killer chasing her?

She shrugged. She didn't want to confess that he'd never arrived. Her mother would demand to speak to 'this Luke character' herself, which would be far more mortifying.

Fortunately, her mother didn't press the matter. She was watching *Ozark*. Jolene wished that she'd watch sitcoms or romantic comedies instead of crime dramas, unless being absorbed in other people's traumas, whether fictional or not, made her feel less alone. She'd been in regular contact with another couple whose daughter had also disappeared in mysterious circumstances, but they'd lost touch a few years ago. Jolene couldn't remember their names.

While she was composing a text to Laura, her phone rang. It was Laura's landline, but it wasn't Laura calling. It was Laura's mother.

'Hi, Mrs Sykes.'

'I don't suppose Laura's with you?'

'She isn't, no. Is everything okay?'

'She never came home from work this afternoon and no one seems to have seen her. It isn't like her. She usually lets me know if she's going to be late or she's staying with a friend. If she contacts you, will you please call me?'

'Of course, Mrs Sykes.'

When she glanced up, her mother was staring at her blankly. Jolene recalled Cora staring blankly through the lounge window at a world that she was no longer part of, Gilbert's venomous eyes searing into her.

'It's Laura. She hasn't come home.'

Her mother's gaze returned to the television.

'It's happening again,' she told Jason Bateman. 'Don't say I didn't warn you. Another girl disappearing who'll never be found.'

Surely this wasn't like that, Jolene thought. The start of another family's nightmare. There must be a simple explanation. Laura wouldn't just disappear.

The Second Girl

Rose

I'd been watching her watching me for a while before she finally approached me. It was raining and I was sheltering beneath the canal bridge. 'My name's Rose, Rose Wray' she said, holding out her hand. 'Do you mind if I sit here?' I didn't shake her hand but I nodded. I only liked touching skin that was lifeless. She sat down next to me on the towpath, black ankle boots but no tights, her legs crossed in front of her like chopsticks. I asked her if she was cold and she shook her head. She was wearing a pea-green duffel coat with black toggles, as easy to see as a lime. She asked me about the fish in the canal. The canal was like tar, a black bean oil slick snaking its way towards the estuary. I doubted whether anything could live in it, although it was surprising how many things thrived in the darkest of places.

She sat fiddling with the toggles on her duffel coat, rolling a chess piece between her fingers that she'd pulled from one of the pockets.

I asked her if she played chess. She said that she only had the one piece, a rook, so no. You didn't tell me your name, she reminded me. I told her that I didn't have a name. Everyone has a name, she replied. She thought for a moment and then she said, 'I know, I'll call you The Thin Man,' which I quite liked. It meant that I could be fleshed out by others. I could drape their skin around me like a new winter coat.

Whenever I saw her she was always alone. Sometimes I wondered if I'd invented her. I'd never had an imaginary friend before and my internal dialogue was becoming somewhat predictable. I discovered that she wasn't imaginary when Geordie Janice accused her of stealing dog food. Sherlock, her Jack Russell, had died months earlier, but she still kept cans of dog food inside her sleeping bag, seemed to think that he was coming back, even though we'd all watched her bury him in a forgotten corner of the churchyard.

After that we mostly met in Clover Wood, where it was always dark, even in summer, a canopy of trees so tall that they hid the sky and so wide that they turned day into night, creating their own timelines. They were like soldiers marching by our side, marching to a beat that only they could hear, morning and night. I like to think that Rose Wray loved the darkness as much as I did.

During our brief time together I taught her how to build a shelter from leaves and twigs and how to make a fire. I thought that I was teaching her resilience and resourcefulness, providing her with valuable survival skills, but really I was just fattening her up before I killed her, although I didn't realise that then. Contrary to what you may think, I didn't always know that I was going to kill someone. Sometimes even I didn't know how it would end.

What I did know, however, was that whenever I looked at her I saw my younger self staring back at me. She reminded me of loneliness and neglect. And I wasn't that person anymore. I'd been reborn for what felt like the thousandth time, peeling away the flesh from my bones until every memory was erased. Like Owen, who could have been several oceans away or still languishing in the place where he'd been born, the place where he'd been stolen, carried out of our lives like a parcel.

Sadly, the novelty of being somebody else quickly fades. I suppose it's like being a character in a play – twelve months of touring and you're desperate to wear your own clothes again. Currently, I was 'between lives', modelling outfits and highlighting my hair in petrol station toilets, wondering if the real 'me' might step forward if I removed enough layers. He never did, thankfully. He was too deeply buried, too far away to see with the naked eye.

I then began to wonder what it would be like to build a person from scratch instead of wearing someone else's skin – to invent an entirely new person to walk the earth, especially as I'd recently learned that there was a tall man asking about a mother and her son – Derek, I assumed. A father will search the ends of the earth for his missing daughter, I've since discovered.

The winter snowfall was heavy that year, the year that Rose Wray died. Our feet sank into the snow as we climbed the incline that led to the lumberjack's hut on the eastern side of Clover Wood, the trees ghostly versions of themselves, a skeleton army. Rose Wray had given me a Christmas present, a colourful scarf that she'd knitted that I'd promised always to wear. I gave her two chess pieces that I'd carved out of wood, a king and a queen. She now had three chess pieces. It was unlikely that she'd get to hold any more.

Normally, the wood was dark and silent, but that day a tangerine sun reflected orange pools of light onto the falling snow *and red-breasted robins shook frost from tree branches fringed with icicles chiselled like daggers.*

Later, I imagined Rose Wray beneath the snow, in the spot where I'd left her, her face gradually reappearing like a winter sunrise as the snow slowly melted.

Chapter Eleven

WANTED, DEAD OR ALIVE

DS Cathy Daniels was sitting in the passenger seat of the police car humming. It was intensely irritating. Rex didn't even like the radio on in the car, but Cathy insisted on humming and singing her way through the entire day, songs from musicals mostly, *The Book of Mormon*, *Hairspray*, *Elaine Paige on Sunday*.

Rex knew far more than he needed to know about musical theatre. Yesterday, she'd been listening to a West End playlist at her desk when she should have been typing up witness statements and he'd had to remind her not to play music in the office. It distracted the other officers. Colin Kent had cried, 'Thank God!' He was going to shoot himself if he had to hear *Mamma Mia* one more time. Dale Allen had asked her to play it again.

'We saw *Hamilton* last weekend, sir,' she told Rex, as they were driving along the dual carriageway. 'It was amazing. Even Matt enjoyed it and he hates musicals. Says it's weird when actors suddenly burst into song. I've seen *Wicked* seventeen times, although once was one time too many, according to Matt. But they're so uplifting, don't you think?'

'What's *Hamilton*?'

As soon as he'd asked the question Rex realised that he wasn't particularly interested in the answer, but by then of course it was too late. A detailed account of the plot swiftly followed. Couldn't he have just nodded, changed the subject, let her switch the radio on? They arrived at the Sykes home just as Hamilton was embarking on an affair with Maria Reynolds at the beginning of Act II.

'I'll tell you the rest on the way back to the station, sir. I promise not to sing *all* the songs.'

Rex didn't want to hear *any* of the songs.

The crunch of white gravel on the Sykeses' driveway announced their arrival. He'd need to polish his shoes before he climbed back into the car. They were now covered in a chalky residue.

'So many homeowners replace their gardens with gravel driveways nowadays,' Cathy observed. 'We like our cars far more than we like watering plants or mowing grass. The gravel industry must be raking it in.'

How long had she been waiting to say that, Rex wondered?

'Very good,' he replied, as if he was marking a geography test paper.

He rang the doorbell, a cheerful jingle at odds with the sombre occasion. The woman who opened the door introduced herself as Miranda Sykes, Laura's mother, and invited them inside.

As a DI, Rex wouldn't normally attend a home interview, but his office was starting to feel like an extremely tight shirt collar, although he'd prefer that they'd been called to a burglary or a brawl rather than to the home of a missing person, a crime that could be swiftly resolved with a caution and a night in a police cell.

Miranda's mother, Gloria, was sitting on the sofa dabbing at her eyes with a tissue and greeted them with a barely audible whimper. Miranda's husband, James, was apparently in Geneva at a global business and economics conference and she hadn't yet been able to reach him. Rex took a seat, while Cathy hovered by the bay window. She preferred to stand. Rex wasn't sure whether it was meant to be authoritative, a show of subordination or whether it gave her a better vantage point when surveying her surroundings.

She was especially interested in the psychological aspects of a crime, regularly requesting permission to attend profiling seminars and criminology courses. She was currently studying the photographs on the mantelpiece, searching for the hairline cracks that you had to look closely at to prise open. Ornaments obscured every surface, a family of wooden giraffes, a trinket dish shaped like a seashell, a glass angel, a bronze hare... Rex contemplated the amount of dusting entailed, the Mr Sheen. Dust collectors, his mother used to call them, clutter.

Families often found these preliminary fact-finding missions exasperating. They wanted you out there, searching, not sipping tea on their sofa, repeating the same unanswerable questions over and over again. They didn't realise that the wheels of law enforcement were already turning, although in Laura's case those wheels wouldn't be turning quite as industriously as Miranda Sykes might have hoped without evidence of a crime being committed or Laura being categorised as high risk.

An adult could come and go as they pleased. If they wanted to walk away without saying goodbye then they could.

Rex remembered his mother buttering toast as if it was another ordinary day, but then a seemingly ordinary day became 'The last time that he ever saw his mother'. And he didn't care that she was an adult and that it might have been her decision to leave. He wanted to know where she was, how she was. He wanted the police to search for her like they would a minor or a vulnerable person. She was similarly loved and missed and he had no idea whether she was dead or alive. He thought of those posters nailed to fence posts in Westerns. Wanted, Dead or Alive. He of course hoped that she was the latter.

Miranda Sykes was trying not to cry, her sea-glass green eyes glacial and still, her pale skin the colour of milk. It was as if a pin was the only thing holding her steady. Rex knew all about pins: the office stationery that kept the case files on his desk and the photographs on his office walls in place, kept the faces that stared back at him safe, kept them alive.

He wondered how Miranda Sykes would fare in front of a camera. Those closest to the victim weren't always their greatest allies. He remembered Carla Salmon. She'd looked like she'd been up all night, but not because her son was missing. It was more of a 'falling in from a night out' kind of tired. She was wearing a red leather miniskirt, black fishnet tights with additional holes and a see-through pale blue blouse. The parting in her bleached hair was black and her lips were red, a different shade of red to the miniskirt and a different shade of red to the varnish on her chipped fingernails. There'd been too much red. And it had looked too much like blood.

She'd been chewing one of her chipped nails, which had highlighted the cold sore on her top lip and the frosting of cocaine around her nostrils. She hadn't looked like someone's mother. She hadn't acted like someone's mother. Rather than upset, she'd seemed irritated. Rather than frantic, she'd seemed impatient, as if there were a million and one other things she'd rather be doing. She'd fanned the inferno instead of abating it. The media and the public had sharpened their talons. Did she have something to do with her son's disappearance? Why wasn't she crying? Surely she should be crying. I don't like the way she's looking at the camera, the way she's not looking at the camera. First impressions mattered. People liked to see a tearful mother. And Carla Salmon wasn't a tearful mother. Even psychologists, who insisted that trauma affects people differently, couldn't repair the damage. Her son was never found and fourteen years later she's still considered the prime suspect.

Towards the end of a police visit Cathy would orchestrate an 'intermission', while Rex continued to gather 'intel' (Cathy's choice of words), which generally consisted of a request to use the toilet, primarily to determine the layout of the bedrooms and inspect the contents of the bathroom cabinet, or five minutes' fresh air, when she'd scan the back garden for evidence of soil disturbances, recent landscaping, patio repaving or new decking. A bathroom cabinet can reveal a surprising amount about a person, she'd tell him.

When Cathy came back downstairs Rex asked Miranda Sykes if they could see Laura's room, aware that Cathy would have already taken a cursory look. Clothes lay crumpled in unrecognisable shapes on the carpet, shed like the skin of a snake, slipped into and stepped out of. Magazines were strewn around the room as if they'd been used as Frisbees or thrown in a rage. Open bottles of nail polish sat solidifying on an IKEA desk, a glittery peach satin bubble glistening like a coloured contact lens.

When Rex glanced at Miranda Sykes she seemed embarrassed, as if she'd had no idea how untidy Laura's room was. Rex checked the desk drawers while Cathy searched the wardrobe but, apart from a laptop lying on a nest of bras coiled like vipers beneath the bed, there appeared to be nothing else of evidentiary value.

'Is it okay if we take the laptop?' Rex asked.

Miranda Sykes nodded.

'We've asked Laura's phone provider for permission to access her phone records and they're triangulating data for a possible location. Did Laura have a boyfriend?'

'I'm sorry, I don't know. You could ask, Jolene. Jolene Edwards. They've known each other since primary school.'

'We'll need Jolene's address and telephone number and if we could also have Laura's toothbrush.'

'Her toothbrush?'

'For DNA purposes.'

Rex didn't elaborate. He didn't want to be drawn into offering assurances that it was purely routine and making promises that he couldn't keep, so he drew the conversation to a close.

'I think that's everything for now, Mrs Sykes. A family liaison officer will be in touch with you shortly and a team of officers will be back to conduct a more thorough search of Laura's bedroom, but don't hesitate to contact us if you think of anything else.'

He left his contact details and a receipt for the laptop and toothbrush.

After dropping Cathy back at the station to complete the paperwork, Rex made his way to the hospital. He'd hoped to escape the conclusion of *Hamilton*, but once Cathy had articulated her thoughts on what might have happened to Laura Sykes and what she'd gleaned from the home (a dichotomy of personalities culminating in a variety of dissociative disorders – he suspected that she'd been reading too many profiling blogs – her mother takes diet pills, her father erectile dysfunction medication. I suspect Laura just needs some space), she resumed her detailed synopsis. Every traffic light had been on red and on every street corner he saw Laura Sykes walking away from him linking his mother's arm.

When he arrived at the hospital, his wife, Denise, was sitting in a high-backed chair reading a magazine.

Rex watched her for a moment, committing the image to memory, and then he walked over and kissed her on the cheek.

'To what do I owe the pleasure?' she asked him, smiling.

She wasn't expecting him for another four hours.

'Andrew Lloyd Webber.'

The person who'd popularised musical theatre.

'Andrew Lloyd Webber?'

'Just Cathy being Cathy,' he clarified, which he realised didn't clarify anything at all.

'Who else should she be?'

Rex was reminded how empty the house felt without

Denise. It was like a seashell with nothing but the rush of the sea swirling through it. When he'd told Denise this a few weeks ago, not that he was living inside a seashell, but that the house felt so empty without her, she'd pointed out that he was rarely there, so how would he know? But he knew. Every time he unlocked the front door and switched on the hall light, no matter how late it was, no matter how infrequently he was there, the emptiness was like a screaming mouth that might devour him if he stepped inside.

Denise winced.

'Shall I get a nurse?'

'No, it'll pass.'

One day it wouldn't pass. One day it would stop completely.

'What case are you working on at the moment?'

Denise had been a DC so she took more than a passing interest in his cases. And even though he didn't tell her everything, particularly if it involved a gruesome death, he told her far more than he should have. But they both considered it a necessary distraction. It diverted focus from the gunman planning to execute *her* – a different type of assassin – your own body turning against you. A routine smear test that had not proved so routine after all, his wife now diagnosed with terminal cancer.

He briefly mentioned Laura Sykes and then they sat reminiscing – the present was just too painful – the U2 concert where they'd been so close to the stage that they'd almost touched Bono's left leg and a holiday in Santorini where a guest at the taverna where they were staying had been convinced that he recognised them and became extremely argumentative when they'd insisted that they weren't Sian and Peter Woodcock from Dagenham, the production of their passports failing to appease him. He'd ultimately concluded that they were in a witness protection programme and, winking conspiratorially, assured them that their secret was safe with him.

After an hour of reminiscing Rex reluctantly kissed his wife goodbye. He needed to get back to the station. They'd be wondering where he was.

But not before he'd locked himself inside one of the toilet cubicles in the hospital foyer and let the tears that had threatened to fall in front of Denise fall in private.

He was in desperate need of a pin of his own.

Chapter Twelve
MY HAPPINESS DEPENDS ON YOU

Laura was still missing the following morning.

Jolene had barely slept. After learning that Laura hadn't come home, Jolene's first instinct had been to help search for her – driving aimlessly around town was surely more constructive than doing nothing – but Jolene's mother had insisted that the police knew what they were doing, which of course she didn't believe at all. She'd spent years telling people the police couldn't find a missing person if the missing person walked into the police station and told them they were missing.

So instead Jolene had spent the night texting Laura's mother until she realised that every time Laura's mother's phone pinged with a new message she must have thought that it was Laura and then been deeply disappointed to discover that it was just Jolene asking if there was any news. Just Jolene. She'd been Just Jolene more times than she cared to remember – *'Is it Dolly?'*, *'No, it's Just Jolene'*.

The moon had glistened like a coin in her bedroom window

and she'd wondered if Laura could see it too, if she was looking at it at that very moment. She'd hoped so. She'd hoped that wherever she was she could at least see the moon. But there'd been a tight knot in her stomach that suggested otherwise, a knot woven from omens and prophecies and her mother's fateful warnings.

She'd always refused to acknowledge how devastating it must have been for her mother to watch Dolly leave the house and never return. Not to know where she was or what had happened to her, the blade of a guillotine unexpectedly slicing their lives in two. She'd been too concerned with how Dolly disappearing had affected her own life, how she'd been the one made to suffer. Dolly not being there had meant that her mother hadn't been there either and that was the part Jolene had had to wrestle with the most, empty spaces where the people she loved should have been standing. The different ways you could fall.

She didn't want to make allowances for the way her mother had behaved since Dolly's disappearance, excuse her actions, absolve her, forgive her for suffocating her and scarring her, for turning every stranger into a predator and making her small life even smaller. But the knot inside her stomach was growing and the wave of empathy she was feeling for her mother was building.

Laura was on the morning news. She'll hate that photograph, Jolene thought, but she supposed there hadn't been time to flick through photo albums and scroll through Laura's social media accounts looking for the most flattering photograph. It was so poorly cropped that the elbow of the man standing next to her was still visible. It wasn't even a photograph of her. She was a guest at another person's wedding, a narrow sliver of a much larger picture.

Jolene turned to her mother.

'We'll visit the Japanese gardens another time,' she told her.

Her mother's thoughts didn't follow those of normal people.

'I'm going to spend the morning looking for Laura. And then I'll join the search party that Laura's mother has organised for later today. They're meeting outside the town hall at four.'

Surprisingly, her mother didn't offer her services. She was usually the first person reaching for her coat in the hope that searching for another missing person might somehow lead her to Dolly. She didn't try to dissuade Jolene either and she was always the voice of caution, reminding you of the possible pitfalls ahead, as if disappearing was as prevalent as pulling on socks. She seemed different today, happier almost. No, not happier, that wasn't the right word. She couldn't be happier if she'd never been happy. It would have purely been guesswork had Jolene thought her capable of an emotion such as happiness. But it was as if someone else disappearing had made her own life fractionally more tolerable, reminded her that she wasn't so special after all. These things happened to other people too.

'A police officer called earlier, asking to speak to you. The number's on the coffee table.'

Jolene took the piece of paper into the back garden and returned the call. A speckled bird sat watching her, as she was placed on hold, its eyes like raisins. DI Spencer and his colleague DS Daniels would be with her shortly. They wanted to speak to her about Laura. Jolene would have preferred not to speak to them in front of her mother, who was always so critical of police officers, and would inevitably bring the conversation back to Dolly when today was about Laura, not Dolly. But it was less formal than a police station, she supposed.

She wondered whether to call Laura's mother. There might have been a development since she last spoke to her – perhaps the news bulletin had reminded someone of something – but she'd immediately think Jolene had spoken to Laura when she hadn't, her hopes rising and falling within the space of a breath.

A solitary daffodil swayed back and forth in the breeze; a symbol of hope among a forest of weeds, a yellow starfish on a pebble beach. Her mother did barely any gardening, but flowers continued to bloom year after year, new life emerged, undeterred. Some things you just couldn't kill no matter how badly you neglected them, while other things were as easy to slice through as butter.

When she told her mother the police wanted to speak to her about Laura and that they'd be arriving soon, she expected her to rush upstairs to retrieve Dolly's scrapbook and, while one of the police officers was politely turning the pages, she could remind them that Dolly was still missing and that the same person could be responsible and shouldn't they reopen her case. That's what the look had been earlier, Jolene realised. A kernel of hope, a seed sown. It was expectation and anticipation. It was the prospect of Dolly being unearthed again, her twenty-year-old smile in the spotlight once more. When a person disappeared, previous investigations were re-examined, connections explored, the presumed dead were brought back to life.

But she didn't collect Dolly. Instead, she offered to make tea.

While the older male officer, DI Spencer, took a seat, the younger female officer, DS Daniels, remained standing, her eyes combing the room, presumably in search of something that might be construed as incriminating or suspicious, her trained eye spinning everyday possessions into secrets and lies.

Jolene wondered whether she should be wearing her expressionless face or the face she used in interviews. She'd recently come to realise that she could produce several different faces and none of them were hers. She didn't want to appear unconcerned because she wasn't. She was distraught. Laura was her friend. But she didn't want to cry either in case they questioned the authenticity of her tears. She supposed the police always had that effect on people, made you doubt your emotions, made you feel guilty when you'd done nothing wrong, assumed you were hiding something when you'd told them everything. She did wish her T-shirt hadn't got a toothpaste stain down the front of it though and that her jeans weren't ripped. Although appearances didn't matter to her, they mattered to other people.

Her mother returned carrying a silver tray. The gold leaf Coronation tea set that had belonged to Jolene's grandmother and that her mother usually only allowed visiting vicars and journalists to drink from rattled like loose teeth as she walked. DS Daniels didn't want anything to drink, but DI Spencer nodded. He was gazing at the photograph of Dolly on the mantelpiece, Dolly smiling warmly back at him. No doubt he knew all about the Edwards family. Everyone knew her mother or knew of her. While Jolene preferred anonymity, her mother basked most brightly in the glow of an audience.

After pouring DI Spencer's tea her mother sat at the dining table, pretending to sift through jigsaw pieces. Rome, Jolene noticed, still hadn't been built, didn't look like it was ever going to be built. Asked when she'd last seen Laura, Jolene admitted they hadn't seen each other in a while due to work commitments, so they normally communicated by text or Facebook. Didn't everyone? DI Spencer asked her where she worked, nodding thoughtfully when she told him.

DS Daniels was studying her closely. She reminded Jolene of the stone statues of Admirals and Dukes in the park that she could see from her father's kitchen window. Sensing Jolene's gaze, DS Daniels glanced at her watch and asked if she could use the toilet. Jolene suspected she just wanted to take a look upstairs. Not that she'd find anything incriminating or revelatory. There were very few personal items in Jolene's room (a North Face backpack containing her passport and five hundred pounds in cash all that she'd rescue in a fire) and the other two bedroom doors would be locked.

Still, it was ten minutes before DS Daniels returned and, carelessly, she hadn't remembered to flush the toilet, but by then Dolly had joined them, her mother taking full advantage of the lengthening silence, as she slid Dolly's scrapbook from its hiding place beneath the jigsaw box and walked briskly across the room.

Chapter Thirteen

HOLLYWOOD ENDINGS

Sunday at Sunset House was like most Sundays. A leisurely morning reading the Sunday supplements, a roast beef dinner and an afternoon movie matinee, interspersed with perhaps more toilet visits, the occasional emergency and on this particular Sunday two hours of arts and crafts. The residents had been making Easter cards and Will was tidying away tubes of glitter and rolls of felt (flecks of glitter were sparkling like grains of sand on the lounge carpet days later). A care home, he'd discovered, was essentially a primary school minus the homework and the bullying.

While Jolene preferred late shifts and overnight shifts, Will preferred the slower pace of weekends, but mostly he was just relieved that Janette didn't work at the weekend. He didn't like her touching his elbow or patting his knee and he didn't know how to ask her to stop. When he next saw Jolene he'd solicit her opinion 'on behalf of a friend', although she'd probably realise that it was him and tell him to stop being so ridiculous and to stand up for himself. Was he a man or a mouse?

A mouse, a voice inside his head squeaked. Maybe he should go directly to the source of his discomfort and talk to Janette himself, although how you told someone to stop touching you, in a polite but forthright manner without offending them, he had absolutely no idea.

The deputy manager on duty today was Rob Ford, who you rarely saw (he was usually in Janette's office watching YouTube videos), which Will thought one of the more desirable requisites of a manager – only contactable in the event of an emergency. He liked to think he knew what was expected of him without the need for supervision, although Jolene would no doubt disagree. She was so impatient that she'd frequently elbow him aside and finish a task herself. Admittedly, he'd been a little slow to react when Sheila had suddenly slithered to the floor like cut rope, but all he could see was his mother lying on the kitchen parquet, wondering if *her* pupils had ghoulishly rolled beneath her fluttering eyelids, leaving just the whites of her eyes visible.

After collecting the tea and coffee that had been left to go cold, the residents having fallen asleep in the middle of drinking them (a standard occurrence), Will returned to the staff desk by the window to complete his shift notes before the Sunday afternoon visitors started arriving. He hoped that Martin Williams wouldn't be one of those visitors. He was someone else who'd started to make him feel uncomfortable, even more so after their last encounter. Gilbert was the one talking to him, he'd wanted to tell him, but he'd been too terrified to respond.

Gilbert and John were reading crossword clues aloud, John tasked with filling in the squares. The lenses of John's glasses were smeared with what looked like custard and he kept wiping them with his cardigan sleeve, making them worse. Unable to bear it any longer, Will went over and rinsed his glasses under the tap. When Will later collected the newspaper for recycling, he noticed that various girls' names had been written in the squares. He tore out the page and slipped it into his notebook.

Yesterday, he'd spent the morning in the reference room of the local library browsing microfiche and microfilm newspaper holdings for missing Naomis, but without more detailed information it had been like searching for one of those missing flecks of glitter. It would take weeks, possibly months, to review the last fifty or sixty years. He'd asked the library assistant, a man wearing a Ramones T-shirt who was reading a copy of *Kerrang!*, if there was anyone who could help or whether there was a search index that he could consult, but the unhelpful Ramone had merely shrugged and told him that the librarian wasn't available at the weekend. He'd have to call back on Monday.

Ordering an Americano and a jam doughnut from the café next door that was run by a group of visually impaired volunteers (where he also purchased a wooden wind chime that was a tangle of sandpapered discs and varnished pipes from a selection of handmade gifts by the till. He thought he might hang it on the yew tree beside his mother's grave), Will had considered his next step.

Opposite, the automatic glass doors of the police station had been repeatedly sliding open and closed (often when there was no one entering or exiting) and he'd wondered whether he should inform the police of Gilbert's remarks.

They had access to far more resources than he did – national databases, forensic reports, DNA records. Will's skills paled in comparison. Would they believe his allegations, express their gratitude, or would they think he'd been listening to too many true crime podcasts and dismiss his concerns without investigating his claims, consider him deluded, a time-waster? They were always understaffed or underfunded according to news reports and it wasn't as if he had any actual evidence of a crime having been committed. No one else had heard Gilbert say these things. It was his word against Gilbert's. And Gilbert was a frail and vulnerable seventy-nine-year-old man who had no idea what day it was (although that was to be expected when every day was the same as the last).

Sometimes, Will wondered if he'd imagined Gilbert's comments, rewritten his past for dramatic effect, but he wasn't a Hollywood scriptwriter. He didn't have the creative skills necessary to lay responsibility for fictitious crimes at the feet of elderly care home residents. And he'd never be able to forgive himself if what Gilbert had been saying was true and he could have provided closure for the victims' families. Surely it was better to know the truth than to envisage a progressively more distressing succession of endings, each one more horrifying than the last. He'd made that mistake once before, kept the ending to himself.

By the time he'd finished his doughnut, he'd made his decision. He'd report what Gilbert had been saying to the police and then they could decide how best to proceed. He'd of course continue to update them with new information, as and when received. He'd also continue with his own research should they choose to ignore his concerns (foolish in his opinion).

The police station reception area had been as riotous as a protest rally, a rising crescendo of exasperation culminating in general uproar. Like most establishments their busiest time was lunchtime when staff were taking their own lunch breaks. But Will had expected a little more decorum and a little less swearing. If the police couldn't coordinate a queue of customers in a police station foyer, then how effectual would they be when faced with a genuine emergency?

An Alsatian had been barking in the corner, a man carrying a cycle helmet had started to raise his voice about a summons that he'd received and a woman with neck tattoos and a bruised wrist had been showing a female employee the inside of what appeared to be an empty handbag.

Will had contemplated returning later, but wondered if he would actually do so once he'd left, so he'd taken the last remaining seat by the window and patiently waited. More people had arrived as he was re-reading the posters on the walls, *Online Fraud, Reporting a Crime, Zero Tolerance Policy*. The man with the summons had then started yelling and the woman with the neck tattoos had positioned herself on the floor by the door and was refusing to move. The victims of crimes were now, it seemed, the perpetrators.

When it was finally Will's turn, the officer behind the glass had sighed wearily and, without acknowledging him, had reached for a blank form. Worried that what he was about to divulge would languish in someone's in-tray indefinitely, Will had asked to speak to the police officer in charge, in person.

It was urgent. It was regarding two possible murders. That's right, *two*. There was a sudden hush behind him.

Fifteen minutes later another police officer was asking him to follow him into an interview room. The wind chime in Will's jacket pocket had jangled like a cursed talisman. An interview room? Were they planning to interrogate him? Did they think that he was reporting two murders that *he'd* committed, that he was the one who'd abducted the two girls?

His palms began to sweat. He wiped them on his jacket. What if they didn't believe him? Did he need a solicitor? He wished he'd stayed in the café across the road, ordered another Americano, eaten another doughnut. He wished he could retrace his steps back to the exit. But that was now impossible without attracting further suspicion.

He'd hesitantly sat down opposite the police officer, a DI Rex Spencer, glancing anxiously at the one-way glass. He could see shadows moving behind the glass. He tried to steady his nerves. He hadn't done anything illegal – he hadn't stolen a priceless gemstone, he wasn't carrying ten grams of cocaine in his lower intestine.

And, taking a deep breath, he'd let his perspiring guilt pool innocently (until proven guilty) at his feet, momentarily forgetting that he wasn't entirely innocent, that everyone had something to be ashamed of if you looked closely enough. The past was often much darker than it first appeared.

Chapter Fourteen

THE ICE PALACE

Rex was sitting in his car in the police station car park studying the photograph of Laura Sykes that her mother, Miranda, had handed to him. When he'd asked for a recent photograph of Laura she'd passed him a sealed white envelope, having anticipated the request, and said that it was one of her favourites (hers or Laura's, she didn't specify). 'Such a happy occasion,' she'd murmured, wistfully.

Whenever Rex held a photograph in his hands nowadays it was either of a smiling missing person or a blood-spattered crime scene. It was only ever bad news that he got to hold. He hoped there were still photographs of Denise in the loft. He didn't want to have to search for her on his phone. He remembered the ruthless way she'd sifted through their wedding photographs, tossing aside the ones she'd disliked, condensing two hundred into a tolerable fifty-six, how they'd take camera films into Boots to be developed and two days later collect twenty-four images of themselves with eyes mostly closed or Martian red. No second chances.

The photograph of Laura had been released a few hours earlier and the switchboard had already been inundated with calls – the customary hoaxes, three from local psychics and the remainder from people who were either genuinely mistaken, intentionally misleading or unnecessarily abusive. One person had even wanted to know if they could 'tag' the clothing brand of the dress that Laura was wearing. Another had asked if that was Weymouth Harbour they could see in the distance.

Rex had never understood why people claimed to have seen a person in a Belgian market three hundred miles away or working as a croupier in a Reno casino when they hadn't. Or that they'd killed someone who'd not been killed or *had* been killed but by someone else.

Jacob Lyons was a prime example. He regularly professed responsibility for a disappearance, even though he was currently serving a six-year prison sentence for attempting to run over his stepson in a Volkswagen Golf. Rex imagined him tirelessly raising his hand as a child – a small boy requiring a man-sized amount of attention. *It was me, sir. I'm the one who did it.* Did he expect a pat on the back, a handshake? He was what was commonly referred to as a serial confessor and, unofficially, 'a pain in the arse'. You were expected to accept his assertions that he'd maimed or killed someone from the confines of his prison cell as entirely plausible, but there was never any definitive evidence of his involvement. No monosyllabic telephone calls or encrypted correspondence or visiting hitmen for hire. He was always irritatingly vague and knew no more than what had been reported in the media. Rex wondered if one of the prison guards was letting him out after lights out and then letting him back in again the following morning, but even in a world where nothing surprised Rex anymore, it seemed too fanciful a notion.

It was a peculiar practice – doing something for the thrill of it without financial gain or notoriety – unless it was the prospect of deceiving the police that was the biggest thrill of all. They still had to check every lead, follow every sighting. And while they were pursuing those false leads and sightings the person who was missing was getting further and further away.

And he now had two more possible abductions or murders to investigate, that might or might not be connected.

The police station reception area had been unusually busy when a flustered Craig had rushed over to him and told him that a Mr Will Cavanagh would like to speak to someone urgently about two murders. A man wearing a hi-vis jacket had been aggressively shaking a letter at Craig minutes earlier and an Alsatian that should have been tied up outside had been barking in the corner. Alison Sinclair, who normally manned the switchboard, had been trying to persuade an inebriated woman who'd been blocking the doorway to get up off the floor, while two teenage boys had been videoing the woman on their mobile phones. Sort this chaos out, he'd told Craig. It's like a chimps' tea party in here.

'Would you like to follow me?' Rex had asked the man reporting two murders, leading him into a nearby interview room when he nodded. 'Sorry we haven't got anywhere more comfortable, but at least it's private.'

It wasn't. There was a one-way mirror across one of the walls and anyone could have been sitting behind it eating their sandwiches, listening. Rex had even thought he could smell corned beef.

'Please, take a seat.'

Pearls of sweat had begun to form on the man's forehead.

'So ... how can I help?'

Afterwards, Rex had asked Cathy to do a background check on both Gilbert Williams *and* Will Cavanagh.

'And contact The National Crime Agency for any missing Naomis or Joannes listed on their database, no surnames as yet. They don't appear to be recent crimes if they're crimes at all and, although they may not be local disappearances, check the paper files we keep in storage just in case. Maybe Mr Cavanagh is trying to make his life a little more interesting than it really is. Or maybe his intention is to mislead us and he knows more than he's telling us. Either way, see what you can find.'

Cathy had nodded enthusiastically. It would mean spending several hours in the part of the station she liked best – the windowless basement they called 'The Dungeon', where clouds of dust particles were expelled like icy breaths when the metal cabinets were opened, releasing the ghostly spirits of the missing people they contained or the puffs of smoke they'd left behind when they disappeared.

Current cases can often be traced back to historic cases (she never referred to them as cold cases, called it disrespectful), she would tell Rex. Crimes are like family trees, their origins almost always buried in the past.

A few hours later she'd knocked on his office door.

'Nothing on a Naomi as yet, sir, I've gone back as far as the 1970s, but there are several possible Joannes, five so far. I'm working through them now.'

'Mr Cavanagh's alleged Internet research produced the same result,' Rex replied, despondently.

When online investigative journalism was as informative as official police records he wondered where that left procedural justice.

'There's very little on Gilbert Williams, the usual parking tickets, an altercation outside a Methodist chapel in his teens. One interesting fact, his wife committed suicide when she was forty-three, hung herself from a tree.'

Not a family tree then, but an actual tree.

'Mr Cavanagh mentioned that too. Take a look at the coroner's report. There must be something that can't be found by typing keywords into Google.'

'Do you think we should speak to Gilbert Williams, sir? There may be a simple explanation.'

'He's currently in a care home, displaying early signs of dementia, so we'll need to seek permission from the family before talking to him. I'll give the care home a call. Mr Cavanagh would prefer that we didn't mention that he was the one who contacted us, which I've agreed to – for now. He doesn't want to upset the family, but they're obviously going to be upset when we start asking Mr Williams about his possible involvement in the disappearance of two girls. Anything on Mr Cavanagh?'

'Nothing yet, sir.'

Rex was scrolling through photographs of Denise on his phone when it rang. It was the manager of Sunset House confirming that they would be able to speak to Mr Williams tomorrow morning in the presence of his daughter. Before heading into the station, Rex took one last glance at his screensaver, a photograph of Denise in the Lake District, Buttermere, rain dripping from her jacket hood, splashes of mud on her left cheek. She was dissolving before his eyes. She isn't dead yet, Rex reminded himself, as he blinked away a tear. She might not die at all. Doctors don't know everything. New discoveries and medical breakthroughs are being made daily. Admittedly, such thoughts were designed to precipitate hope, but it didn't mean that they wouldn't one day yield results.

Only this morning he'd discovered a link between Will Cavanagh and Laura Sykes. *Jolene Edwards*. And he'd wondered whether Will Cavanagh had brought Gilbert Williams to their attention in order to distract them from the investigation into Laura Sykes' disappearance. And was Jolene's missing sister, Dolly, connected in some way? Or was it simply a coincidence? Rex found coincidences endlessly fascinating.

When fifteen-year-old Dolly Edwards was first reported missing Rex had been undertaking hostage training, which he'd ultimately decided was a little too specialised for his tastes. He preferred a 'Jack-of-all-trades' approach. Not a script that needed to be followed closely – one wrong word and you'd killed someone. Rex didn't flourish under that kind of pressure. And it would have sounded insincere on his lips. Some people were just better at bullshitting than he was. He had however read the case file. And he had of course come into contact with Dolly's mother on several occasions over the years – most recently holding a 'Justice for Dolly' placard outside the police station and a few days later on the town hall steps where she'd been giving a disparaging television interview about police inertia.

A couple of years ago he'd been called to one of the candlelight vigils she organised each year. A car headlight had been smashed and she'd scratched Liam Cole's cheek. She'd always believed that Liam, Dolly's ex-boyfriend, who'd been several years older than Dolly, was responsible for her disappearance and she'd been cautioned numerous times for mentioning his name in interviews and trespassing on his father's farmland. And although someone *had* actually claimed to have seen Dolly arguing with Liam that day, Liam had never been considered a suspect, possibly because he had an uncle who was a DCI and a brother with links to organised crime and the person who'd claimed to have seen him was considered an unreliable witness. Dolly's father, Anthony, became a person of interest for a while, immediate family routinely the primary focus of police investigations, but there'd been no evidence to indicate his involvement.

Every time Rex drove past the ice rink he thought of Dolly Edwards and the metallic silver padded jacket and blue woollen gloves decorated with snowflakes she'd been wearing that night, one snowflake fewer on the right glove. It had been called The Ice Palace then, a smokescreen of Swarovski crystals, pink champagne and teenage dreams. Now it was just The Ice Rink, the place where Dolly Edwards was last seen.

Cathy was at her desk flicking through a box of case files when Rex walked into the office.

'Sunset House are happy for us to speak to Gilbert Williams tomorrow morning,' he told her. 'Have you discovered anything else?'

She shook her head.

'Has the televised appeal with Laura Sykes' parents been arranged?' she asked him.

'It's scheduled to be broadcast tomorrow afternoon.'

Rex hoped it wouldn't be another Carla Salmon fiasco. Miranda Sykes seemed relatively normal, hovering somewhere between genuine grief and hysteria, but he was yet to meet her husband, James.

Chapter Fifteen
JESUS JONES

'Nice sash windows,' Cathy remarked, as they were walking towards the entrance of Sunset House. 'I've always wanted sash windows, but Matt says they're a nightmare to maintain. That's Matt though, always stamping on your dreams with his size elevens.'

Rex wasn't sure if Cathy was talking about something other than sash windows, but chose not to enquire further. He seldom engaged in personal conversations unless absolutely necessary, assumed that if an employee had a grievance they'd report it officially and he could deal with it through the appropriate channels.

'Let's hope we don't find anything grisly,' she said with a grimace.

On the rare occasions when she wasn't immersed in a broth of jazz hands and tap shoes she was downloading true crime podcasts. Consequently, she had a tendency to expect the worst. She wasn't someone who you went to for an unbiased opinion. A contusion on a forehead was from an angry fist, a bruise on a wrist a violent grip. There's probably a dead body buried in most gardens, she told him, matter-of-factly. It was unsettling how she could be singing 'supercalifragilisticexpialidocious' one minute and then listening to *Missing Maura Murray* the next, a summer sky turning to winter frost in seconds. But she had had a violent ex-boyfriend so she was more attuned to potential high-risk situations than most officers.

Unusually, for someone so unguarded, she rarely discussed her ex-boyfriend in any significant detail, said that giving him a platform was just fuelling the fire, but Rex had seen his arrest photograph. An unflattering image (weren't they all?) of an ordinary-looking man with blue-black shadows beneath his eyes, who was currently in prison for murdering his girlfriend. There but for the grace of God, thought Rex, wondering how one girlfriend survived and another died. What made you less fortunate? A single word or glance triggering an explosive rage? Or an accumulation of small things culminating in a violent confrontation?

Cathy had once volunteered at a women's refuge and fervently believed that if someone wanted to find you, they'd never stop searching, no matter how long it took. You can't run for ever, she said. And you can never disappear completely, there's always a trace of you somewhere. While railway stations might facilitate the absconding process, allow you to view other possibilities and make different choices, you still have to step off the train at some point.

In Rex's experience, finding people was akin to a seemingly impossible feat of engineering or a baffling magic trick. It relied on luck and determination, on those involved confessing, on so many things that had little to do with everyday policing. 'The Missing' were by their very nature an elusive group of protagonists. Fraud or Vice were far easier crimes to navigate, networks you could infiltrate and manipulate, sting operations and undercover assignments you could coordinate. It was far less convoluted than chasing swirls of smoke and thin air.

Cathy recalled Caroline, a colleague, arranging a small collection for Tracey (not her real name), one of the residents, who'd decided to return to her husband after only two weeks, presenting her with a relaxation CD compilation ('a one-way ticket to the moon, had funds allowed, might have been more welcome') with the money raised. Tracey returned with a black eye and a fractured rib four days later, her husband that same afternoon. He'd followed her to the refuge, kicking open the back door and aiming a gun at Caroline's head. Caroline had only called in to change the door codes, a monthly practice to ensure there were no security breaches. Tracey wasn't there. She'd said she was going to church, which for Tracey meant she was meeting her drug dealer, Jesus Jones. There was no guessing when she'd be back.

Her husband of course didn't believe she wasn't there and no one was brave enough to mention Jesus Jones so they were all herded into the lounge area at gunpoint, while Caroline was instructed to 'Find the fucking bitch!', and when she didn't he shot her three times in the chest.

Tracey felt the need to increase her church visiting hours after that and died of a drug overdose a few months later.

They were let in by Janette, the care home manager, and asked to sign their names in the visitors' book. The care staff looked harassed and ill-tempered. In the reception area there was a spoonful of what looked like mashed potato on a clock on the wall, concealing both the five and the six, a slice of sponge cake in a glass vase precariously positioned between the stems of three tulips, and a baked bean on one of Van Gogh's sunflowers.

Gilbert Williams' daughter had apparently been delayed, but had confirmed that the informal chat could go ahead without her, providing that Janette was present. Gilbert was in his room, his hair dandruff-white, his skin the texture of tree bark. He was sitting in a chair in soiled trousers, sobbing. Rex had witnessed generations of men yell and lash out and then fall silent for days, sometimes weeks – his father had been one of those men – but he'd seen very few men openly sobbing.

Janette, noticing the state of his trousers, said that she'd deal with it immediately and then swiftly disappeared.

Rex and Cathy glanced at each other. They should really wait for her to return before speaking to Gilbert, but they needed to get back to the station. Laura Sykes was still missing.

'Is it okay if we have a word, Mr Williams?' Rex asked.

He didn't appear to have heard him.

'Mr Williams?'

This was hopeless.

He seemed to have forgotten all the words that he'd spent a lifetime learning.

The sobbing continued.

A woman stood in the doorway, watching them.

'Doesn't say much, does he? That television's mine by the way. We shook on it.'

Rex noticed an adhesive label on the flat screen television with the name Nelly Quinn written on it. He presumed that she was Nelly Quinn.

Cathy, meanwhile, was examining the room as if Gilbert Williams was already guilty (and without a warrant). Even though she often scanned a room before introducing herself, was the human equivalent of antivirus software, she wasn't usually this brazen. She was currently peering inside the wardrobe, sliding coat hangers along the rail as if she was deciding what to wear.

'Some of his clothes have other people's name tags inside them. This cardigan belongs to Cressida Bailey,' she told Rex, holding up a beaded cardigan with embroidered flowers on it.

He wasn't sure what she was implying. Was she disappointed in the laundry service provided by the care home? If this is happening heaven knows what else is going on. Or was it something more sinister? Who was Cressida Bailey and was she still alive?

Rex glanced across the courtyard into another resident's room. A woman with red hair waved back at him. Or maybe she was beckoning him over, asking for help. 'I want to go home,' he imagined her pleading, clutching his jacket sleeve when he tried to leave. Rex turned away. He couldn't rescue everybody. Christ, he couldn't rescue anybody. He'd have to give her another police officer's contact details.

When a laundry assistant entered Gilbert's room, Cathy passed her the beaded cardigan.

'I think you'll find that this belongs to Cressida Bailey. Is she still here?'

She couldn't help herself.

'That's my television,' Nelly Quinn told the laundry assistant. 'I've told them not to touch it.'

The assistant rolled her eyes and glanced at Rex.

'She's already got three televisions. I'll have a word with Janette.'

'Excuse me, are those odd socks?' Cathy asked the assistant, pointing at the pair of socks that she was about to place in a drawer. 'And Mr Williams' trousers need changing. The manager was supposed to be dealing with it. We've had to open a window.'

She was enjoying the effect that the police uniform that she wasn't obligated to wear was having on the staff.

A few minutes later a care assistant appeared with Gilbert's medication. It was like Piccadilly Circus, and yet nobody was willing to address (or undress) the most immediate issue, the soiled trousers. The staff appeared unable to multitask. And as quickly as they'd arrived they'd departed, with barely a word to Gilbert.

After finishing Gilbert's biscuits ('I left my Nākd bar at work') Cathy continued with her in-depth inspection of the room. She walked over to the chest of drawers and began picking up framed photographs and putting them back down again. Before Rex could stop her she was taking photographs of the photographs on her mobile phone, particularly interested in a photograph of a supposedly much younger Gilbert, wearing drainpipe trousers and a shoelace tie. He looked like a young Elvis Presley.

The woman next to him, his wife Ruth, Rex assumed, was wearing a white mini dress and white ballet pumps. There was a gap between her front teeth and she looked a little like

Marianne Faithfull. Rex tried not to picture her hanging from an oak tree with a broken neck.

According to the coroner's report Ruth Williams' cause of death was suicide by hanging and Rex doubted that the family would grant them permission to exhume the body for a second autopsy. Or whether an autopsy was even possible on such degraded remains.

Rex wondered how many photographs of the same smiles you needed to have on display in order to convince yourself that you'd been happy. Gilbert Williams had twenty and, strangely, none of them were recent. Cathy began removing the photographs from their frames so that she could take a closer look.

'Let's not get carried away,' he told her.

'I'll be quick,' she replied. 'My finger dexterity is excellent. I do a lot of gaming. And I've always found the practice of writing names and dates on the back of photographs extremely informative.'

Reluctantly, Rex moved towards the door to keep watch. He'd speak to her later.

As Cathy was methodically working her way along the portrait gallery ('I'm not convinced that the man in these photographs *is* Gilbert Williams'), Gilbert Williams suddenly started yelling at her to stop touching his things. And then he began to make a strange high-pitched beeping sound, as if he was reversing.

Rex abandoned his position by the door and walked over to him with the intention of calming him down, relieved that he'd at least said 'things' plural because he wouldn't want Cathy to face charges of molestation. Seconds later two care assistants were in the room forming a protective shield around Gilbert and glaring at them both. Rex wondered if they were usually this quick to respond, but suspected not, considering the condition of Gilbert's trousers.

'I'm terribly sorry,' Cathy said, a picture frame dismantled in her hands. 'I was just admiring Mr Williams' photographs. They look so professional. I wondered if the name of the photographer was stamped on the back.'

Cathy could fabricate a lie in a matter of seconds. She'd easily pass a polygraph. It made Rex wonder what else she lied about – probably the actual number of times that she'd seen *Wicked*. I've got tickets for *Joseph*, she'd told him earlier. My sister's never seen it, would you believe? He could believe. And she loves Jason Donovan, so double the excitement.

'Gilbert doesn't like anyone touching his things,' one of the carers reiterated, glancing around the room to see if there was anything missing.

She even stared at Cathy's handbag for several seconds. Rex had to concede that it did seem like a thief's paradise. Anyone could walk in and help themselves to whatever they liked. They could have been professional care home thieves pretending to be police officers. Nobody had checked their IDs. At least Nelly Quinn waited for you to die before she took what wasn't hers, even wrote her name on it.

'Evidently,' Cathy agreed, securing the back of the photograph frame that she was still holding. 'I'll pop it back where I found it, shall I?'

When Janette, the manager, returned, there was an awkward silence.

'I'm so sorry to have kept you. There was a problem with one of the fire exit doors. Now where were we?'

She waited for someone to enlighten her, but no one spoke. It was as if she'd stumbled upon something clandestine.

Frowning, she glanced around the room, trying to ascertain what had happened in her absence.

'I think it might be best if you left,' she told Rex. 'Mr Williams seems overly tired today.'

'Do you think they sedated him before we arrived?' Cathy asked Rex, as they were leaving.

He didn't answer. He'd received three missed calls from the hospital.

Chapter Sixteen

BUFFALO WINGS

The news that two police officers had been in Gilbert's room that morning was like an Elizabethan banquet for the Sunset House care home staff, who feasted on a scandal as much as, if not more than, the next person.

And while Will was of course relieved that the police had seemingly chosen to investigate his concerns more thoroughly, he prayed that his name hadn't been accidentally mentioned in the process. He didn't want Gilbert's son and daughter to learn that he was the one responsible for the allegations and hoped that the police had used every non-committal and vague sentence at their disposal to protect his identity – 'It's come to our attention', 'We're talking to everyone' – even though Will doubted that the police had managed to tease anything useful out of Gilbert if they *had* tried to speak to him. They'd need to work backwards. They'd learn far more if they could unlock the young Gilbert, the Gilbert in the photographs in his room, who might have been abducting and murdering people for much of his adult life.

Will wondered if it was a coincidence that someone else had now disappeared, a Barclays bank employee named Laura Sykes, or whether he'd unintentionally initiated a chain of events that had led to another person's abduction. Was someone attempting to prove Gilbert's innocence or were they attempting to replicate his crimes? It definitely hadn't been Gilbert. He'd had a migraine all weekend, or so he'd claimed, and hadn't even joined them for afternoon tea in the garden, although Will had a sudden vision of him pulling on thermal socks and the tan suede loafers that he sometimes wore and climbing out of the window. But it seemed something of a stretch, pretending to be in ill health and senile so that you could roam the streets at night searching for people to abduct.

Will had been so anxious about his name being mentioned that he'd had to eat two lunches to settle his stomach; his own packed lunch, consumed by eleven a.m., and a serving of cod in parsley sauce followed by homemade rice pudding courtesy of Enid, who'd been collected by her sister without prior notice. When Will had expressed an interest in Enid's meal, Alison had told him to 'knock himself out' so he had. It wasn't exactly Michelin-starred cuisine and it was practically pureed, but it would hopefully address the unease that he was feeling.

His compulsion to overeat began three days after his mother's death. Food, he discovered, was like a balm, a sedative. It alleviated the pain. If he was eating then he wasn't remembering and if he wasn't remembering then it didn't hurt quite so much. The grief didn't claw at him day and night, drawing blood. Quietly and purposefully he bandaged those memories with calories, and no one was particularly interested in any underlying cause.

As he was swallowing the last mouthful of rice pudding a sharp pain suddenly mushroomed into a well of agony inside his chest. He thumped his sternum with his fist, tried to dislodge whatever had accumulated there in a Windsor-tight knot, waiting for the pain to pass (it usually did), blaming it on indigestion, on the fact that the cavities inside him were not fully sealed and he needed to insulate his arteries more effectively, provide padding where there was just air. But the pain didn't ease. He felt breathless and lightheaded. There was a fluttering inside his chest, like the flapping of butterfly wings. Or perhaps they were Buffalo wings. That seemed more likely.

Jolene walked into the staffroom as he was searching for an indigestion tablet in his locker and dramatically clutching his chest. She glanced at the empty dinner plate and the empty dessert bowl, both dishwasher-clean.

'Enjoy your lunch?' she asked him.

She always made him feel as if he was doing something wrong. He'd been given permission to eat Enid's lunch, he wanted to tell her. He hadn't just taken it.

'Not really,' he grimaced.

'You look terrible,' she told him. 'You should know not to eat the food in here. It's worse than prison food. I bet the main course was the same colour as the pudding.'

It had been, but that wasn't currently his most pressing concern.

'It's just a bout of indigestion. I'll be fine in a few minutes.'

'So said the man who died seconds later,' she remarked, unhelpfully.

It didn't seem to be easing. If anything, it was getting worse and he couldn't find any indigestion tablets in his locker. Sensing that he wasn't being melodramatic and was actually in pain Jolene unexpectedly took pity on him.

'I've got an aspirin somewhere. Sit down. You look really sweaty.'

He obediently swallowed the aspirin offered and then completed the breathing exercise that she instructed him to do – *inhale for a count of four, hold for a count of seven and exhale for a count of eight. Repeat four times.* He wasn't sure that breathing exercises aided indigestion, but as she was trying to be supportive he felt it only polite to comply and after two or three minutes of breathing and counting, the pain did seem to be lessening.

'Are you sure it wasn't a panic attack?'

'I'm pretty sure it was indigestion.'

'You need to watch those calories. They are not your friends.'

There was a loud knock at the staffroom window. It was Luke Trent.

'Just what I need,' Jolene said, snapping the blinds closed.

Later that night, as he was angling his telescope towards the sky, Will thought about his mother. Sometimes he'd search for her among stars sparkling like fireflies and it was as if everything he could see through the lens of his telescope belonged to him because he was the one who'd selected it, because he was the one who gazed at it most.

And he now had other things to look for, things that were

beyond the scope of his telescope, the span of his eyeline. And he really wasn't sure where he might find those things.

He unscrewed the telescopic lens and retrieved the preserved eye hidden inside it, rolling it around in his palm like a worry bead. He'd never been particularly squeamish; an eye was just an eye whether it was still in its socket or not. He'd found the eye (gravel-grey, owner unknown) on Striding Rise and even now he still wondered whether he should have handed it in to the police. He'd smeared chocolate on it, he remembered, as he was wondering where the other eye was. He couldn't see it on the grass. Perhaps a bird had flown away with it.

He would have liked to have returned the eye to its owner, given the police something to look into and the victim something to look out of, but two hikers had suddenly appeared on the ridge, their Nordic sticks spearing fallen leaves into autumn kebabs.

After carefully screwing the eye back inside the telescope, he reached for the shoebox beneath his bed and, removing the lid, unwrapped the peacock brooch. One of the metal claws that secured the petrol-blue gemstones on the plumes of the peacock pricked his finger. He wiped away the blood with the hem of his T-shirt, before rolling his thumb along the bevelled edge of the rose gold horseshoe earring and the prong of the silver belt buckle. He couldn't now remember what had made him want to collect these things, but whenever he saw something fall from a pocket he'd pick it up and place it in his own pocket. He didn't consider it stealing. He was merely keeping these things safe. Some of the items that he'd found over the years had been carefully buried, others loosely trampled into the earth; they didn't belong to the people he'd followed, but he kept them just the same.

Finally, he untied the aubergine velvet pouch decorated with an embroidered seahorse in ocean blue and tipped out the contents – a silver charm bracelet with a star so sharp it could pierce a heart like a dagger, his most cherished possession.

Chapter Seventeen

TEARS IN GLASS JARS

When Jolene arrived at Sunset House on Monday she assumed that Laura would be the main topic of conversation but surprisingly it was Gilbert. Apparently, two police officers had been in his room earlier that morning, although Janette wouldn't reveal why and Alison had a multitude of outlandish theories. Jolene wondered if it was something to do with Will, indebted to him if it was, because it meant that no one was discussing Laura and the mascara that she'd just reapplied would remain as advertised for a little while longer.

She'd spent the last thirty minutes locked inside the disabled toilet, all her tears seemingly falling at once – new tears, recycled tears, tears that had been placed in glass jars like pennies and kept on a kitchen shelf for just this type of occasion.

After she'd spoken to the police yesterday she'd filled the car with petrol and commenced her own search for Laura, wondering if she might see her tenpin bowling with Hannah or sharing a tub of salted popcorn with Rebecca outside the swimming baths, and it was all a dreadful misunderstanding. She'd driven along the route that Laura would have taken to work and then she'd extended her search to the outskirts of town, checking the passenger seats of cars as they overtook her, the backseats after they'd overtaken her, the drivers sounding their horns and mouthing obscenities at her due to her sluggish speed, after which she'd parked the car at a Pay and Display car park and continued her search on foot.

With mounting trepidation, she'd searched the woodland behind the golf course, praying that she wouldn't stumble upon Laura's remains. She didn't want to find her dismembered beneath a carpet of wet leaves wrapped in tarpaulin. She wanted to find a living Laura, a 'sorry-for-not-calling' Laura. At one point she'd even thought she was being watched, the same feeling she'd had on Saturday night walking to the multistorey car park, and she'd almost turned back. She didn't want to be subdued with a chloroform-scented handkerchief or restrained with a length of rope; to be abducted herself while searching for Laura.

While following a trail beside a stream she'd spotted Glen Taylor in the distance, stooped over something. She'd recognised the navy-blue zipped anorak with tartan lining that he always wore, something that his father might have worn. Perhaps it had belonged to his father. She remembered him walking past Wetherspoons twice on Saturday night. He was someone you saw several times a day.

He hadn't noticed her until she was almost behind him and she'd clearly startled him. Most people thought him strange, always alone, always there, but Jolene didn't mind people's eccentricities. And he seemed harmless.

'Found anything exciting, Glen?'

He'd walked towards her, shielding whatever it was that he'd been looking at with his body.

'A dead bird. I was just burying it.'

'Very Springwatch. I'm looking for Laura. I don't suppose you've seen her on your travels.'

When he'd shaken his head, his dark-rimmed glasses had slipped down his nose. He'd pushed them back into position with an index finger. He should really do something about those glasses, Jolene had thought. She wondered if they'd also belonged to his father.

'How's your mother?'

His mother was agoraphobic and never left the house.

'Still breathing.'

Unsure whether he was experimenting with humour or whether his reserves of sympathy and compassion had reached critical levels, she'd quickly changed the subject.

'Thanks for attending Dolly's vigil, by the way.'

Everyone who attended the vigils deserved a 'thank you' in Jolene's opinion, although her mother said that standing in the cold for a few hours once a year was the least they could do.

'Any time.'

He seemed to be waiting for her to leave.

'I'll let you get back to your burial.'

Did people usually bury the dead birds they found while out walking?

Before crossing the stepping stones, Jolene had watched him return to the spot where he'd been stooping. He must see so many unusual things when he's out walking, she'd thought, things that he probably doesn't even know are unusual until it's too late.

The search that Laura's mother had arranged for later that day had been another unrewarding and tense few hours. Laura's father had refused to join them, even though he'd arrived back from Geneva earlier than expected, upsetting Laura's mother, while Jolene's mother *did* decide to join them, but kept trying to guide them in the direction of Beech Cliff Farm, where Liam Cole's family lived. She was convinced that Laura was being held captive there. And that they'd find Dolly too. *But they needed to go now, while there was still time.*

When Jed Myers, a local councillor, had declared the search routes already decided, her mother began to sulk, eventually drifting away from her assigned group, and didn't return home until dawn.

While mopping one of the corridor floors (Iris, one of the cleaners, was on long-term sick leave), Jolene noticed Luke watering the rosebushes. He'd texted her yesterday evening to apologise for not meeting her as arranged on Saturday night, asking for a chance to explain. She hadn't replied. She wasn't usually so churlish or childish. She wasn't someone who censored their words. She was normally more forthright. But she really didn't want to speak to him. End of.

When she re-entered the lounge Laura was smiling back at

her. It took her a second or two to realise that it wasn't real-life Laura, but Missing Laura and her wedding-guest smile on the one o'clock news. That's what people will think she looks like, thought Jolene, but she was at a wedding. No one looks like themselves at a wedding. Maybe she still doesn't look like herself. She could have dyed and restyled her hair and they're looking for someone who no longer exists. Jolene would often think she'd seen Dolly in Poundland or at the checkout in Morrisons, but it was the Dolly on the landing or in the hallway. It wasn't the Dolly she would have looked like now.

She recalled her last conversation with Laura. They'd been sitting in Starbucks streaming music on Spotify when Laura had asked her if she'd ever read the Bible. Jolene had shaken her head and asked why. 'No reason. I just wondered.' And then she'd steered the conversation back to Dua Lipa. Jolene supposed it was normal for everything a person last said to become magnified in hindsight. You were left with a desperate need to analyse every syllable, dissect every pause. It didn't always have to mean anything. She wondered whether she should mention it to the police.

Laura's parents were bookended by DS Daniels and a Superintendent Forrester during the televised press conference. Jolene was surprised that DS Daniels wasn't standing. Alison increased the television volume as Laura's father read a short statement, staring belligerently into the camera lens. Jolene imagined him silently threatening whoever was involved, 'If she isn't returned to us immediately, there'll be serious consequences' or perhaps it was Laura whom he was threatening, 'If you don't come home now, I'll kill you myself.' Or, worse, and to no one in particular, 'No one will ever find you.'

Jolene didn't know Laura's father well, she'd only met him a handful of times, but Laura was always happier when he was in a different country. How ironic it would have been if Laura was now the one in a different country, forcing her father to return home.

As James Sykes' combative expression intensified with every 'we have no further comment at this time' response from Superintendent Forrester, Laura's mother appeared to be slowly dissolving, her outline growing fainter as her husband's overbearing presence became more defined. The incessant nose-blowing and throat-clearing, as if she wanted to say something but was unsure what to say, were the only indications that she wasn't a computer-generated hologram. But not everyone was as comfortable as her mother or Laura's father in front of microphones and cameras.

When the appeal was over Alison muted the television and switched channels to *Tipping Point*.

'That female police officer was one of the police officers in Gilbert's room this morning,' Jolene heard Alison telling Jean, as they were clearing away the lunch dishes. 'I don't know what they said to him, but he was extremely agitated. I've never seen him like that before. He was making siren noises.'

'Perhaps he was pretending to be a police car,' Jean quipped.

Jolene wondered why DS Daniels had been in Gilbert's room.

Did it have something to do with Laura? She'd assumed

that it must have been something to do with what Gilbert had been saying to Will, but perhaps not.

She was still thinking about Laura as she lay on Cora's bed later that afternoon. Cora was in the activities room playing bingo and her room faced a wall, so Jolene had decided to take advantage of the silence and the privacy. She'd switched on the television and was currently watching *Escape to the Country* – where, predictably, there was no escape to the country because nothing was ever good enough – while she helped herself to some of Cora's grapes, although she soon spat them out when she discovered they were seeded ('who the fuck buys seeded grapes?').

And resembling one thing but being another – the similarity between black grapes and black olives for example – was clearly duplicitous.

Was that what she was doing, being duplicitous?

She was certainly ashamed of herself for hiding. She'd never considered herself cowardly, but now it seemed that as well as never knowing how other people might behave, she could barely predict her own behaviour. How long would it be before Luke gave up trying to explain? He didn't strike her as overly persistent, but who knew? Perhaps it had been a matter of life and death why he hadn't turned up or been able to text, and she would now never know, although he hadn't looked particularly grief-stricken earlier. She was annoyed that she was now thinking about Luke and not Laura.

Where *was* Laura? Jolene had absolutely no idea. Was that a reflection on her? Had she not been listening properly? Had she missed something? Laura could be miles away by now. She could be anywhere. That was the worst thought, that she could be anywhere. No, the worst thought was that she was nowhere. But what if it wasn't an abduction at all? What if she'd just walked away? What then?

She felt as if she was having a panic attack. The second one today. Will had been having some sort of panic attack in the staffroom earlier, gulping the air as if he'd climbed ten flights of stairs. Or maybe he'd been having a heart attack and she should have taken it more seriously than just handing him an aspirin that had probably been in her handbag for the best part of a year. She didn't like suggesting that he might want to eat a little less – he was apparently on his second lunch – but sometimes it was a necessary evil if you didn't want someone dying in front of you. Her first-aid skills were exceptional, if she did say so herself, but she couldn't perform miracles. She couldn't bring a person back from the dead.

She'd have thought it was attention-seeking behaviour had he not been alone in the staffroom at the time. Her mother would similarly paw at her chest and start panting, claiming to be having a heart attack, usually when Jolene was planning to meet friends. But as soon as Jolene reached for the phone to call for an ambulance it was suddenly heartburn or low blood pressure. Jolene wondered what sort of mother did that to a child. A disturbed one, most definitely. In primary school it wasn't so mortifying that her mother was always peering through the school gates. But when she was a teenager it had felt far more intrusive. It had felt like she was spying on her.

When her breathing exercises didn't appear to be having any effect, Jolene transported herself to Canada instead. That was where she travelled to now when she needed to quiet the screaming inside her head. She'd been googling Ontario on her phone, the area that her father was planning to move to; scrolling through images of the Great Lakes and the boreal forests, where there was so much more space to breathe and the landscape was so vast that no one, not even her mother, would ever find her.

Cora's door opened as Jolene was white-water rafting on the Madawaska River.

'Don't mind me,' Cora said, glancing at her depleted bag of seeded grapes.

'Sorry, Cora, I just needed five minutes. It's been one of those days. If you promise not to tell anyone, I'll fetch you a Jaffa Cake.'

'We can do better than that. There's a box of After Eight mints and half a Swiss Roll in that cupboard.'

Chapter Eighteen

LIONEL AND HIS TRIPOD

Rex had been ambushed by Superintendent Forrester at the vending machine and summoned to his mahogany-panelled office, where a self-congratulatory collection of framed photographs of the Superintendent in uniform accepting awards and shaking hands with dignitaries at ceremonial luncheons and black tie events lined the walls. The Superintendent's Long Service and Good Conduct medal glittered like a gold tooth in a glass cabinet, like a velvet bow attached to a parcel – aesthetically pleasing, but it was the Sellotape that was doing the heavy lifting, his subordinates the unacknowledged heroes of his glittering career.

Twirling a silver and green ballpoint pen between his thumb and forefinger, the Superintendent suggested that Rex might wish to reconsider his decision not to take the three days' compassionate leave that had been offered. Rex again declined the 'kind' offer with a 'that won't be necessary, sir' and, asking if that was everything, he returned to his desk to reread the first sentence of the missing person file that he'd requested until the words blurred in front of him and then disappeared completely, like the person on the page.

He'd never felt so angry. Angry at Will Cavanagh for wasting his time. Angry at the hospital for not contacting him sooner. But mostly he was angry with Denise for dying. And if he heard 'So sorry for your loss' one more time, he thought he might actually taser someone. He hadn't lost her. He'd known exactly where she was. He just hadn't been able to reach her in time.

When he'd called the hospital back Denise was already dead. A nurse named Mai had held his dying wife's hand and she didn't even know her. He didn't even know her. Reheated rage began to swirl around inside him like a cyclone as he mentally listed more people to blame: the doctor with the beard who never explained anything, the inebriated driver of the car that hit Denise when she was seventeen. Didn't cancers often develop after traumatic incidents?

He thought of Laura Sykes, neither dead nor alive, but somewhere in between. Wasn't that the definition of missing, being neither dead nor alive, until proven otherwise? He was starting to talk in riddles, like Cathy.

There was a knock on the door (his usual 'open door' policy now a 'permanently-closed door' policy). Rex had been reading the sympathy cards that had been left on his desk, even though he didn't want to know how sorry people were, how he was in their thoughts – 'sorry' was a word he could happily live without, a glib word, an all-purpose word, a word for every occasion. But reading the messages had brought a definite lump to his throat. He hadn't expected that. He hadn't expected his resolve to lessen. He'd expected to be unmoved, his fury too mutinous an emotion to be temporarily pushed aside.

He quickly slipped the cards back inside his desk drawer, out of sight, and cleared his throat.

'Come in.'

Cathy stood in the doorway, not sure whether to approach him or not, not sure whether he might be dangerous. They'd no doubt heard the slamming of desk drawers and the sound of staplers hitting walls. Signs that he wouldn't be dealing with his grief in a professional and reflective manner.

For one excruciating moment he thought she was going to burst into song. Something from *Les Misérables* perhaps. He then sensed what was coming next. Not a song, but something else. That word again. He couldn't stop it.

'I'm so sorry about your wife, sir. If there's anything you need.'

The lump in his throat was rising. He didn't want to cry. Not here. At his desk. In front of a colleague. He didn't want to make Cathy feel even more uncomfortable than she already did. And what did he need? He needed his wife not to be dead. And if that wasn't possible then he needed to be able to travel back in time so he could say goodbye. And no one could make either of those things happen.

He swallowed his grief.

'Thank you, Cathy, but I'm fine.'

Denise's brother, Terry, had flown over from New Zealand for the funeral. His wife, Helen, and their two teenage daughters, Rachel and Louise, were buttering bread in Denise's parents' kitchen for the funeral buffet that was being held at The King's Arms. Rex was sitting on a bench in the garden when Terry joined him. He quickly extinguished the cigarette he'd been smoking in the ornate glass ashtray by his feet, noting the disparity between the craftsmanship of the ashtray and its contents. He'd unfortunately recently returned to his twenty-a-day habit, but he supposed that it was preferable to alcohol; you could still walk in a straight line after smoking, lead police investigations.

They both gazed awkwardly into the distance, listening to the squeals of schoolchildren in the playing field beyond the hedge. An uneasy silence stretched between them, but before Rex could comment on the unseasonably warm weather, Terry had bypassed the usual introductory topics of conversation and gone directly to the elephant on the bench, Denise's cancer. And once he'd started he couldn't seem to stop – why hadn't they spotted it sooner, had they sought a second opinion, alternative treatments? You shouldn't be dying of cancer in this day and age. Well, why was it that people were? Rex had wanted to ask him.

On and on Terry sermonised, like a rising tide, like he'd been saving up all his questions for this moment, questions that Rex didn't know how to answer. He wasn't a doctor. He googled his symptoms like everyone else. And cancer was the last thing Rex wanted to talk about today. It was the reason why they were all here, buttering bread and waiting for the hearse to arrive. He wondered if he was the one being blamed. He wanted to say, and where were you when Denise was dying, when the shit was hitting the fan? I didn't see you demanding second opinions and driving her to hospital appointments. I didn't see you sitting with her while she vomited and cried and didn't want to die.

'She's here,' Denise's mother called from the doorway, and for a brief moment Rex expected to see Denise waving at him from the kitchen window, until he remembered that she'd never wave at him again.

He'd decided not to travel with the funeral procession and was making his own way to the church. He didn't want to be assigned the task of ensuring that Denise arrived. It already felt as if they were disposing of her, and perhaps they were, albeit in a lavish and respectful manner.

Rex wondered what kind of funeral service Denise would have chosen, had she known she would die much sooner than anticipated, had a small part of her not believed it was all a terrible mistake. He'd tentatively broached the logistics of dying with her (cremation or burial, probate, etc.) when she was first diagnosed, in the blasé way that people did when they didn't expect it to happen so quickly, and she'd said that she didn't care whether she was buried or cremated or whether it was a religious or non-religious service. Five minutes' silence in a motorway café or ten days of mourning. The decision's yours. It's for your benefit, not mine. I'll be dead. I won't care. Just don't scatter my ashes in the sea. You know how much I hate swimming. And any donations should be forwarded to the PDSA. I don't want flowers or wreaths. They'll just die. I want to save an animal's life.

At least she hadn't said, 'I want it to be a celebration, everyone in fancy dress and a few disco classics.' He wouldn't have been able to bear it.

Terry stood up.

'Smoking again?' he asked Rex, accusingly.

Again? How did Terry know that he'd smoked before? He lived over eleven thousand miles away. Was he now judging Rex's lifestyle as well as his medical expertise? Rex could feel the anger rising, bubbling like volcanic lava beneath his sternum. Surely he should be allowed to grieve however he chose to.

'See you at the church,' Rex replied sharply, lighting another cigarette.

When he arrived at St Swithin's a man in a straw hat was photographing the bell tower. It was Norman – the bell tower, not the man. The man was Lionel, Lionel Smart. He was a features editor at *The Community Gazette*, a local newspaper, and wrote a column called 'Once Upon a Time' that was popular among the older generation, who liked to remember the past and how things used to be – the air-raid shelter beneath the village hall, the housing estate and leisure centre complex that had once been a speedway track. Nostalgia was like catnip to the over-fifties. Rex even began a sentence with the phrase 'In my day' himself sometimes, much to his dismay.

St Swithin's was on the crest of a hill, surrounded by a moat of wildflower meadows and a panorama of uninterrupted sunsets. The graveyard sloped down to a river that sparkled like champagne. Rex would often sit on the riverbank and stare at his reflection, fish swimming across his face and distorting his features like a fairground mirror.

Lionel was lying on the grass, clicking feverishly. Lionel and his tripod had captured every seasonal depiction of the bell tower over the years: the bell tower iced with snow, bathed in autumn sunlight, glistening with summer rain, at dawn, at dusk, pink and lilac, yellow and golden.

Today it was the place where Denise would be buried.

Inside the church, Rex's breaths became increasingly more strained (possibly due to the nicotine in his lungs and the proximity of Denise's family). He wished he could have sat towards the back of the church, near the door, where there were fewer mourners. And the interior of the church was so dark and depressing he wished there *was* a disco ball hanging from the chandelier and Earth, Wind and Fire instead of Pachelbel's 'Canon in D Major' on the CD player.

He stared at the coffin as if it was some cruel prank, as if Denise would suddenly start knocking on the coffin lid pleading to be let out. He wondered if she was even dead. He hadn't been there. He hadn't heard her last breath. What if her pulse had been unusually faint or her heart had only temporarily stopped beating or she'd fallen into a coma and the physician on duty had announced her time of death without double-checking, Denise already on her way to the mortuary. Rex hadn't checked whether she was definitely dead either. She was his wife. She wasn't a murdered stranger whom he'd never met. He hadn't wanted to see her lying in a casket, couldn't even bring himself to select an outfit from her wardrobe, the blue dress that her mother had chosen, a dress that he didn't remember Denise ever wearing.

He wondered whether to stop the service so he could

confirm she really was dead, find a chisel from somewhere and prise open the coffin lid, but, before he could raise his hand, the church organist was playing the first chord of 'How Great Thou Art' and everyone was rising to their feet and he couldn't hear if Denise was hammering on the coffin lid or not.

After the service Rex remained by the graveside. He didn't want to go to The King's Arms with Denise's family. He wanted to be with Denise, not her family. He didn't want to see her father wiping his glasses for the umpteenth time or listen to her mother organising which sandwiches went where. He didn't want to have to answer questions about his failings as a husband and why he hadn't researched cervical cancer more thoroughly. He didn't feel any connection to her family whatsoever, now that there was a Denise-shaped ravine between them.

The sky was a swirl of coral and saffron. Gravediggers were quietly chatting behind him. Rex thought he recognised one of them, Raymond Bryant, whom he'd arrested for receiving stolen goods a few years earlier. When he saw Rex staring, he lowered the brim of his cap. Rex wondered what illegal activities he was involved in now. He hoped that it wasn't grave robbing or organ trafficking. He glanced at the row of strangers that Denise would now be joining – the 'Gone Too Soon's and the 'Sadly Missed' – and then he dropped the envelope that he was holding onto Denise's coffin. He'd read that writing a letter might provide some comfort. It hadn't.

As he was staring at the envelope, wondering whether to climb down and retrieve it, a bird swooped down, leaving muddy footprints across the envelope. What was he thinking?

It wasn't as if Denise would be able to read the letter. She was dead. *Wasn't she?* And shouldn't he have told her these things when she was still alive? He listened one last time for tapping or scratching from inside the coffin and hearing nothing but the sound of the bird's claws on the cherry-effect wood he turned and left.

Leaving the car where it was parked he exited the churchyard on foot and followed a lane dappled with clouds of elderflower. A flight of steps led down to the canal towpath. Left or right? Rex wondered. Left took him back into town, past the marina. Right took him deeper into the countryside, through cattle fields and woodland. Right, he decided, a darker, less travelled path. He didn't want to see anything picturesque. He wanted to see moorland mists, flooded plains and the steelworks in the distance. A barge drifted past, a Border Terrier captaining. A cyclist sounded a bell behind him, swerving past in colourful Lycra.

Pausing to smoke a cigarette beside Lock 56 he heard rustling in the hedgerow behind him, a bird possibly, or a wild hare. He crushed the cigarette beneath his foot and climbed over the stile, following a path that ran parallel to the towpath. At the point where the path forked right something caught his eye. A bird to the left of him was pecking at what looked like a piece of red fabric. To anyone else it might have looked like blood dripping from its beak, the unravelled intestine of a mauled animal, but Rex could see the fabric's frayed edges. A dropped glove that had been shredded by a nocturnal rodent? Or something more ominous? It was always best to assume the latter, particularly in his profession.

As he stepped closer the bird released what it had been

holding in its beak and flew away. There was more red fabric behind a nearby tree. It was as if the soil was bleeding or something bloody had been unearthed.

Finally, close enough, he saw a human skeleton, mostly intact, in a shallow woodland grave – slivers of red fabric clinging to the bones like ribbons.

The Third Girl

Joanne

While I was creating an entirely new person, I continued to impersonate existing people and steal their identities. I could be anyone I wanted to be, anything I wanted to be, and I took advantage of that. There seemed to be no limits to the life that I could lead. It started small. I'd adopt accents, assume names that I'd heard, walk with a different gait, change my handwriting – sloping the letters to the left rather than the right. I watched people constantly – their mannerisms, their habits, how they shook their hair from their eyes, how they smiled, held a coffee cup. I'd listen to them speak and then swallow their words and make them my own. Their voice became my voice. That's how it usually started. And then I would slowly take everything else.

Sometimes it troubled me that I would rather be someone else. It made my own life seem inadequate and inconsequential, which of course it wasn't. How many people are able to wear so many different disguises? I was no one and yet I was everyone.

Initially, I merely wanted to live as many different lives as possible. I liked the idea of being the sum of a series of moving parts, a chameleon assuming a façade that suited a particular situation or circumstance. I liked the idea of being a person that another person had spent a lifetime waiting for – becoming the very thing that person desired. I'd browse obituaries and headstones for new identities, ask my contact to create fake passports and birth certificates. And for a while I'd live that person's life, enrol on college courses, apply for jobs with false references and qualifications – until I lost interest. It seemed that everybody's life became tiresome after a while – even those that I'd woken from the dead.

The one role that I hadn't yet played and was most looking forward to, however, was that of a family man. I'd often wonder what the mother of my children might look like. Was that her drinking G&Ts outside Caesar's? Or was it the woman in the denim pinafore dress who withdrew money from the cashpoint next to the bookmakers? It didn't take long for me to find out. It seems that there are plenty of women willing to marry monsters.

My wife was seven months pregnant when the Collins family moved in opposite. I spent hours watching their daughter, Joanne, from the bedroom window. Her suede tasselled shoulder bag with the World Wildlife Fund badge that rhythmically patted her right hip when she walked, her caramel-streaked hair that almost reached her waist. I absorbed it all.

One afternoon when I was mowing the front lawn I saw her drop something on the pavement as she was climbing into a white car. I waited for the car to disappear and retrieved what had been dropped.

It was a silver front door key attached to a keyring shaped like a cassette tape, the letter J in gold printed on the label. I slipped it into my trouser pocket.

When Joanne disappeared a few months later, I would often come home to find her mother Maureen in our living room sobbing. My wife would be rocking a crying baby to and fro trying to comfort them both. Perhaps she's working as an au pair in The Hamptons or teaching English to Japanese businessmen, my wife would tell her. And even if she has been brainwashed by a religious cult or is suffering from amnesia like the newspapers suggest, then at least she's still alive. There was always hope, always something else she could be doing, somewhere else she could be, the hint of something vague stretched into a distinct possibility.

And I could tell that a small part of Maureen believed my overly optimistic wife, believed that Joanne wasn't gone, but was everywhere, doing amazing things, even though she didn't have a passport, because there was no evidence to suggest otherwise. When Maureen was in our living room, it was a room of Happy Ever Afters, the one place where Joanne was still alive.

Once when I came home from work Maureen and her husband Malcolm were sitting in the living room drinking coffee.

'How was Greece?' I heard my wife ask them, as if they'd just been on holiday.

Neither of them looked particularly tanned.

'Usual dead-end,' Malcolm said. 'She did look a little like Joanne, I suppose, but she was at least fifteen years older. French, I think she was, or Turkish.'

'Maybe it's time to stop looking, go to Greece on holiday instead,' my wife proposed.

I think she was getting a little tired of Maureen and Malcolm by then. She was running out of suggestions as to where Joanne might be.

'We'll never stop looking,' Malcolm assured her.

'He's got a computer now,' Maureen said, changing the subject. 'For spreadsheets. He locks himself away for hours at a time.'

'Hardly hours.'

'Spreadsheets?' I asked.

'Among other things.'

You really wouldn't think that they'd been to Greece at all, I remember thinking.

'Has anyone else been in touch recently?' my wife asked.

'An Irish doctor claims to have seen her outside Limerick. I'm planning to follow that lead next,' Malcolm said, as if he was planning his next holiday.

She wasn't outside Limerick, of course. She was where I'd left her. And where I continue to leave her. She's the only one of my victims that I move from time to time. I like being close to her. She reminds me of happier times, of long hot summers and sea lavender. Of being a family man.

On the day that Joanne disappeared, she'd spent the morning talking to Kevin Masters, the hot dog kiosk owner's son, now and then reaching down to throw a tennis ball across the shingle beach for her dog, Sasha. She didn't know that I was watching her, that Sasha had recognised me and was burrowing her wet nose in my palm and dropping the tennis ball at my feet. Nobody ever noticed me, until it was too late. Not once did she turn round. Not once did she feel that prickle of unease. She must have felt invincible, Sasha watching me watching Joanne watching Kevin as he wrapped hot dogs in greaseproof paper and shook mustard and ketchup bottles like tambourines. All part of the same watch chain.

Afterwards, I devoured every mention of her. I did everything in reverse – I killed her and then I got to know her. Her friend Samantha was interviewed for a television documentary and said that Joanne had argued with someone a few weeks before her disappearance, a man who'd been savagely kicking his dog in his front yard. Joanne had told him to stop, threatened to call the police if he didn't.

'It all got quite heated. He told her that he'd slit her throat if she called the police. She said that he must have a really small penis if he got off on hitting defenceless animals and told him to go fuck himself – if he could with his really small penis. She wasn't afraid of anyone.'

She'd been afraid of me.

'I told her not to get involved, we'd contact the RSPCA when we got home, but she'd already opened the gate, intent on rescuing the dog. And then a woman appeared at the front door with a rifle – I don't know if it was real or if it was even loaded, it looked ancient, like it had been on a wall or in a display cabinet – but she aimed the rifle at Joanne and told her that she'd blow her fucking head off if she didn't leave right now. Joanne reluctantly retreated, but before she left she turned to the dog and said, "I'll come back for you, I promise." And she'd have gone back if she could. I know she would.'

In a newspaper article Maureen detailed her own version of events that day.

There'd been nothing out of ordinary, nothing to suggest that she'd never see her daughter again. Joanne had taken Sasha for a walk along the seafront, finalised arrangements to attend a music festival with Kevin Masters and then later that afternoon she'd changed into white denim shorts and a red T-shirt to meet a group of friends at

Chapel Cove, although her friends had insisted that there'd been no plans to meet up that day, their individual recollections seamlessly intertwined, each other's alibis, while Kevin was confirmed to have spent the evening helping his father, Bernie, replace the brake pads on his motorcycle. Which had left Maureen's husband, Malcolm.

No one could corroborate his whereabouts that day. He'd claimed to be at derelict factory premises – the council had planning permission to build a hundred new houses on the site and he was allegedly conducting a risk analysis assessment – but nobody reported seeing him there and the council had no record of a risk analysis assessment having been requested. He didn't arrive home until eleven o'clock that night, insisting that he'd been in The Red Lion, but nobody remembered him being there either. He was a man you didn't always notice, he told police, but that didn't mean he'd murdered his daughter.

Psychics predicted that Joanne was in deep water (metaphorically, certainly), prison inmates claimed responsibility for her disappearance or claimed to have been involved or to know who was involved. Anonymous letters were received. For eight years an overseas postcard arrived each year with the words 'I'm still dead' written on the back. And even though her parents didn't recognise the handwriting, the police disagreed, believing that if her father hadn't killed her then it must be Joanne who'd sent the postcards.

Only I knew what really happened that day. Only I knew that a huge expanse of indigo sky had stretched above us like a gloved hand, that the car headlights across the headland had glistened like a thousand stars, that the moon had shone like a polished medal pinned to a military lapel and that, although I couldn't see them, I imagined the harbour boats bobbing up and down like coloured beads on a bracelet.

The waves crashed beneath us. A police siren screeched like a seagull in the distance. A whispering breeze rolled along the coastal path gathering secrets.

But all I could hear was the blood rushing through my veins, echoing in my ears.

Chapter Nineteen

WELCOME TO THE HOTEL PARADISO

'Jolene, we have a new guest in room thirty-nine, a Mr Knowles,' Janette informed Jolene brusquely, handing her an A4 sheet of paper. 'Can you please ensure that this questionnaire is completed by lunchtime?'

The questionnaire flapping in her hand, Jolene made her way to Mr Knowles' room. She sighed. The less she knew about people, the better. She didn't particularly want to spend thirty minutes probing a pensioner. And she was getting increasingly tired of Janette's controlling and unorthodox management style. She now seemed to think she was a hotel manager. She'd recently started calling the residents 'guests', hoped they were enjoying their stay at Sunset House, and was leaving feedback forms in their rooms, which inevitably ended up in adjacent litter bins or used as coasters.

The residents weren't particularly interested in a more varied menu or a games night every other Friday or whether staff helpfulness was poor (Jolene) or outstanding (Will). They favoured the familiar, which Janette would have known had she read the dementia advice guidelines instead of attending motivational lectures (a particular passion) and customer service seminars on branding, where renaming customers and premises apparently elevated a company's profile, distanced you from similar organisations (Janette couldn't seem to accept that a care home was still a care home no matter what you called it), although Jolene supposed it was a hotel of sorts.

No one was expected to make their own bed or clean the showerhead. And two-course meals appeared promptly at set times. You didn't have to rely on Jamie Oliver for inspiration. There was even entertainment – if you could call waistcoated organists and schoolgirl Adeles entertainment. If she heard 'Someone Like You' once more she was going to strike the next schoolgirl Adele across the face with the microphone. *Sing something else!*

She collected a cup of tea that didn't appear to have been introduced to a teabag from a passing refreshment trolley and knocked loudly on Mr Knowles' door.

'Room service,' she called.

She might as well keep up the hospitality façade, welcome him to the Hotel Paradiso (which was what Janette often called it, somewhat facetiously, Jolene thought).

There was no answer, so she opened the door. She'd be there until Christmas if she waited for someone to say 'Come in'.

Crosby Knowles was listening to an audiobook – Tom Clancy or Lee Child. Both disc cases lay on his lap. Jolene wondered why he didn't just download them, briefly forgetting that the older generation weren't iPhone literate. They still listened to albums on vinyl and read paperbacks.

They didn't realise that everything was now at your fingertips, your whole life on one device, instantly available (and instantly deletable) at the click of a button. She assumed that they'd all be deletable at the click of a button at some point in the near future.

He was wearing a diamond-patterned golf jumper in pink and cream and lime green tracksuit bottoms and he was smiling at her with his teeth *and* his eyes. She didn't think anyone had ever smiled at her like that before, like they were genuinely pleased to see her.

He already had a cup of tea (a perfectly brewed D4, as illustrated on the Tea Chart pinned above the kitchen drainer in the lounge), so Jolene settled herself on his bed and risked a sip of the cup of tea (tepid water) that she'd brought with her. Ironically, he did actually look like a hotel guest. There was a metallic grey suitcase with wheels beneath the window, a striped navy blue and maroon dressing gown hanging behind the door, and a collection of miniature toiletries had been arranged on a bathroom shelf in size order. Jolene noticed that there was already a feedback form on the bedside table, even though as yet there was very little to feed back. It looked like Janette had recently discovered Clip Art.

She dropped the form into the litter bin and introduced herself, loudly. She automatically assumed that all new residents had poor hearing, although they often tried to trick her by not wearing their hearing aids.

'Welcome to Sunset House. I'm Jolene and I'm here to learn a little more about you,' she enunciated slowly and clearly.

She sounded like the manager of a health spa or a tutor teaching English to overseas students, failing to appreciate that saying something louder didn't make it any more comprehensible.

'I'm not sure that I'm worth getting to know. I'm only here for two weeks,' he replied, at a normal decibel.

His hearing seemed fine.

'Everybody's worth getting to know, Mr Knowles, even if it's only briefly. Some of my favourite people I've only known for minutes,' Jolene confessed, her voice still too loud and too corporate.

There were few people whom she wanted to be in the company of for more than five minutes.

'And two weeks can easily become two years,' she continued. 'Ask Graham Whittaker. Actually, you can't ask Graham Whittaker because he died last month. But he was only supposed to be here for three weeks and that was four years ago.'

What on earth was she saying? Why did she always have to be so brutally honest? She swiftly added a caveat.

'That won't apply to you, of course.'

It was possible. He seemed normal so far, able to respond appropriately, and he hadn't fallen asleep yet, which was a positive sign.

'Let's hope so. I'm in the middle of painting the kitchen.'

'That's the spirit. Shall we start?'

'Do you always talk this loudly? My heart might be defective, but there's nothing wrong with my hearing.'

'Sorry, force of habit.'

Jolene worked her way through the list of banal questions that Janette had compiled. It was no *Question Time* debate. Sometimes, she imagined she was a journalist interviewing a politician or an actor, other times she threw in a curved ball – so, favourite sexual position, drug of choice? – insisting that they'd misheard her if they were openly horrified. It made the terribly mundane questions such as 'What's your favourite meal?' or 'What's your favourite television programme?' slightly more tolerable, but Crosby Knowles had led a genuinely interesting life, his answers far more fascinating than the usual 'cottage pie' or *Midsomer Murders*' or 'I've absolutely no idea.'

He was a semi-retired private investigator, a somewhat dangerous profession, it transpired, his clients often refusing to pay him or accusing him of lying and doctoring evidence because it wasn't what they wanted to see or hear and even, on occasion, attempting to kill him.

'One man tried to run me over in his four-wheel drive. While I was clinging to a hawthorn hedge on a grass verge, he kept trying to reverse.'

His wife Dolores, who'd recently died, had been a midwife.

'She wanted me to retire, said that I was too old to be clinging onto hawthorn hedges, and being semi-something was like being only half-interested in a thing anyway, but any assistance, no matter how sporadic, is always worthwhile. When I first set up Crosby Investigations I naively believed that I was going to change the world, that each case would follow the structure of a detective novel, the scene-setting, the cast of characters, the twists and turns, the mounting tension and then bam' – he clapped his hands together – 'the final curtain. Case solved, hands shaken. But it isn't like that at all. Often you're just treading water waiting for something significant to float to the surface that hopefully isn't a body, but at least you're there if it ever does.'

According to his medical notes Crosby had suffered a minor heart attack while driving and was now at Sunset House for two weeks' rest and recuperation because he had no relatives to care for him.

'No one?' asked Jolene.

'No one.'

'Everyone should have someone.'

Jolene had a sudden vision of her mother gasping for breath, in genuine pain. If Jolene relocated to Canada (she'd yet to broach the proposal with her father, too afraid that he'd say no), she'd have no one too, no one to call an ambulance, no one to hold her hand and comfort her. Would it be Jolene's fault if her mother died and she wasn't there?

'I have someone,' he said, sadly, a single tear sitting in the corner of his right eye. 'She's in here.'

He tapped his chest.

And then he introduced Jolene to his dead wife.

'Before she died she said that it was important that I moved on – with one proviso: under no circumstances should it be with Toni Bennett from number forty-seven, who apparently has absolutely no qualms about stepping into a dead woman's shoes while they're still warm. She was convinced that Toni had been slowly poisoning her with the homemade ginger cake that she kept leaving on the front step that Dolores insisted on eating because it reminded her of home.'

Jolene found herself actually listening and she rarely listened. Normally, she instructed and interrupted or, worse, ignored. She hoped that he wasn't the same private investigator who'd slept with her mother and stolen all her savings. She hoped that his wife's name *was* Dolores.

She asked him about his career as a private investigator.

'Most of my work is low-level surveillance,' he told her. 'Infidelity, mainly. I once received a top-of-the-range security system in return for following a man's wife to the Manor House Hotel on Wednesday nights and documenting her in various stages of undress with the man's brother. Never my favourite assignments, following adulterous husbands and wives, it's always so tawdry and unnecessary, but it paid well, and the promise of a hi-tech gadget was an added bonus.'

So he wasn't as unacquainted with technology as she'd presumed.

'Did you ever solve any missing person cases?'

'Not as many as I would have liked.'

'What if a missing person doesn't want to be found?' Jolene asked him.

'I can be creative and evasive if I need to be. Some people have their reasons for disappearing.'

'Any high-profile cases?'

'I'm afraid I'm not at liberty to say. It's a profession that relies on discretion.'

'Excellent hashtag.'

She hesitated.

'My friend Laura is missing. You've probably seen it on the news.'

He nodded.

'And my sister, Dolly, too.'

She continued, 'I wouldn't be able to pay you, but would you be able to take a look at their cases? I'd make sure that you had extra gravy at mealtimes and a spare blanket. It gets cold at night. Janette, the manager, turns the central heating down after lunch. She says that it's hotter than the Sahara Desert and gets annoyed when residents fall asleep in the middle of a singer's setlist or a comedian's stand-up routine. She considers it disrespectful. Personally, I think the blame lies with the acts themselves. There's a reason why they don't do it professionally.'

He was yawning.

Was she losing him?

'Admittedly, a care home isn't the most ideal location when conducting a criminal investigation, the Wi-Fi's temperamental and you'll be expected to participate in group activities, but any assistance offered will be gratefully received – if you feel well enough, of course. I don't want to impose, but, believe me, when you've seen the other residents you might be grateful for the distraction. They're even worse company than me. They make me look like the life and soul of the party and I assure you that I'm neither.'

She'd won him back.

He was intrigued. She could tell. She felt like an angler reeling in a prize-winning bream.

'Do you still have sources and contacts?'

'I have a guy.'

'I love that there's always a guy.'

'There's always a guy – a computer guy, a police guy, a prison guy, a handwriting "expert" who's an old poker buddy – sometimes it's the same "guy".'

He'd no doubt be able to extract information from the

unlikeliest of sources. He still ran an informant who apparently 'owed him' – 'info for life', he called it.

As he was retrieving an A5 spiral notepad and a pencil from a drawer, Jolene sensed that whatever she said in this room was going to be the start of something mutually rewarding and momentous. This was the reason why she'd been sent to Crosby Knowles' room with a questionnaire, not to find out whether he preferred tea or coffee, but to find Laura and Dolly.

Goosepimples speckled her bare arms.

'Begin at the beginning. Tell me everything.'

So Jolene did. She went back to the beginning, to the day that Dolly disappeared. No one at Sunset House knew that she was Dolly Edwards' sister. She never spoke about her. She didn't trust them to keep her secret. But she trusted Crosby Knowles. He wrote down everything she told him, everything she knew. She'd never realised before quite what a weight she'd been holding onto. Afterwards, she felt lighter, her shoulders straighter, as if she'd completed the first leg of a relay race and passed the baton onto someone else and it was no longer her responsibility. She was no longer expected to carry it; both Laura and Dolly were in Crosby's safe, baton-carrying hands.

She glanced at the clock on the bedside table, a small square travel clock that sat in a protective red leather case that could be clicked shut and slipped into a pocket when it was time to leave. She'd been sitting on Crosby's bed for over an hour.

'I'd better get back. But a word of warning before I leave. Keep your door closed. If Cora sees you she'll want to waltz with you and if Theo Winchester sees you he'll pass you a floor plan highlighting all possible escape routes.'

Chapter Twenty

THE GIRL WITH UPSIDE-DOWN FLAMES IN HER HAIR

'Have you been following anyone interesting recently?'

Will and Sophie were at The Riverside Shopping Centre having lunch at The Upstairs Café, chicken pesto paninis and cappuccinos. Sophie had been on a second date with Harrison, the man with a surname for a first name, whom she'd met online. Second dates for Sophie were unheard of. 'What's wrong with me?' she'd ask Will. 'Am I not thin enough or blonde enough?' She was both of those things. She was generic, a warehouse mannequin, a carbon copy of a million other girls her age, having swapped her fiery dark hair and individuality for blonde extensions and breast implants. If anything, she was *too* blonde, *too* thin. It was like living in a futuristic *I, Robot* world sponsored by *Playboy*.

He missed the original, feisty and opinionated Sophie, the Sophie with the upside-down flames in her hair. This Sophie had not only undergone a physical transformation, but had also seemingly been relieved of valuable brain cells during liposuction or some other cosmetic procedure. She often now veered towards the shallow and the superficial, the reality shows and the No.7 cosmetics counter in Boots. She'd just spent the last hour deciding between a Luna and a Stargazer lip gloss, eventually selecting the Luna one and then slipping the Stargazer one into her coat pocket (Will had pretended not to notice, relieved that some of the original Sophie still remained).

On previous Saturday mornings he'd have found her in Vinyl Heaven browsing through obscure Def Leppard albums and Van Halen memorabilia and in the afternoons in independent bookshops searching for first edition poetry books. She used to be able to recite several Emily Dickinson poems. Now all she wanted to talk about was *The Real Housewives of Beverly Hills* and Harry Styles.

Her panini remained untouched. When she told him that she'd already eaten, which he suspected was a lie, he reached across and transferred it to his own plate.

'I've told you. I don't follow people anymore,' Will replied (wanting to add, 'Just like you don't steal').

When he bit into the panini, he felt as if he was taking a bite out of Sophie, gnawing at the last remaining slivers of flesh on her bones and attaching them to his own frame, Sophie slowly disappearing while he grew larger, the disturbing image of a half-eaten Sophie seemingly not enough to prevent him from finishing the panini, which was both delicious and hugely disappointing. Instead of helping himself to Sophie's lunch he should have been encouraging her to eat it. Eating was the one thing he was good at. He suspected it was her mother, Elspeth, who'd triggered her eating disorder. Whenever she finally staggered home after three or four days on someone's sofa she'd tell Sophie she couldn't afford to keep feeding her, as if she was an insatiable, unnecessary extravagance. All he ever saw Sophie eat now was shredded lettuce and cucumber, which, as Sophie had recently informed him, was 96 per cent water.

A psychologist specialising in eating disorders had visited Sunset House a few months ago. Janette requested various in-house and external training sessions for both residents and staff, from stress management to drafting wills (a recent interest) to origami. If there was a course on something, then Sunset House would be one of its first attendees. This particular course had been more relevant than most because one of the residents had been refusing to eat, and it was unclear whether it was a medical condition, an emotional response to a past trauma or a means of gaining some measure of control over the fact that they'd been moved into a care home against their wishes. 'Emotional' was the consensus. Certain foods were reminding her of a traumatic incident in her childhood.

Will wondered if overeating was a means of gaining control over his own life, but it seemed more likely that he was losing control of it. He was no longer able to sensibly ration his portions and his health was deteriorating rapidly. There seemed to be a permanent fluttering inside his ribcage, possibly his thin self trying to escape. The effectiveness of taste buds declines as we age, the psychologist had told them, and it's often only the sweetest things that we are able to taste. Savoury foods may therefore benefit from the addition of herbs and spices.

Flavour wasn't a priority for Will. It was the size of the spoon that made most difference.

'Yeah, right. I have seen you, you know.'

What had Sophie seen?

Swiftly changing the subject, Will asked how her second date with Harrison had gone, but she seemed reluctant to discuss it, asking him if he wanted another cappuccino. He shook his head, introducing her to Gilbert instead, but he could sense that she wasn't listening. She was staring at something or someone behind him. Will turned round to see what she was staring at.

A group of teenage boys were inspecting the inside of each other's carrier bags outside GAME and several shoppers were gathered around The Body Shop entrance, watching a beauty demonstration. It could be that, Will supposed. Sophie was highly susceptible to a longer-lasting mascara or a coconut body lotion.

Minutes later, Sophie still seemed transfixed.

'Everything okay?' he asked her. 'Is there a sale on at Greggs that I'm missing?'

She didn't smile.

'Do you mind if we go to the cinema another time? There's something I need to do.'

Before Will could ask her what it was that was so urgent, she'd pulled on her coat and was negotiating a flight path around what appeared to be a hen party. The bride-to-be was wearing angel wings and singing 'I Will Survive', somewhat inappropriately, while the rest of the party had formed a conga behind her, chanting, 'Charlotte's getting married' and urging spectators to 'climb aboard'.

As he was reaching for his wallet he noticed Sophie had left a ten-pound note beneath her saucer and became even more convinced that something was amiss. She never paid. He checked his wallet. There was no cash missing. Perhaps she'd stolen it from the man at the next table. A leather wallet was tantalisingly jutting out of his trouser pocket.

Will quickly paid the bill and took the lift to the ground floor.

While he was queuing for popcorn in the cinema foyer, he saw Martin Williams walk past the glass doors. Will held his breath, hoping that he wouldn't see him. He didn't strike Will as someone who would consider three recent sightings a coincidence, even though they had all been coincidences.

Or a sign that Will really should start following him and there was no time like the present.

Abandoning his popcorn order, Will hurried out of the cinema foyer and began his pursuit. Following people on foot was something of a novelty nowadays when everyone drove everywhere, and tailing someone in a vehicle didn't provide the same level of jeopardy or excitement, unless it involved a high-speed police chase or was fuelled by road rage.

Martin Williams was wearing an oversized black leather jacket. Will imagined it squeaking with every step. If he was closer he'd be able to hear it. He quickened his pace as he crossed the road at the traffic lights. He felt the familiar exhilaration that always surfaced when he was following someone who had no idea they were being followed: the anticipation of learning their rituals and routines, of living their life, wearing their skin. How easy would it be to step into their shoes and carry on walking? he wondered. How easy would it be to be that person?

He wasn't sure where Martin Williams was going, but it wasn't in the direction of Gilbert's property, which he'd assumed was where he was now living. He was walking briskly, too briskly. Will wished he hadn't had that second panini. His heart was racing from both the adrenaline and the exertion. He hoped it wouldn't be much further. He didn't want to have to start incorporating an exercise regime into his daily schedule to increase his stamina.

He noticed a girl in a mink coat (fake, he hoped) walking a few metres in front of Martin Williams and he wondered if Martin Williams was following her, which would have made Will a stalker stalking another stalker, although that wasn't a term he ever used, of course. He was simply curious, inquisitive, collecting the minutiae of people's lives, the traces of themselves that they left behind. The term 'follower' had a similarly negative subtext, synonymous with cults and social media, which begged the question – what was he and what was he doing? It was a difficult question to answer, almost impossible to explain.

On the corner of Madison Avenue, Will almost collided with someone walking in the opposite direction. Fortunately, it wasn't Martin Williams doubling back to confront him; it was Luke Trent.

'All right?' Luke asked.

Will wanted to say, 'No, I'm not all right. I've recently accused an elderly man of abduction and murder and I'm now following his son,' but he just nodded.

Over Luke's shoulder Will watched Martin Williams unlock

the front door of a terraced property, glancing left and right before stepping inside and closing the door behind him. The girl in the mink coat who'd been walking ahead of him had disappeared.

Luke fell in step with Will as he headed back to the cinema.

'I don't suppose you know if Jolene's working today?' Luke asked him.

'Probably,' Will replied.

She'd been working more hours than usual over the past few days, spending most of her time with a new resident, Crosby Knowles. Janette had pulled her aside during a morning meeting and told her that staff weren't allowed to have favourites (they all did, of course, even him, it was only natural to gravitate towards like-minded individuals) and if she didn't divide her time equally between residents then they'd have to let her go.

'Only I really need to speak to her…'

Will wasn't listening. He was wondering why Martin Williams had keys to two properties. Did he live in both? Was he leading a double life? Two homes, two families. Was he a landlord with a glowing portfolio of rental premises?

During the next few days Will spent a total of seventeen hours following Martin Williams without him noticing, but his life had seemed even less remarkable than his own, although as well as dividing his time between two dwellings, occupants unknown, there was also a third, smaller and more remote, residence. A triangle of real estate. Will didn't know if he was simply gluttonous (not in a calorific way like him, but entrepreneurially and materialistically) or whether he merely liked the symmetry that these three geometrically aligned points provided.

All that he did know was that he needed to gain access to all three properties. Maybe people (he pictured a terrified Laura Sykes chained to a bedroom wall, her floral print dress blood-stained and torn) or possessions were being surreptitiously moved from one residence to the next.

Like chess pieces.

Like father, like son.

Chapter Twenty-One

DREAMS ABOUT DEAD GIRLS

Retracing his footsteps along the towpath to obtain a phone signal, Rex called Cathy. When she didn't answer her mobile he dialled the police station switchboard and was put through to Connor Raine, a reasonably competent officer, but one who rushed into situations without first assessing the risk factors. His parents were from Tucson, Arizona, and he seemed to have inherited an American single-mindedness that was doubtless admirable, but sadly misplaced in an English town where ambition was regarded with some suspicion. Rex had once caught him swivelling on his, Rex's, office chair, trying it out for size. He'd also interrupted him reprimanding an imaginary employee on his office phone during a Boxing Day game of Trivial Pursuit, 'If that report isn't on my desk in an hour, there'll be hell to pay!' – something that Rex couldn't remember ever saying. He'd never considered himself a managerial cliché, an office caricature.

Rex asked to speak to Cathy, forgetting that she'd booked a day's annual leave.

'*Sister Act The Musical*, sir,' Connor said by way of reminder, adding, 'Isn't it your wife's funeral today, sir?'

There was a tense silence.

'Can you gather a team of officers together? I've uncovered human remains down by the canal, Lock 56. We need to cordon off the area ASAP. I'll call Glenda.'

As a senior crime scene investigator Glenda Clough's role mostly entailed waiting for the dead to reveal themselves, secure in the knowledge that they would reveal themselves eventually, whether it took months or decades, avalanches or earthquakes. Over the years she'd sacrificed several family holidays, weddings and christenings in favour of crime scene preservation and evidence recovery, and one of the first things she'd ever said to Rex was how carefully you had to listen to bones to hear what they were saying because understanding how a person had lived was as important as determining how they'd died.

Her empathy for the dead far outweighed her affection for the living, which in Rex's opinion was problematic because the dead, like the living, were often unreliable narrators. They didn't always speak the truth. They didn't always know the truth. They could be blindsided like everyone else.

'Whenever I look at someone now I always imagine what they'd look like dead,' she'd told him morbidly at one of the station's Secret Santa gift exchanges. 'I never see the amber flecks in their irises or the pink sheen of their lips. I just see the pale wash of death as I peel back their skin and begin weighing their organs.'

Such lyricism from such wretchedness, Rex remembered thinking, as he was unwrapping a Spice Girls calendar.

Predictably, Glenda could barely contain her enthusiasm.

Rex returned to the shallow grave and lit a cigarette while he waited. As expected, Glenda was the first to arrive. Zipping up her protective jumpsuit she offered her condolences and then knelt down beside the remains with a camera and a collection of evidence bags. She'd also requested lighting and a cotton canopy. The wood was so dark that Glenda was astonished that Rex had spotted the remains at all. He was loath to admit that the more impressionable part of him had wondered if the remains were a parting gift from Denise, a cadaver exchange, a balancing of the scales. Denise would have known he'd need some kind of distraction today.

Or that he'd had a strange feeling.

He didn't have strange feelings very often, almost never – just once really, when he knew that missing six-year-old Amanda Jennings was at the bottom of a forest lake. He never told anyone that he'd seen her slip beneath the rippling water, her ponytail the last part of her to disappear, that he'd dreamt about her, because who does that, dream about dead girls?

No, it was best he didn't mention dead girls and corpse swaps and talking bones. He was already half-deranged with grief.

Connor eventually arrived with his chalk-white magazine smile and a roll of crime scene tape, trailed by Colin and Dale, and, wrapping the tape around the lock and the stile, they temporarily cordoned off the towpath while the area was examined.

Rex wondered how the body had been transported there.

By narrowboat, seemed the most likely scenario, certainly the most efficient. The incline was slippery and steep with no clear footpaths.

Alternatively, of course, the victim may have been killed at the burial site, an argument escalating into violence, a night sky concealing the crime. Rex was already assuming that it was murder even though Glenda had given him no indication of cause of death, but that was always a police officer's first instinct. Expect the worst and then you won't be surprised.

Glenda made no such assumptions. *Cause of death is for the pathology lab to determine. Mistakes at this stage are costly. The examination of a crime scene is as important as the subsequent investigation.* Rex could recite Glenda's customary responses verbatim. For someone who claimed to be able to hear the whispers of the dead, she was unusually fixated on rules and regulations.

Connor was still smiling, sanguine and unfazed, even when dealing with human remains. Rex was surrounded by so many cheerful and dedicated officers that it was akin to working at a holiday camp. He often felt like the pantomime villain. There were rumours that Connor was sleeping with Suzanne, the Superintendent's wife. Normally, station gossip bypassed Rex completely. He wasn't fond of it so he didn't listen, but this particular rumour seemed to have unintentionally reached his ears. He wished that it hadn't. It made him judgemental. It made him look at people differently. It made him wonder what lay behind Connor's porcelain veneers and Suzanne's homemade brownies.

His mobile phone vibrated inside his pocket. A text from Denise's mother. He ignored it. He couldn't tell her that he'd rather oversee the recovery of a stranger's remains than attend his dead wife's wake.

Back at the station Rex spent the remainder of the afternoon watching police officers flick elastic bands across the open-plan workspace outside his office door, reflecting on how little everyone else's lives had changed and how someone might lose an eye if this juvenile behaviour continued, but too emotionally distraught to put a stop to it. Connor was sitting on Alan Shenton's desk leaning over his computer. He considered himself something of an IT expert. Big Al, they all affectionately, and ironically, called five foot three Alan. All except Rex, who just called him Alan, or DC Shenton if he needed to be more formal, which, recently, was becoming more and more necessary. Alan had a habit of using undue force on detained suspects and Rex had had to remind him on at least four occasions that this wasn't how they did things here, or anywhere else for that matter. 'I'm a Londoner,' Alan had responded with a shrug. 'I'm used to Big City crimes and Big City ways of dealing with them.'

Those Big City ways had recently resulted in him breaking a suspect's wrist, allegedly accidentally, when the suspect had tried to attack him with a razorblade, but the razorblade was never recovered and the suspect denied ever having a razorblade, claimed that DC Shenton had twisted his arm behind his back with such force that he'd actually heard his wrist snap.

Christian Andersson, a Swedish police officer, whom they'd

naturally christened Hans and who was new to the station, new to the country in fact, confirmed Alan's assessment of the incident and Alan was given a verbal warning. Police officers closed ranks, no matter where they were from. It was a universal unspoken rule. But it was only a matter of time before events escalated and a broken wrist became murder and murder became a prison sentence and a prison sentence became a death sentence because Alan's fellow inmates had discovered that he was a police officer.

Connor suddenly leapt off Alan's desk and began walking towards Rex's office. Rex's gaze immediately returned to his computer monitor, in the hope that Connor would veer right in the direction of the vending machine. He'd seen enough of that smile for one day. It was giving him toothache. Unfortunately, he didn't veer right. He walked straight into Rex's office without knocking. Even when the door wasn't closed most people still politely tapped on it, but for Connor an 'open door' policy (Rex had recently reinstated said policy after a brief hiatus) meant that he could walk in whenever he pleased without prior warning.

'A few of us are going for a drink after work, sir, if you're interested.'

Rex hadn't been expecting this. An invitation. To join them.

'I appreciate the offer, Connor, but I need to catch up on a few things.'

He actually needed to start a few things.

The security footage obtained from Barclays, Laura Sykes' place of work, hadn't shown her leaving the bank on the day she disappeared, even though it had captured her arriving, and none of her colleagues could remember seeing her leave. She'd either left via another exit, the security camera had temporarily malfunctioned or she'd never left. Rex imagined her trapped behind one of the bank walls, locked inside an unused vault, her fists bruised and bleeding. *The Girl in the Wall. The Girl who Never Left.* He'd requested a copy of the original floor plan of the building to check for other possible exits and false partitions, even though Superintendent Forrester had questioned whether that was absolutely necessary.

He was also planning to re-interview Nathan Sparks, the deputy bank manager. He'd been unusually unconcerned about Laura's disappearance, confident that she'd reappear once she'd 'cooled down'. When Rex had asked him why she'd need to cool down, he'd claimed that it was just an expression. It didn't mean anything. Sometimes you just need to take a breath. And why would Laura need to take a breath? Rex had asked him. No reason. Cathy had similarly mentioned a need for space. Not everyone who needs five minutes to themselves vanishes into thin air, thought Rex. There are plenty of perfectly adequate toilet cubicles and designated smoking areas available.

And while Colin and Dale had been diligently working their way through hours of camera footage, Rex had been staring at the world map on his office wall, surprised at how little of the world he'd seen and wondering if now might be a good time to book a round-the-world cruise (after they'd found Laura Sykes, of course), until elastic bands started flying past his open door.

'Cathy's coming. You'll be able to hear all about *Sister Act The Musical*.'

The last thing that Rex needed was an encyclopaedic

re-enactment of a musical about singing nuns. Or maybe he did; every last detail. He glanced at the doodle of a seashell (with nothing but the sea rushing through it) on his jotter, pictured a pale-skinned Denise wheeling a drip through the house like a terminally ill ghost while a Tesco ready meal lay congealing on his lap. Everywhere and yet nowhere.

'Why not?'

'Great, we're meeting at The Watering Hole at seven thirty. See you then.'

It almost felt like a prank, like Rex would be sent to The Watering Hole and everyone would be in The Skylark. It was the smile, Rex thought. It made a lie seem believable. But surely they wouldn't do that to him on the day of Denise's funeral. Send him on a wild goose chase.

It wasn't a prank. Most of the station's off-duty police officers were there. In fact there were so many police officers there that it was like being back at the station, but with a bar and Bon Jovi on the sound system. There didn't appear to be any regulars. But police officers did that, Rex supposed, emptied a pub as soon as they walked into it, slowed down cars, curbed tempers. That was their superpower. Few people acted like themselves in front of police officers, which was perhaps a blessing. Rex had been on the receiving end of more than enough drunken punches and obscene taunts during his career. He'd seen people reach for weapons, witnessed fellow officers being stabbed and shot. He'd much rather a person walked away than stood their ground.

Cathy waved him over – 'I saved you a seat,' she mouthed, pointing at the empty seat beside her. Craig and Dale were playing darts in the corner, while Connor and Alan stood by the pool table, chatting, their cues planted between their feet like flags. Karen Long and Perry Saunders were ordering drinks at the bar. Karen asked Rex what he was drinking. A Heineken, thanks, he told her. Maybe a Heineken would make *Sister Act The Musical* more palatable, and by the time Cathy had concluded her monologue today would be tomorrow and it would no longer be the day of his wife's funeral.

The next morning he woke with a headache that thudded with the persistence of someone waiting to be let in. Although he'd only had three beers the night before he felt as if he'd had far more. He rolled away from the empty space where Denise should have been, a space that felt as vast as an ocean, and stood under the shower until the water ran cold. He was exhausted. Several times during the night he'd been woken by skeletons jangling like car keys and blackboard-chalk fingernails scraping the inside of locked cellar doors. The fourth time he'd woken, at 4.43 a.m., according to the luminous digits of the clock on the bedside table, he'd decided that tomorrow (it was already tomorrow) he was going on a road trip. He'd been thinking about one of the Missing Joannes. In fact he thought that it might have been her scratching her initials on the back of the wardrobe door at 4.43 in the morning.

JC.

Joanne Collins.

Perhaps the dead were now conversing with him; the greater the audience, the more likely that someone was listening.

Superintendent Forrester again urged Rex to take advantage of the compassionate leave that had been offered when Rex called to inform him that he was driving to Anglesey to speak to Maureen and Malcolm Collins. Once again, Rex declined.

'I don't know what you expect to accomplish,' the Superintendent replied, archly, after Rex had briefed him on the case. 'We shouldn't be wasting time and resources on thirty-five-year-old cases. We should be focusing our energies on finding Laura Sykes.'

But were they wasting their time? Cathy's philosophy, that the origins of most crimes lay rooted in the past, was persuasive. Current serial killers influenced by past ones, children replicating the sins of their parents, revenge killings. It seemed to Rex that cold cases were just getting colder. But you still had to keep your foot on the accelerator. You still had to defrost the case file once in a while. There are no new crimes, Cathy had said, paraphrasing Mark Twain, merely new ways of committing them.

And did it matter how long ago Joanne had disappeared? The passage of time didn't invalidate a crime, particularly in light of advances in forensic technology.

'Don't worry, I won't be claiming expenses.'

Superintendent Forrester sighed.

He wasn't going to stop him. He'd just lost his wife.

She isn't lost! I know exactly where she is.

'As you wish, but I'll expect you back at your desk first thing tomorrow morning,' he told him, curtly.

Rex was beginning to wish that he had taken the compassionate leave offered and driven to Anglesey without telling anyone, spent the night on a chilly hotel balcony, gazing at a distant shoreline and an unfamiliar sky, surrounded by people whom he didn't know and who didn't know him.

Cathy texted him as he was leaving.

Hope last night wasn't too horrendous for you, sir.

I've had worse days, he replied.

That's good – not that you've had worse days, but you know what I mean.

I do.

Good news! The Lyceum had a last-minute cancellation for Sweeney Todd: The Demon Barber of Fleet Street for tonight. Restricted view, but still.

Sometimes Rex thought that life would be far easier if he sat through these musicals himself instead of listening to another person's lengthy interpretation of them. He'd at least be able to fall asleep without anyone noticing.

Chapter Twenty-Two

ALISON IN WONDERLAND

Passing a baton onto someone more qualified wasn't as straightforward as Jolene had anticipated. She'd mistakenly believed that once she'd completed the first two hundred metre leg then normal service would be resumed, allowing Crosby to quietly investigate Laura and Dolly's disappearances alone, but she discovered that she wanted to keep running with the baton. She wanted to keep the finish line in sight, peering repeatedly over Crosby's shoulder, requesting updates.

She'd even purchased a notebook so that she could compile her own notes – a teal soft cover Moleskine notebook with an elastic enclosure that she'd purchased from Ryman's. It was far more professional than the notebook that Will had been using, which had been appropriated from Janette's stationery cupboard (with or without Janette's consent, Jolene didn't know, although it probably didn't matter. Will could get away with murder, as far as Janette was concerned. Jolene, meanwhile, had once been reprimanded for picking up a pen).

Jolene hoped her notebook gave the impression she looked for people all the time, cemented her role as Crosby's assistant, regularly dispatched on preliminary fact-finding missions and undercover assignments and, when she was fully trained, carrying the baton permanently. She didn't mind working pro bono initially, while they built a client list and a reputation for solving the most complex cases. Displaying a charitable and altruistic side was a shrewd career move.

Jolene and her notebook were currently sitting on Crosby's bed waiting for him to finish a phone call. Big day for the notebook, she thought, wondering if she should have chosen myrtle green rather than teal, a new silver Gel pen positioned between her fingers like a tabloid journalist.

'Who was that?' she asked him, when he'd ended the call.

'A retired police officer who was part of the original investigating team when Dolly first disappeared,' he told her.

'Really?'

'Don't get too excited. His memory's a little hazy. He's going to take a look at his notes and call me back.'

'Talking of notes, what do you think of my new notebook?'

She didn't feel that he was paying it the attention it deserved.

'You do know that it's what's in the notebook that matters?' he replied.

Why can't it be about what's on the outside for once, Jolene thought, the pleasure gained from something being aesthetically pleasing?

She humoured him.

'Of course. But first impressions matter too. You don't get to make a first impression twice.' (This sounded like a quote from a self-help book. In fact it probably was a quote from a self-help book; her mother had several books on positive thinking and manifestation that Jolene flicked through occasionally.) *And* it cost £11.99.'

'Well, it's very … stylish.'

'Thank you. I knew you'd be impressed.'

The notebook appropriately complimented, Jolene reached down and removed her mother's scrapbook from its carrier bag, handling it as if it was an ancient scroll. She was terrified of damaging it or losing it. Her mother didn't know she'd borrowed it and Jolene prayed she'd never find out. Her mother had taken the scrapbook to Laura's mother's house a few nights earlier and pored over each article with her to see if there were any similarities. But it was twenty years ago. There were very few similarities, apart from the ice rink still being open and both their daughters having disappeared. She could only imagine Laura's mother's frustration as she had to sit through another mother's twenty-year-old grief.

After Dolly disappeared her mother had alternated between two opposing emotional states – mania and despair. Today, she'd probably be diagnosed with bipolar disorder, but back then it had been considered an unusually extreme reaction to loss and treated with a course of antidepressants.

During the manic episodes when her mother would be roaming the neighbourhood in an agitated state befriending drug addicts and sex workers and the homeless, sometimes pretending to be homeless herself so that she could move among them more freely as she tried to gain their trust, inching closer to the ringleaders, the people who knew everything (her obsession with Liam Cole came later), Jolene would be sent to stay with her grandmother.

And then, just as Jolene and her grandmother had acclimatised themselves to the unexplained absences and erratic behaviour, a shawl of despair would wrap itself around her mother's shoulders and she'd lock herself in Dolly's bedroom and sleep for eighteen hours a day. It wasn't actually Dolly's bedroom, of course. Dolly had never lived there. When her parents separated and the marital home was sold, her mother had brought Dolly's bedroom (minus Dolly) with them, painstakingly reproducing it from Polaroids. All that was left of her, a shrine. Jolene wondered if Dolly's Room would now follow them like a wave; as necessary as a bathroom or a kitchen.

Jolene would sometimes visit the mausoleum her mother had created and defiantly move Dolly's possessions a few millimetres to the left or the right. She'd replace the apricot lip gloss on the dressing table with a cherry one or rearrange two items of clothing in the wardrobe that were the same colour, nothing her mother might immediately notice. It made her feel more visible, more commanding. She'd only ever removed something from the room once – a *Just Seventeen* magazine. She never did it again. Her mother slapped her so hard across the face that she fractured her jaw. She couldn't bear the thought of Dolly's belongings smelling of Jolene and not Dolly, although they didn't even smell of Dolly anymore. They just smelled musty and unloved, coated in decades of dust.

But even though it felt as if the walls had been daubed in pig's blood and they were wading through the cremated ashes of the war-ravaged and diseased, Jolene always preferred the despair to the manic episodes because at least her mother was safe. When she was wandering the streets showing Dolly's photograph to drug dealers and sometimes taking the drugs herself, Jolene imagined all kinds of terrible things happening to her as she navigated the depths of a dark and sinister underworld where shapeless creatures crawled through the pavement cracks and tried to lure her into a panther-black abyss.

Jolene hadn't told her mother that she'd enlisted the help of a private investigator, partly because she didn't want to raise her mother's hopes, but also because there was something oddly prophetic about one sister finding another sister (she imagined the headlines – 'Girl Missing for Twenty Years Found by Sister', 'Dolly and Jolene Reunited').

As she was showing Crosby the faded newspaper clippings that her mother had collected over the years, the scribbled notes in the margins and the typewritten timeline stapled to the back page, Jolene realised that she genuinely did want to know what had happened to Dolly. She wanted the story to end. It was the only way she'd be able to unhook herself from her mother's reins.

And, like Cora, she too had discovered a passion. She wanted to research and examine and analyse something so thoroughly that it became something else and existed independently of itself. She wanted to feel the magnetic pull she imagined all new investigators felt, the universal appeal of an unsolved mystery – the unveiling of clues and red herrings, the growing list of suspects, the drum-roll reveal, the arms-folded satisfaction of a resolution. And if she showed Crosby how serious she was, perhaps they'd eventually become business partners. She'd need a filing cabinet full of stationery then.

The only obstacle in her way was Janette. She'd recently threatened to terminate Jolene's employment for 'spending an unacceptable amount of time with one resident to the detriment of others' and was now regularly coaxing Crosby out of his room by insisting that he join them for the mid-morning crossword and the local secondary school poetry readings and Alison's *Alice in Wonderland*-themed Tea Party, which was four hours long. As suspected, Cora had been desperate to dance with him, pressing a freshly powdered pink cheek next to his, and Theo, shaking his hand, had passed him a hand-drawn map of the care home detailing all possible escape routes. Inevitably, Crosby would then be exhausted and would fall asleep in front of the television, the investigation sabotaged.

Jolene wished that Janette would take extended or unpaid leave, leaving Rob, one of the deputy managers, in charge. He didn't walk along the corridors in a pencil skirt holding a clipboard and pointing out faults. And Janette should have been thankful that she was giving at least one of the residents her undivided attention.

There was a sudden knock on the door.

'Tell whoever it is that you can't do today's chair exercises because you've sprained an ankle, while I hide in the bathroom,' Jolene hissed, sliding the scrapbook beneath the duvet in case it was Janette, but it was a dishevelled Gilbert who stood in the doorway, asking if he could place a bet on the two-thirty at Epsom.

'I'll take him back to his room,' Jolene sighed, as Gilbert's daughter suddenly appeared, apologising profusely, and, firmly grasping Gilbert's elbow, guided him back along the corridor towards his room.

'That's nothing,' Jolene confided in Crosby when they'd gone. 'You should hear the things he's been saying to Will. It's obviously nonsense, look how confused he is, but apparently he keeps mentioning killing someone and repeatedly referring to a Naomi and a Joanne. Two police officers were in his room last week and, between you and me, I suspect that Will had something to do with that. He takes everything so seriously.

Crosby suddenly became pensive, so pensive that Jolene later asked Will for an update on Gilbert, but Will brushed her questions aside, agreed that it was probably nothing, although Gilbert had recently made some remark about a Winter Rose, but that could be a flower rather than a person.

'Do you get roses in winter?' Jolene asked him.

'I've no idea. I'm not a gardener. Ask Luke, he might know. He's been wanting to speak to you.'

'Never mind, I'll google it later.'

She asked Will why the police had been in Gilbert's room and he said he didn't know, but Jolene could tell he was lying. He was sweating and he wouldn't look at her.

'You've told them what Gilbert's been saying, haven't you? You think he really has murdered someone.'

'I haven't told them anything,' Will replied, still sweating, still not looking at her. 'They could have been in his room for any number of reasons.'

'I know you're lying. Look, I'm not going to tell anyone, if that's what you're worried about.'

She was definitely going to tell Crosby.

'What else has Gilbert been saying?'

'He says a lot of things. I thought you weren't interested.'

'Yes, well, I've now decided that I am. Why does he only say these things to you?'

'Because I'm the only one who listens?'

'No, that isn't it. It's something else.'

Jolene thought for a moment.

'Perhaps you remind him of someone, a friend, an acquaintance, an accomplice. He still recognises people sometimes, doesn't he?'

'I really don't know, Jolene. Are we done? I need to get Sheila ready for her theatre trip. I don't know why it's suddenly so important.'

'It's important because he may know something. He may know where these girls are. And there may be other girls that he's not yet mentioned.'

'We don't even know if any of these girls are actually missing. And it's in the hands of the police now anyway.'

'So it was you!'

She hadn't meant to be so forceful. She didn't want to trigger another panic attack or mini stroke or whatever it was that he'd been having when she'd found him clutching his chest in the staffroom. But she suddenly needed answers, and being a private investigator meant finding those answers promptly and by whatever means necessary. It might be too late for Dolly but there was still time to save Laura.

Later that evening there was a breaking news bulletin.

'Human remains have been discovered in a densely wooded area alongside the canal. As yet no further details have been disclosed.'

Jolene's skin went cold.

Her mother reached for the phone.

The Anonymous Girl

Faye

'Where's your mother?'

My daughter shrugged, uninterested. My son studied the Rice Krispies in his cereal bowl.

I'd been gone for two days and there were scratches on my neck and soil beneath my fingernails.

I'd been burying a girl with no name. Normally, I liked to know the names of my victims, but the girl had refused my repeated requests that she introduce herself, so I'd killed her in a violent rage and it hadn't gone particularly well. It was chaotic and messy, not at all like I'd imagined. She'd gouged and kicked and spat at me and she'd almost escaped. And now I'd have to wait until she was reported missing to learn her name. I hoped that she was someone who would be reported missing. I didn't like killing people who wouldn't be missed. What would have been the point of that?

My son finished his cereal and went upstairs while my daughter continued to smirk at me.

I'd forgotten that I'd shaved off my beard and was now wearing non-prescription black-rimmed glasses in an attempt to further conceal my identity. I still regularly changed my appearance as a precautionary measure. It was an endless source of delight for my daughter.

'I said, where's your mother?'

'I don't know.'

'You don't know or you won't tell me?'

'She's your wife.'

'And she's your mother.'

'I'm going out. Good luck finding her.'

I loathed being a family man. As much as it masked my true identity, it involved too much responsibility and compromise. But I loathed my children even more. Neither child was particularly fond of me and it had little to do with teenage hormones. I think they'd realised from an early age that the feeling was mutual. If I ever grudgingly picked them up they would scream until they were the colour of a new bruise and then when I'd pass them back to my wife they'd be serenely sucking their thumbs as if it had been someone else screaming. I wanted to see fear in my children's eyes. Instead, I saw hatred and contempt and a thousand other things, but never fear. I wondered if that might change if they knew what I'd done and sometimes I wanted to whisper those things in their ears while they slept. I wanted to tell my daughter that it was her face that I pictured when I killed someone. But then I'd wonder if they already knew.

I was desperate to walk away, but I'd worked hard to appear ordinary. And maybe I'd got used to clean sheets and home-cooked meals. I certainly felt the cold more. To appease my burgeoning wanderlust I'd move my family from one house to the next like pawns. But four people living in the same house, wherever that house might be, was suffocating. I missed sleeping alone beneath the stars, no constraints on my time other than those that I imposed upon myself.

One day, unable to tolerate my dreary suburban existence a second longer, I laced up my boots, pulled on a waterproof jacket and closed the front door behind me. And it was like before, no agenda, no timetable. Just me and whatever lay ahead. I was unreachable for five days. On my return I discovered that my wife had called the police. She never called them again. My wife wasn't arrogant or insolent like my children. She was quiet and timid, accepted any name change or house move that I proposed with an obedient nod. I often caught a tremor in her voice or a flash of fear in her eyes. I expected it. She understood what might happen if I had to repeat myself.

My children, however, were not so compliant. Individually, they were separate parts of me, the worst parts of me, but together they were all of me, a second version of me, a monster. My daughter would glare at me venomously from across the room while my son began to ignore me just as I'd ignored him. My son looked most like me, but instead of feeling an affiliation with him and seeing him as a kindred spirit, a confidant, I could barely look at him. It was like looking at my reflection in a mirror. I spent much of my life walking away from myself, as he did me.

My daughter meanwhile had inherited my more unpleasant traits. She was malicious and spiteful and manipulative. I saw her once pinch the arm of one of the neighbours' children. The child was crying as my daughter twisted their pale skin between her fingers and dug a little deeper. She whispered something in the child's ear before letting them go, no doubt warning them that if they told anyone about what she'd done she'd climb through their bedroom window when it was dark and chop them into tiny pieces. That's what I would have whispered.

When a young child went missing later that year, I often wondered whether it was my daughter who was responsible.

I had frequently speculated over the years whether it was genetics or my unconventional upbringing that had shaped me, and my children seemed to be proof of the fact that it didn't matter how soft your pillows were or how well-stocked your fridge was, a black heart was a black heart and it bled through generations, leaving its liquorice stain. I considered ending the cycle, setting fire to the house while they were asleep inside it, so that I could burn the sneering, cruel side of me that had somehow found its way into the world without me, unintentionally seeped out of me for everyone to see. I wanted to hear ear-piercing screams and terrified squeals. I wanted to see swirling smoke and pounding fists on windows that wouldn't open. I wanted to smell my own flesh burning.

Perhaps one day I would.

I decided to call the nameless girl Faye, after my daughter.

Chapter Twenty-Three

A BEGINNER'S GUIDE TO A LIFE OF CRIME

Will was parked outside the Williams property eating a pepperoni pizza. When Martin Williams had arrived at Sunset House as Will was leaving he'd decided to capitalise on the opportunity and take a look around the family home while he wasn't there. Earlier, he'd asked Gilbert whether Martin had a family, but had been met with a stubborn silence and then a list of girls' names (which may or may not have been related to his initial question, but Will suspected not) that he'd reeled off like an attendance register.

Gilbert was getting noticeably more confused and forgetful and Will couldn't help but feel partly responsible, his relentless questions further dislodging the fragile shards of Gilbert's brain, causing years of fractured memories to come loose, shaken like pill bottles, thrown like dice, until there was nothing left and the memory of these girls' deaths died with him, unsolved. Was he pushing him too far? Perhaps someone more qualified than him would achieve quicker and less harmful results.

Will had nonetheless written the names in his notebook, documented their existence – Esther, Greta, Gina, Heidi and Winter Rose, which could have been a person or a flower (as he'd told Jolene when she'd started interrogating him for no reason). The Winter may even have been a surname, Rose Winter. He'd been waiting for a surname.

There'd also been more descriptive phrases ('a forest of ferns', 'a mountain stream', 'a crescent moon' – burial sites, lines of verse?) and an item inventory ('a keyring', 'a scarf', 'a brooch'. Trophies? Will pictured the peacock brooch beneath his bed, the blood on his finger) woven into the narrative. And it occurred to Will that he might have been listening to the confessions out of context without noting what Gilbert had just been watching or reading or who he'd been talking to. He had to remind himself that both circumstance and setting were equally relevant and, in the interests of providing an accurate account, such observations should be recorded.

Yesterday he'd asked John Thorley about Gilbert when he'd been getting him ready for bed.

'I don't know anyone called Gilbert,' John had said, his crystalline blue eyes glistening like Alpine lakes in the glow of the bedside lamp.

'You talk to him sometimes, play cards.'

'I know a Peter, Peter Rivers, could it be him?'

'Not Peter, Gilbert.'

'Who's asking?'

'I'm asking. Will.'

'I don't like it. I don't like it at all.'

Communicating with the elderly could be as frustrating as untangling Christmas tree lights.

It had been Will's intention to update DI Spencer on any further developments, but he wasn't sure that the DI was taking his concerns as seriously as he would have liked. He hadn't been back to see Gilbert and he hadn't kept Will informed of any progress. For the relationship to work there needed to be transparency on both sides. Will chose not to dwell on the unsettling thought that being in the police force was on a par with welding or finance, some days it was just too difficult to muster up the appropriate level of enthusiasm, but he hoped that the wheels of justice were still turning even if he couldn't hear them.

And although Martin Williams hadn't publicly accused Will of contacting the police, of setting something irreversible in motion, it didn't mean that he wouldn't. Will was a terrible liar, as Jolene had quite accurately pointed out.

Mercifully, Martin Williams had signed his name in the visitors' book and walked straight past him.

It was Cora's son who'd followed Will out, head bowed in reverence as he'd unlocked his iPhone. It didn't matter what time of day he visited, he always looked as if he'd been erecting scaffolding or painting bus shelters. Will had politely held open the door, Cora's son barely acknowledging him as his thumb slid across the phone screen. He didn't seem the type of person to be posting photographs of Michelin-starred cuisine on Instagram or engaging in Twitter rants. Perhaps he was on a dating app. Will wished that he'd glance up occasionally, if only to see the delight on his mother's face when she waltzed around the lounge to, and possibly with, Frank Sinatra, maybe video her on the phone that he couldn't put down.

He'd briefly considered following Cora's son. He often juggled multiple targets; referred to them as Sleepers when he took a temporary leave of absence to re-engage with another target (some of the people he followed were more interesting than others). He certainly wouldn't notice him because he never glanced up, although following someone who only communicated by phone was inherently limiting and an online presence wasn't necessarily an authentic presence. Will thoughtfully watched him climb into a black car and drive away. He was reminded of Harrison, the person whom Sophie had been communicating with online, and had actually met. He hadn't heard from her since their lunch date at The Upstairs Café. He'd text her later.

The house was in darkness. Perhaps it was empty, Martin Williams having finalised the sale of the property, which would make Will's reconnaissance mission easier, but far less productive. Or perhaps, as he'd hoped, Martin Williams lived there alone. The last slice of pizza consumed, Will locked the car and crossed the road. An early evening hush had descended upon the neighbourhood. The golden ears of corn behind the cul-de-sac at the end of the road, which had earlier burned orange, were now blackened around the edges as dusk fell.

A smell of garlic drifted through an open window, Indian spices. Will's mouth watered. He'd call at the Taj Mahal on the way home, order a chicken tikka masala. An aeroplane passed overhead, too far away and too fleeting to notice him.

Quietly opening the gate, he walked along the path towards the back of the house, pausing beside an amber-flecked rotary washing line. Somewhere, a dog barked, but the

Williams house remained silent. Will almost stepped into a small pond, moss-green with algae and lichen, by the garden fence. He wondered how deep the pond was, whether it might contain human bones, but when he measured the depth of the water with a twig he could see that it was too shallow.

Stone steps led down to a mildewed greenhouse where teetering columns of plastic plant pots in varying sizes and breadcrumbs of loose soil populated the glass shelves. The floor of the greenhouse appeared intact. Beyond the greenhouse a low brick wall curved around a domed barbecue and a potholed lawn. Will searched the lawn with his torch and found a silver teaspoon and a Carlton Casino keyring, both of which he put in his pocket. He'd examine the items in more detail later. There might be blood on the keyring, saliva on the spoon.

He then examined the concrete paving that comprised the upper third of the garden, knelt down to check how level it was. There were no apparent disturbances. A couple of bottle tops, a ten pence piece and an earring lay beneath a patio chair. He held the earring in front of the torch's beam and rotated it between his fingers – a gold hoop with a broken clasp. He slipped it into his pocket and then sat on one of the patio chairs, closing his eyes so he could hear the evening more clearly; eliminating one sense brought the other senses into focus, sharpened them. It was something that his mother had taught him. Close your eyes, she'd say. And then none of it will matter. And sometimes it didn't matter. But sometimes it mattered more.

Finally, he approached the back door. All the windows were closed and the upstairs curtains drawn. He couldn't see an alarm. With a gloved hand he turned the door handle, even though the door was unlikely to be open; people rarely forgot to lock doors nowadays. As expected the door was locked. He tried the front door. A double-decker bus rattled past, a plume of grey smoke spluttering from the exhaust, the twilight silence magnifying the roar of the engine. The door was locked.

He returned to the back door and reached into his pocket for a paperclip. He'd spent the past couple of weeks refreshing his lock-picking skills on YouTube, practising with the lock on his bedroom door. It was a skill that every person who followed someone should have. You never knew what you might see, who you might need to rescue.

As he was unfolding the paperclip he became acutely aware of the fact that he was about to cross a line. This wasn't innocently following people. This was a violation of their personal space. This was criminal intent. Will had recently discovered that Crosby Knowles was a semi-retired private investigator and he'd wanted to share his thoughts on Gilbert with him, ask his advice, but before he could introduce himself Jolene had whisked him away like a secret. Will was surprised. He didn't think she'd have had time for someone who pried into people's private lives. She'd surely want to tell them to stop concerning themselves with things that didn't concern them.

When his parents were arguing his mother would always tell him to stop concerning himself with things that didn't concern him, but how could he not be concerned when he could hear them through the bedroom wall? Sometimes things did concern him.

Earlier, Janette had informed him that he would now be in

charge of Mr Knowles' care because Jolene was no longer fulfilling her other duties, and her non-compliance with discriminatory legislation was risking the future of the care home. If it had been anyone else they'd have been commended for their attentiveness, but because it was Jolene, Janette chose to be petty and melodramatic.

'Isn't he going home soon?' Will had asked, recalling one afternoon a few days ago when Gilbert's daughter had been outside Crosby's room, a mobile phone pressed against her ear, a faint smell of chlorine in the air.

'All the more reason to cut the reins,' Janette had said, 'before he gets too dependent.'

Will had assumed the conversation was over, but then Janette had glanced at her watch and told him she had a spare ten minutes if he wanted to discuss the social care course he'd been thinking about enrolling on. He'd forgotten about the lie, the course that he'd pretended to be considering when he'd been caught stealing the notebook from the stationery cupboard but, even if it had been a genuine consideration, he certainly wouldn't have wanted to discuss it with Janette in her office.

Fortunately, before Will could politely decline, John Thorley had fallen to the floor with a thud just ahead of them (not so fortunate for John Thorley, of course), his walking frame rolling along the corridor without him. He'd landed awkwardly and was clutching his elbow, groaning. Janette had rushed over to him. She was only ever truly happy when she was rushing from one crisis to the next, believing herself indispensable and irreplaceable.

John Thorley spent hours walking around the home and,

unlike Will, he didn't seem to need an incentive, such as a carrot or another person ahead of him. Will had asked Janette whether they should commission a local artist to paint Cumbrian hills or Welsh valleys on the corridor walls so that he could pretend (or genuinely believe) that he was outdoors, but she'd said that although it was an excellent idea as always, they couldn't risk exposing the residents to poisonous paint fumes.

It made Will dizzy watching him do countless laps around the lounge, easily accomplishing his daily step count. Will asked him once if he'd done a lot of walking in the past and he'd nodded, said that he'd always liked walking, even as a child. 'I lived on a narrowboat once,' he told him. 'I wouldn't recommend it. It was like sleeping in a floating coffin.' It was only recently that he'd reluctantly started to use a walking frame because his ankles were swollen and he'd been diagnosed with early-stage emphysema. Only recently that he seemed to have no recollection of who Gilbert was, or of the secrets they'd shared.

'This is Jolene's fault,' Janette had muttered, as she was asking John Thorley where it hurt.

How it was Jolene's fault, when she wasn't even there, Will didn't know.

'Up go my "No Serious Incidents" statistics for this month,' she'd sighed. 'Rhonda at Sunrise House will be jumping for joy when she sees an ambulance racing past.'

Finally, he heard a click. He refolded the paperclip and slipped it back into his pocket before opening the door. An owl hooted from its roost behind him. Will stepped into the house and quietly closed the door, the beam of his torch sweeping across the walls like a speeding moon, revealing a long narrow hallway painted in what he thought might be pistachio. Car headlights illuminated the Art Nouveau stained glass panel above the front door.

There were three closed doors along the hallway. The first door led into a kitchen. It didn't look as if the house was being sold. It looked lived in and was tidier than he'd imagined, the dishes washed and stacked on a wire drainer, the bread wrapper neatly secured. He'd expected a dimly lit, germ-infested interior filled with pornographic magazines, takeaway boxes and drug paraphernalia, the inside mirroring the outside. But he supposed even monsters could be organised and house-proud.

He opened the next door. Perhaps the further inside he ventured, the more cluttered and chaotic it would be, like the inside of Gilbert's head, but if anything it was even tidier. On a sideboard there was a photograph of a young girl on a swing, her feet touching the sky, a watery smile. Martin Williams' daughter? Gilbert's daughter when she was a child? Will couldn't imagine Gilbert having young children, pushing them on swings and listening to their rollercoaster screams, and then afterwards pushing strangers' children into meadow dirt and listening to different screams. He hoped that the child wasn't asleep upstairs if it was Martin Williams' child.

An exercise bike and a collection of Haynes Car Manuals occupied the third room alongside unlabelled cardboard boxes arranged like Jenga blocks beside a wood burning stove. It was either a room for storage, the first room to be emptied, or the room's belongings had yet to be unpacked.

Back in the hallway Will noticed another door beneath the

stairs. A cupboard? A cellar? There was a padlock on the door. Was someone being held captive here, on a quiet moonlit street that smelled of Indian spices? Laura Sykes perhaps? Was he about to rescue someone, or discover their body? He placed his torch upright on the floor and retrieved the paperclip.

As he was inserting the straightened paperclip into the padlock he heard the creak of a floorboard behind him.

'What are you doing?' a voice asked.

Chapter Twenty-Four

THE HURTING KIND

Bon Voyage! Cathy had generously texted as Rex was leaving the Welsh mainland, charitably disguising the disappointment she no doubt felt because he was driving to Anglesey without her. Cathy relished time away from her desk. 'We don't get out of the office as often as I'd like,' she'd remind Rex at the end of every staff appraisal, failing to appreciate that a police officer's role was mostly administrative. There were very few car chases and shootouts and all-expenses paid trips to the Bahamas, although her choice of conference or course was often dependent upon its location and they'd once stayed in Ramsgate overnight.

A man who'd been missing for seven months had been sighted on the seafront and Cathy had treated it like a weekend away, purchasing a Kent travel guide and a bottle of Ambre Solaire from a WHSmith at one of the motorway services. Rex had had to remind her that it was a work trip, but she'd told him that sightseeing could be just as productive as perusing a suspect's bathroom cabinet. 'You never know what treasures you might find,' she'd said, turning to the index at the back of the Kent travel guide. 'I wonder if there's a theatre in Ramsgate.'

He'd often thought she'd be better suited to West End set designing than policing, although her crime-detecting skills *were* exemplary, even when she was seemingly preoccupied modelling sunglasses and flip-flops or checking theatre listings and local attractions in newsagents' windows. While she'd been supposedly checking the availability of afternoon boat trips around Ramsgate harbour she'd suddenly nudged Rex violently in the ribs, alerting him to a drug exchange beneath the pier.

And undergoing plastic surgery to evade identification provided no safety net. She'd once been strolling around Lewisham and seen Cliff Palmer and his new nose on the opposite side of the street. They'd been looking for him for three years and he was thought to have been in South America. She'd followed him to a gated community in a leafy suburb and then called it in. He was arrested that same afternoon.

There was a roadside café up ahead. It was actually called The Roadside Café. Rex admired the simplicity. He pulled into the car park and, before going inside, called Denise's mother. He hadn't expected her to answer the phone crying and was immediately wrong-footed. 'Rex, is that you?' Disconnect the call, he thought, don't say it's you. You don't need this. Your own grief is too raw, your capacity for compassion too small. He swallowed. Men weren't supposed to cry, were they? They were tough and resilient. They were just supposed to deal with whatever life threw at them, particularly men who were also police officers.

'How are you, Delia?' Rex finally rallied, pondering the different Days that now lay ahead of him – Days when he might notice the cherry blossom on the trees signalling the start of spring and Days when every thought he had would sear his flesh like a branding iron and cause him immeasurable pain. And then the Days in between, the Days when there was nothing at all, which seemed somehow far worse.

He tried to ignore the desperate sobbing in his left ear and instead watched a man wearing a chef's apron and black and white checked trousers toss a bin liner into one of the commercial waste bins at the back of the café. A muscular-looking monochrome man with his sleeves rolled up, wearing a black bandana with skulls printed on it. He looked like someone who could deal with anything.

Eventually, Delia ran out of words, but the sobbing continued. Rex said he'd call again in a few days. He wasn't sure he would. It was too soon. Maybe it would always be too soon. The café door chimed when he entered. He was the only customer. He ordered a bacon and egg roll and a mug of tea, then sat by the window watching the traffic pass by, wondering who these people were and where they were going and whether any of them were people he knew, people he was looking for.

The waitress – Cindy, according to her name badge, black liquid eyeliner framing her brown eyes – strolled over to the window while he was eating, similarly mesmerised by the passing vehicles. Or maybe she was staring at her reflection. It was difficult to tell.

When he left the café a radiant red sun had been pinned onto a sky as blue as the mouthwash on his bathroom shelf and seagulls were sitting on caravan roofs in the distance like defending sentries. The sea lay just beyond the trees, the air salty and gritty. Behind him a stream glistened like a sequinned ball gown. A tractor rumbled somewhere in the distance.

When he'd spoken to Maureen Collins earlier she'd told him they'd be waiting. Waiting for news, Rex assumed. Why else would he drive all the way to Anglesey if he didn't have something important to tell them? He'd stressed that it was just a routine visit, he didn't want to raise their hopes, but he suspected it was too late for that. Hopes had already been raised.

He parked outside a pebbledashed ex-council house that had been painted white. There was a wire mesh hanging basket to the right of the door, pink and purple begonias spilling from it. The door itself was a glossy turquoise with a glass porthole, the doorknocker a silver anchor, comprehensively polished to within an inch of its life, a slippery thing in his hand. He glanced at the other houses along the street. The house directly opposite was less maritime, more 'haven't got the time' – flaking windowsills, streaks of green paint that had run down the pebbledash like tears, a broken garage door swinging open and closed, and a lucky dip of children's plastic toys scattered across the lawn that looked like they'd been left outside all winter.

He could see a fishing boat in the distance, a net tossed over the side. He pictured himself sailing away, nothing but a thumbprint on the horizon.

A small, thin woman opened the door. Tight grey curls framed her face and she was wearing a pleated tartan skirt and a cream-coloured jumper. Rex noticed a hole on the right sleeve. Rex had always been observant, which Denise had never quite been able to believe. 'What colour shoes was that estate agent wearing?' she'd ask him as they were driving home. 'What song was that busker playing at Charing Cross Station?' She was always testing him, said he wasn't normal. Men didn't notice these things. He did. He didn't want Denise disappearing, like his mother had.

Rex introduced himself with his ID card. He always produced his ID card, even when it wasn't requested. There'd even been occasions when he'd been asked to wait on the doorstep while a sceptical homeowner rang the number on the back of the card. But better that than let a conman walk into your house and steal your life savings. He'd once given a talk at an elderly day care centre on how to deal with bogus callers and distraction thefts, but the women kept asking him if he was married and the men sat snoring. Scheduling the talk after lunch had been an oversight. Attention-spans were poor and guidance on keeping doors locked and not being pressured into letting someone inside your home was like a sedative, like spraying lavender oil onto a pillowcase.

The nautical accents continued inside the property – acrylic fishermen in cable-knit sweaters, fabric doorstops shaped like beach huts, a red and white wooden lighthouse masquerading as a table lamp, and a collection of blue-and-white-striped cushions and throws. A Jack Russell with a sailor scarf knotted around its neck sat watching him from the sofa. On the mantelpiece inside a seashell picture frame was the photograph that had been used in all the media publicity, Joanne with her arms wrapped around her long deceased

Golden Retriever, Sasha. Rex had learned the dog's name when he'd spoken to Ken Dawson, the lead officer on the original investigating team, who was now retired. Rex wondered why a missing person was always expected to smile. It would have been far more appropriate if they were crying or in distress, conveying a sense of gravity and urgency rather than seeming to be enjoying themselves, wherever they were.

Maureen Collins told him that her husband would be home shortly. He'd gone to buy a newspaper. She asked Rex if he'd like anything to drink. He declined, but he did need to use the toilet, and it wasn't an 'I'm going to pretend that I want to use the toilet so that I can take a look upstairs' toilet visit. He actually did need to use the toilet. Besides, there wouldn't be anything in the house that would aid the investigation now, unless Joanne was buried beneath the floorboards. Too many years had passed.

The front door opened as he was coming back downstairs. A folded newspaper was tucked under Malcolm Collins' arm and he was holding a carton of milk. Rex introduced himself with his ID card, somewhat embarrassed that Malcolm Collins would now think he'd been snooping around upstairs.

His wife stood watching them from the doorway.

'I'm not sure why you're here,' Malcolm Collins said, tersely, placing the newspaper and the milk on the console table by the front door and shaking off his jacket. 'How many times do we have to go through this? It upsets Maureen.'

Rex couldn't tell if his wife was upset or not. Her eyes gave little away. But they obviously hadn't heard the news about human remains being found or if they had then they'd dismissed the possibility that it might be Joanne.

She addressed her husband. 'He's just doing his job, Malcolm. And she's our daughter. I'll never stop wanting to talk about her, especially now my memory's trying to hide her from me.'

Malcolm Collins wanted to forget that he'd ever had a daughter. His wife was trying to keep her alive.

Rex followed them into the lounge, scrolling through his phone for the photographs Cathy had forwarded to him, the ones of Gilbert Williams she'd taken at the care home, the ones she shouldn't have taken without Gilbert Williams' consent. She'd also taken a DNA sample that day too, a used tissue she'd had checked against the national DNA database that had returned no results and that Rex had only recently found out about. He hadn't yet decided what course of action he planned to take: a quiet word, a caution, disciplinary proceedings. Cathy was one of his most dedicated and conscientious officers, but she could be unpredictable and didn't always follow protocol, which might ultimately lead to unsafe prosecutions and the collapse of Crown Prosecution Service cases. He'd talk to her when he got back, although he hated those 'Can I see you in my office?' conversations.

Rex explained that, although no new evidence had come to light, they were following a recent line of enquiry and Joanne's case was one of several they were looking into. He suspected they were wondering why it wasn't a local police officer knocking on their door. Joanne had disappeared from her hometown, not hundreds of miles away.

Not that it mattered, of course. While it was true that most serial killers operated within a specific radius, dependent upon mobility and lifestyle, others crossed borders and age ranges and remained active for a number of years.

He handed Maureen Collins his phone and asked if they recognised the man in the photographs. They examined Gilbert Williams in microscopic detail, enlarging the images with their fingers, passing the phone back and forth. Malcolm Collins removed his glasses and peered more closely, eventually shaking his head, although whether from denial or despair, Rex couldn't be sure. Maureen switched on the lighthouse lamp that glowed red like a warning in order to see his face more clearly. She walked over to the window, tilted the phone and then tilted her head. They desperately wanted to recognise him.

'He doesn't look familiar,' Maureen said, handing back the phone. 'Who is he? Does he know where Joanne is?'

And that's when he heard it, the click of a locked door being unlocked.

Rex was both relieved and disappointed. Relieved that their daughter might still be alive, but disappointed that he hadn't been able to establish a connection between the Collins family and Gilbert Williams, although he could still be the one responsible for abducting or murdering their daughter and it was entirely possible that they'd never seen him or met him. He wasn't known to have lived in the area. It crossed Rex's mind that maybe he was searching for people who were alive rather than dead, saved rather than missing. It was possible. Anything was possible. It also occurred to Rex that Gilbert Williams might not have always been Gilbert Williams and that the photographs in his room, the photographs that he'd asked Maureen and Malcolm Collins to take a look at, were, as

Cathy had proposed, of somebody else. He wished Cathy had had the foresight to take a photograph of Gilbert Williams as he looked now.

As he was about to apologise for any distress his visit might have caused, his phone vibrated. Rex excused himself and walked into the hallway. The human remains he'd found had been identified. They belonged to Joanne Collins. *This* Joanne Collins.

He'd had no idea that he'd be bringing Joanne with him.

Chapter Twenty-Five
THE SUNSET HOUSE TALENT SHOW

Finishing the painting of Crosby's kitchen was an offer that Jolene was now regretting.

'I hope you're not expecting a professional finish,' she warned him, gazing despondently at the dove-grey kitchen walls that didn't look like they needed painting at all and then at the whipped cream, Swiss Meringue, peaks in the paint tin by her feet.

How many coats of paint was this going to take?

'Any assistance, no matter how slapdash, will be gratefully received,' Crosby assured her.

He was wearing a rainbow-coloured short-sleeved Hawaiian shirt decorated with cartoon penguins and llamas, butter-yellow socks and jade-green chinos with red trim. He'd spent most of the morning in the garage searching for his notes on Joanne Collins.

Crosby had disclosed his connection to Joanne Collins, whose remains had recently been discovered, on his penultimate day at Sunset House, during the staging of a talent show in his honour.

Janette had insisted they have a leaving celebration. She'd purchased 'We'll Miss You' balloons and a 'Good Luck' card and a selection of cupcakes from The Cupcake Emporium and she'd allocated herself the role of head judge for the talent show that she'd spent the previous two days organising. Sheila had just finished a soprano rendition of 'Dancing Queen' and a new resident, Herbert, was next to perform with his ventriloquist dummy Jeffrey, when Crosby had revealed that he'd been hired by the Collins family when Joanne Collins first went missing. He'd been living in Anglesey at the time, about to start work on a child custody dispute.

Unfortunately, however, after completing preliminary interviews with several neighbours and four of Joanne's schoolfriends, and discovering that a man who'd threatened Joanne when she'd accused him of mistreating his dog had been in police custody on an unrelated matter at the time of her disappearance, and was not considered a person of interest, Joanne's parents unexpectedly terminated his contract – influenced, he later learned, by a couple who lived opposite, who'd developed a close bond with the Collins family shortly after Joanne's disappearance.

During the talent show finale, Cora recreating 'The Dance of the Little Swans' (or rather Swan, singular) from *Swan Lake* in a pink tutu, Theo telling insulting *Sunday Night at the London Palladium*-style mother-in-law jokes and Enid playing 'Wonderwall' excruciatingly badly on the ukulele, Jolene had seated Crosby on the chair vacated by John Thorley next to Gilbert so that he could converse with him, determine whether he recognised him at all, but no positive identification could be confirmed, and Crosby had ultimately brushed the encounter aside.

'It was a long time ago,' he told her. 'And Joanne's a common enough name. There's no doubt an innocent explanation.'

Not when someone has confessed to murder.

For a private investigator, Crosby could be remarkably dismissive.

For Jolene, a hunch or a feeling often felt like enough.

She'd received the same lacklustre response earlier when she'd shown Crosby one of the photographs in Gilbert's room.

And then the afternoon had spiralled into further disappointment when Janette had declared Enid the winner of the talent show, causing Cora's face to contort in confusion. She wasn't accustomed to losing. Jolene had had to gently steer her towards Crosby and a consolatory red velvet cupcake, glaring angrily at Janette as she'd presented an undeserving Enid with a bouquet of chrysanthemums. Noel Gallagher's ears must have been bleeding after being subjected to the torturous scraping of Enid's ukulele strings, thought Jolene.

'No cause of death has yet been established, according to my police source,' Crosby was saying, as he browsed his emails. 'But I suspect the remains will be too degraded.'

'What about the retired police officer? Did he get back in touch?'

Since the announcement that human remains had been discovered and subsequently identified, her mother had left a series of increasingly frantic messages and voicemails for the officer in charge of Dolly's case (even though there wasn't actually an officer in charge of her case), demanding to know what steps were being taken to find Dolly in light of this new development. She seemed physically incapable of letting another mother grieve for her dead child. And whoever the messages and voicemails had been passed on to, if indeed they had been passed on, seemed to be actively avoiding her calls.

Jolene meanwhile had been searching Dolly's Shrine for something that might have been overlooked – a coded message inside the pages of a diary, random letters underlined in biro in favourite novels – even though her mother would have already forensically examined what remained of her missing daughter with a magnifying glass.

Silver branch-like creases graced book spines and crescent-sharp indents where page corners had been folded down with thumbnails bookmarked specific passages, but there was no teenage anguish, no secret admirer. And the diary that Jolene had found was mostly blank, just two dental appointments and a reminder to purchase train tickets. She'd even read Dolly's school reports, filed neatly in year order. Dolly had been far more academically gifted than Jolene. She was going to cure cancer, discover life on other planets. She was going to make a difference, be somebody, unlike Jolene, who would amount to little. Everyone agreed. Dolly was the 'one to watch'.

It was unfortunate they hadn't been watching her on the night she disappeared.

Jolene often thought *she* should have been the one to disappear because she wouldn't have been such a loss to the world. She wasn't worthy of a shrine or a mausoleum, which made it all the more puzzling that her mother even cared where she was and who she was with, although there'd been many times in the past when she hadn't.

'He did,' Crosby replied. 'He's forwarded copies of his notes. Liam Cole was questioned twice by police, mainly at your mother's insistence, but he was never considered a suspect, despite Dolly's friends claiming that he was jealous and controlling.'

Crosby plugged in his laptop charger and continued.

'There are noticeable similarities between the two cases – age, appearance, opportunity – suggesting that it could be the same perpetrator. Serial killers can easily extend their reach nowadays, crossing oceans and continents, changing their identity to avoid detection. Few people spend their entire life in one place, or kill in one place, and solitary, transient professions such as long-distance lorry driving or sales, where you can be away from home for weeks at a time without attracting suspicion, are a convenient way of facilitating criminal behaviour. But even though the world is geographically smaller and more technologically advanced, there are still plenty of blind spots. And of course there's no evidence to suggest that Dolly was actually abducted so I would suggest keeping an open mind.'

'What about Laura? Have they traced her phone yet?'

'It was switched off on the day she disappeared and there's been no activity since.'

While arranging a packet of shortbread fingers into petals or sunbeams, or maybe neither, on a dinner plate, a jammie dodger in the centre, Crosby mentioned that Toni Bennett had left a chicken curry on the doorstep a couple of days ago.

'A chicken curry?' Jolene asked, trying not to sound alarmed. 'You didn't eat it, did you?'

She remembered his wife Dolores insinuating that Toni Bennett had been trying to poison her with homemade ginger cake. Would she poison Crosby if he spurned her advances?

'No, I wore it as a hat. Of course I ate it, well, most of it – it was delicious.'

'You should be careful about eating things that have been left on doorsteps. You don't know what might be in them.'

'Chicken, I would hope. And the neighbours left all manner of things on the doorstep when Dolores died, casseroles, lasagnes, stews. It's called being neighbourly.'

'People could have life-threatening peanut allergies. It's not neighbourly. It's irresponsible. Let me know next time she leaves something.'

'This investigation is making you paranoid.'

'I'm not paranoid. I just don't trust anyone.'

'So said the person who most definitely *is* paranoid.'

When Crosby went into his study Jolene wrote 'doorstep chicken curry' in her notebook to remind her. She'd take a look in his kitchen bin later and retrieve what he hadn't eaten. Didn't he know that undercooked chicken could kill him?

Returning with a handful of files, he asked Jolene if she'd like a brief demonstration of the hi-tech security system that he'd been given in exchange for obtaining photographic evidence of a husband's adulterous wife.

She wasn't especially interested in security systems, but she was even less interested in satin paint so she followed him into his study.

It was how she imagined the flight deck of a Boeing 747 to look, a console of dials and buttons and levers and red warning lights. Four CCTV monitors, capturing images from multiple locations, were attached to the far wall above a series of control panels, and the system beeped like a heart monitor on a hospital ward, interspersed with occasional buzzing, like electrical currents running through overhead power lines.

Smaller monitors at the back of the room provided a more extensive view of the neighbourhood – an elderly woman wearing a patterned headscarf walking along the pavement carrying two carrier bags of shopping, an empty van parked outside the house opposite, *Expert Roofing*, a man pruning roses in his front garden, a window cleaner stroking a cat on a windowsill. It was a voyeur's paradise. And the picture quality was exceptional. It was like watching Netflix.

'When foxes pad across the back lawn, you can see every strand of fur, the detail's amazing,' he told her.

You'd have thought he lived in perpetual fear, but Jolene couldn't imagine Crosby being afraid of anyone, although she had noticed him glancing over his shoulder a couple of times when she'd walked him to his front door. And he'd confessed to having been in prison, although he hadn't told her why.

She noticed the time on one of the monitors. She was working an overnight shift later, not because she'd managed to persuade Janette to change the rota, but because a flu virus was working its way through the temping agency that she used. Jolene told Crosby that she'd finish painting the kitchen tomorrow and made him promise not to eat anything else that had been left on the doorstep.

Before leaving she removed the liner from the food waste caddy and told him she'd pop it in the recycling on her way out, instead placing it on the passenger seat of the car.

Her mother wasn't in when she arrived home. Jolene hoped she wasn't sitting in the police station foyer accusing the police of conspiring against her, of cherry-picking evidence to suit a theory, of getting it wrong. She was that critical voice in your ear late at night – *you're pathetic, you're worthless, you're a fucking useless piece of shit.*

Jolene hid the potentially poisonous chicken curry leftovers in the outdoor storage shed – she'd research online poison detection kits tomorrow – and quickly showered and changed.

As she was stirring a saucepan of tomato soup the doorbell rang. It was no doubt her mother. She often rushed out of the house without her keys. However, when Jolene opened the door it wasn't her mother looking flustered. There was no one there. A white cardboard cake box wrapped in red ribbon had been left on the doorstep, Jolene's full name written in black felt tip capital letters. Before picking it up she glanced along the street, but the only person nearby was Callum Whitehead, who lived across the road. He was wheeling his bike along the pavement. It looked like it had a flat tyre.

She called him over and asked him if he'd seen the person who'd left the cake box, but he just shrugged and said he didn't know anything. Of course he must have known *something*, his own name at the very least, but he always seemed to think you were trying to trick him in some way. Jolene was all for people keeping themselves to themselves, but Callum took it to another level. Perhaps it was a prank and he was part of it. Never mind, she told him.

She wondered if Toni Bennett knew where she lived. She liked leaving surprise packages on doorsteps. Jolene picked up the box and listened. She couldn't hear ticking. And it didn't smell of chicken curry or ginger cake. She carried it into the kitchen and, placing it on the table, untied the ribbon and lifted the lid.

Two dead rats lay in the box like a gift that no one had ordered. They had name tags wrapped around their necks that read 'Dolly' and 'Jolene'.

Chapter Twenty-Six

SWEETWATER LAKE

Sixteen Years Earlier

'What are you doing?'

Angelina Merry was staring straight at him.

Will had been following her for the past four hours, ever since she'd left the school nurse's office, and today she'd led him on even more of a 'Merry' dance than usual.

As he'd followed her out of the school gates, Derek Shannon, his geography teacher, had been arriving.

'And where do you think you're going?' he'd asked him, neglecting to call after Angelina to ask her the same thing. He just watched her leave.

Will invented an excuse about his father being ill and because it was still only a few weeks since his mother had died he hoped that the sympathy and the 'of course you cans' would continue for a while longer yet.

'Have you informed the school office? You can't just leave the school premises whenever you feel like it.'

Will nodded distractedly as he watched Angelina getting smaller and smaller over Derek Shannon's left shoulder, too afraid to blink in case he blinked her away. Fortunately, Hannah Turner then appeared on the school steps in her much-shorter-than-allowed school skirt and, finding her far more appealing than a dishevelled teenage boy who'd just lost his mother and who'd not in fact been given permission to leave the school premises, Derek Shannon abruptly finished whatever it was he'd been about to add and sauntered towards her, tossing Tic Tacs onto his tongue. He was always shaking Tic Tac containers like maracas. Will imagined that most teenage girls found the sound of Tic Tacs rattling around inside Derek Shannon's trouser pocket as terrifying as lone whistling at dusk.

He caught up with Angelina at the inlet of shops that joined the high street, the shops that, like him, were on the periphery, easily missed if you didn't know they were there. She stood outside Crystal Vision, gazing at the moonstone dreamcatchers and the Tiger's Eyes in the window. When she pushed open the shop door the sleeve of her blazer slid down revealing the eight scars on her right arm. She'd had the scars since primary school, but because the teachers were always treating grazed knees and bruised elbows and searching the playground for lost milk teeth to place under pillows for the tooth fairy, they went largely unnoticed. And no doubt no one considered she might be self-harming at such a young age.

Where would she have learnt to do such a thing? From her mother, her sister? From television programmes she shouldn't have been watching, magazines she shouldn't have been reading?

Even the bruises that blossomed like petals across her arms and legs were seldom remarked upon, any possible cause promptly dismissed – *'Foolish girl, as unsteady as a newborn lamb'*, *'Heavens, not again! She's worse than Mr. Bean'*. The rumours came much later – *'Her father likes using his fists'*, *'She cuts herself with razors'*, *'Kirsty saw her at the abortion clinic on Thursday'*.

Will preferred it when she'd been branded careless and accident-prone and tried not to listen to the more hurtful rumours, spun like spider's webs, even when she bandaged herself in black fabric in summer and stared blankly out of windows misted with condensation in winter, her eyes two pools of fathomless raven-black ink, but he did wonder how the rumours had started, from which mill they'd spilled, why the worst things to happen to you should be passed around like Fruit Pastilles.

He couldn't now remember why he'd chosen to follow Angelina. Maybe he'd felt an affinity with her. He'd just lost his mother and Angelina seemed to have already lost so many things, if the rumours were to be believed. But whatever the reason, he discovered he liked viewing the world through Angelina's eyes. She took him to places he'd never been to before, showed him things he didn't know existed. She knew the area in so much more detail than he did, the secret passageways no wider than a ruler, the private parties held in a dilapidated Jacobean mansion behind the racetrack every third Wednesday of the month, the market hall stall that sold Roman coins and Victorian doll's house furnishings.

When Angelina reappeared, Will couldn't tell if she'd purchased anything or not, but if she had it would be inside the denim backpack she always carried, which was covered with self-help stickers such as *The Only Obstacle in Your Way is Yourself* and *Believe and Achieve*. He wasn't sure whether she was being intentionally ironic and confronting the rumours directly or whether she truly believed in such affirmations. Personally, Will had had his fill of trite sayings.

He'd been seeing a bereavement counsellor named Jeremy Crofts, a man who recited clichés as if they were going out of fashion and sat on two silk cushions for the sole purpose of reinforcing his seniority. A white paper bag filled with white chocolate mice lay open on the table between them like a bribe as he made listless assurances that none of this was his fault. Although the less Will spoke, the more chocolate mice he was able to swallow, a whole litter of them each week, so ultimately, he supposed, the victory was his.

He'd recently stolen a bicycle because he wanted to feel something other than grief. He wanted to feel ashamed and exhilarated and unstoppable. And he was eating so much because he needed to fill the echoing emptiness inside him that his mother had hollowed out. And that Angelina Merry later scooped out further. Surely this was normal behaviour in the circumstances. He didn't need a bereavement counsellor to parcel up his feelings with string and hand them back to him.

Will followed Angelina into the shopping centre (chain stores and fast food outlets layered like four-tiered wedding cakes, buildings that she rarely entered), where she took the escalator to the third floor and disappeared inside Burger King. He wished he could walk over to her like a normal person and ask if anyone was sitting in the seat opposite. But he couldn't. What if she said no? What if she laughed at him, swore at him, called him weird? At least this way he wasn't humiliated and the pedestal on which he'd placed her remained intact.

Often, he wondered whether he even wanted to talk to her at all or whether he was content to simply observe her from afar. Perhaps that was enough.

He hoped Sophie wasn't in the shopping centre. She'd often unexpectedly appear like a genie from a lamp and tap him on the shoulder, and he'd told her he wasn't following Angelina Merry anymore.

She reappeared fifty-six minutes later. He'd spent most of that time on a teardrop-shaped marble bench outside Clarks, listing chocolate bars alphabetically and seeing how many knots he could make in his school tie before tying it around his head like Rambo. Unlimited patience was an essential requirement when following people, a quality he had in abundance, and he'd have considered MI5 a potential career choice if they didn't allocate specific targets and explicit instructions. He preferred things to unfold organically and to follow who he felt like following. On the whole though, he did prefer his subjects to keep moving.

Returning to the ground floor, Angelina left the shopping centre and walked through the archway towards the revolving glass doors of the art gallery. Will wished he'd had more than the sausage roll and the steak pie he'd purchased while waiting outside Clarks, hidden behind the fronds of a plastic palm tree. It was obviously going to be one of his longer pursuits. Sometimes he preferred shorter, brisker commutes, a final destination within striking distance, instead of labour-intensive expeditions, requiring advanced levels of concentration he didn't currently have.

Angelina took the stairs to the second floor of the art gallery, where she spent an inordinate amount of time in Room 12 among the soot-stained factory chimneys and bottle kilns, bleak scenes depicting an industrially oppressive past that could have just as easily been an apocalyptic future.

Will lingered in the adjacent room, Room 11, where the infants were fair-haired and pale-skinned and dressed in taffeta silk.

As he was gazing at the peach ruffles and frills, stifling yet another yawn, a class of primary school children ran across the tiled floor behind him screaming. A flustered teacher tried to shush them, gathering them in a semicircle beside an interactive display.

'Pull out your sketchbooks and pencils, *quietly please.*'

The obligatory unzipping of zips, rustling, sighing and rolling around on the floor (*'Stop that, Ben!'*) ensued.

When Will next peered into Room 12, Angelina was gone. He'd allowed his concentration to lapse, become distracted by pastels and pencils and pupils misbehaving. He quickly searched the other rooms, which included a display of anatomical drawings, a collection of Italian landscapes and an exhibition featuring portraits of local war heroes, and then lastly the cafeteria and the toilets. He eventually found her in the gift shop, purchasing a postcard. Relieved, he followed her outside. It was raining heavily and Will hoped that might be as far as they'd go today and she would finally head home. But she pulled an umbrella from her backpack and began walking towards the bus station. He wondered if she was planning to leave, to climb on a bus and disappear, and he'd be the last person ever to see her, but she turned left along a lane that led to Sweetwater Lake.

That wasn't the actual name of the lake. Will didn't think it had a name, and it certainly wasn't sweet. The path that ran around it was laced with brambles and nettles and difficult to navigate and the water was the colour of pine cones, although it was allegedly unusually deep. The locals referred to it as a nature reserve, but Will had never seen so much as a mallard on the stagnant water. It had been called Sweetwater for as long as Will could remember. His mother once told him that it was in honour of wartime couples who were 'sweet on each other' and who would pledge their undying love beside the water's edge. It wasn't always a mud pit, she told him. Couples certainly still frequented the area, but being 'sweet on each other' wasn't quite how Will would have phrased it.

Used condoms hung from tree branches like miniature paper lanterns and in a small clearing to his right a single syringe had been stabbed into the ashes of a fire. At least Will hoped they were the ashes of a fire and not the ashes of a person.

He followed Angelina down to the lake. She picked up a pebble and tossed it into the water. It ricocheted across the surface, sinking without trace. As he was reflecting upon the familiarity of a person's silhouette, how he was able to recognise their less obvious features, the slope of their shoulders, the curve of their ankles, the shape of their neck, she turned around and asked him what he was doing. She'd lured him here in order to confront him. He was hiding behind an apple blossom tree a few metres away from her, sufficiently concealed, or so he'd thought, his right cheek blurred by the rain. He didn't move. He didn't breathe. Perhaps she'd walk on and he could slip quietly away, undiscovered. She didn't.

A seashell-white petal fell from the tree, landing on his left shoe.

The white of surrender.

'Why do you keep following me?'

This was going to be difficult to explain. What could he say? You're mistaken. I'm not following you. I was just here. And you were there. We like the same things. They didn't. He didn't like bottle kilns and affirmations and sweetwater lakes.

Clearly outmanoeuvred, he slowly revealed himself.

He didn't think he'd ever been wetter.

'You're shit at following people. I noticed you hours ago.'

Her words stung. He'd thought he was skilled at staying unnoticed. He likened himself to a shadow, able to move stealthily and quietly in a person's wake.

'Everyone knows. They think it's creepy. They think you're creepy.'

'Everyone knows?'

'Everyone. That's Will Cavanagh, he follows people, but don't worry, he's harmless. Are you?'

'Am I what?'

'Harmless.'

He didn't know, but he thought so.

Unfortunately, it seemed he was also creepy too. Didn't she know he was keeping her safe?

Foolishly, he'd imagined that if she ever did notice him, it would be an amusing 'How did the two of you meet?' anecdote they'd recycle for family and friends. He certainly hadn't imagined this.

He didn't answer.

She sighed.

'Go home, Will. And stop using your mother's death as an excuse to be weird.'

He envisioned the whispers, the sneers, the unconcealed disgust that would inevitably result when she told everyone that yesterday he'd followed her for four hours. He couldn't let that happen. He'd have to keep seeing that patronising counsellor. He'd have to keep swallowing all those white chocolate mice that were starting to make him feel sick and listening to his tedious platitudes. Sometimes, it *was* your fault. And how dare she blame his mother. *He* was allowed to attribute his behaviour to his mother's death, but that didn't mean other people could allude to it.

Even now he struggles to understand what happened next, how the broken branch lying by his feet was suddenly in his hands and Angelina, who a moment before had been standing beneath her umbrella, ridiculing him, was now in the lake. He doesn't remember hitting her and can only assume she lost her balance and fell in, but he does remember the panicking, the spluttering that she couldn't swim, which of course he should have known. She wouldn't have wanted to wear a swimming costume in public.

He wonders why he didn't try to save her, why he watched each of the cuts on her wrist disappear beneath the surface of the water like markers … 8, 7, 6, 5 … until every trace of her was gone.

Why he unhooked the bracelet that had somehow attached itself to the branch and placed it in his pocket, a bracelet with lightning bolts and musical notes and a smear of dried blood on a sharply pointed star as if she'd cut herself one last time before falling into the water.

Why he hoped her backpack would keep her weighted down.

Had he wanted to watch her die? He hadn't been there when his mother died, but he could be there for Angelina. And sometimes he wondered whether Angelina truly wanted to be saved, whether she wasn't in fact panicking, but had surrendered willingly, letting the murky water lure her to its darkest depths. Perhaps she was waving, not drowning. He waved back, picked up the umbrella and left.

Over the coming weeks and months, while he nervously waited for her body to surface or for an angler's fishing line to attach itself to an item of her clothing or one of her trainers, his overeating escalated. He couldn't blink away the image of Angelina drowning. Some days, he wanted her to be found so that the excessive eating would stop, considered accidentally finding her himself so that her family would know where she was. Other days he convinced himself that she'd pulled herself out of the lake after he left and caught a bus to the coast.

He waited for Sophie to say something, to jokingly ask if Angelina Merry's disappearance was something to do with him. But she never did. He still dreams about Angelina sometimes. She's being hoisted out of the water like a shipwreck, rising to the surface like the *Mary Celeste*, her skin covered in barnacles and sediment, reeds and algae entwined in her hair, free at last.

The Next Girl

Fern

When my wife unexpectedly died, I was surprised by how much I missed her and not solely for her domestic and childcare duties. I genuinely did miss her. She'd been supportive and loyal, although admittedly I was there so infrequently, had we spent longer together I might have revised my opinion. But if we hadn't had children I like to think that our lives might have been different, I might have been different, and not chosen occupations that took me away from home for months at a time and allowed me to kill more easily. I was currently employed as a delivery driver, which I was finding too inflexible, the owner of the company more mindful of timekeeping than any of my previous employers.

I appreciate the irony. Children are something of a necessity if you wish to be a family man. Otherwise you're simply a couple and a couple don't have the same leverage as a family. They don't provide the same camouflage.

Fortunately, my wife's parents had also recently died, a few *months earlier in a car accident, leaving a sizeable inheritance, and I was soon able to resign from my delivery driver post and spend more time at home, which was tolerable now that my teenage children were either in their rooms or staying with friends and I rarely saw them.*

Neither child seemed distressed by their mother's death and I'd often wonder why. Whenever I'd seen my wife and children together they'd appeared cordial, their relationship certainly more natural than mine, but of course I didn't know what they were like when I wasn't there. I remembered a slight friction between my wife and daughter occasionally, but nothing to cause concern or not attribute to adolescent mood swings.

My daughter refused to attend the funeral.

'What does it matter? She's dead. She won't care whether I'm there or not.'

'I care.'

'Really? You want to go there?'

I didn't. I watched her leave the house and climb into a red van that was parked in the driveway.

I wondered if they blamed their mother for my absences, if they saw her weakness and subservience as a weapon with which to punish her and loathed her for it. Or did they blame me for her death? I expected my daughter to see how far she could push me, safe in the knowledge that I couldn't retaliate because a second death in the family would raise too much suspicion, but she barely acknowledged me. If you could call us a family. I appeared to be a family man without a family, without a safety net. And that's how it remained for the next few years, the three of us living separate lives, like strangers, my impulses allowed to escalate without parental or spousal responsibilities.

The next girl I killed looked exactly like my daughter. I'd spent months *looking for her. I'd let other girls live, so that she could die. Her name was Fern and she was yet another secret that I was forced to keep.*

The brake lights ahead of me were blurred red by the pouring rain, warning signs that I chose to ignore. I slowed down and opened the car window.

'Can I give you a lift somewhere?' I asked the girl with rainwater dripping from her fringe.

She nodded gratefully, falling onto the backseat like a wet stone.

'Where are you heading?' I asked.

I noticed a scab on my chin when I glanced in the rear-view mirror.

'South.'

'I'm David,' I said with a smile.

I hadn't used that name in a while.

'Fern,' she replied, her ballet-slipper-pink lips unravelling like an Easter ribbon.

Chapter Twenty-Seven

THREE THINGS ABOUT LUCAS

Maureen and Malcolm Collins' forest green Alfa Romeo was a funereal presence in Rex's rear-view mirror, soon to be joined, according to Superintendent Forrester, by a DI Sheena Kendrick and a DS Lucas Granger from the Welsh police with a special interest in the case. Rex had rolled his eyes when he'd heard the name Lucas Granger, even though there was no one to witness the eye-rolling.

He'd met Lucas once before on a two-day profiling conference in Ipswich. He'd practically taken over the entire two days talking about 'synergy' and 'deep diving' and 'rubber meeting the road' and just when you thought that he'd run out of corporate clichés and impossible maths percentages, he'd irritatingly impart another one.

And he was never punctual. Anyone else would have quietly slipped into the back of the lecture theatre unobserved. But not Lucas. He'd bluster in as if he was the keynote speaker and demand to be brought 'up to speed'.

That was the first thing to know about Lucas Granger. He

followed his own schedule, always waylaid by something or someone far more important than you.

His hand had been permanently in the air asking for further clarification or expansion on a particular point or to voice his grave concerns (his concerns were always grave, they were never just normal concerns), annoyingly usually when they were just about to take a break or were so hungry that they actually felt faint.

The second thing to know about Lucas Granger was that he liked the sound of his own voice.

It was early evening when Rex and the Alfa Romeo arrived back at the station, the sky a blaze of apricot and claret, and it soon transpired that the Welsh police would actually be leading the investigation, rather than merely assisting. They'd even arrived ahead of him, making it look as if he'd been Sunday-driving with no sense of urgency whatsoever – which, forensically, there wasn't. The canal bones were unlikely to reveal cause and manner of death, no matter how closely Glenda listened.

Rex sighed. It was patently clear that there would be no moving forward for Rex on this case. If anything Lucas Granger would be holding him back.

That was the third thing to know about Lucas Granger. He held you back. He was someone who tied your shoelaces together when you weren't looking, a long-distance runner who boxed you in and jostled and elbowed you until you tripped over your own feet or another set of feet so devious that they couldn't be identified.

While Maureen and Malcolm Collins were being introduced to a Family Liaison Officer, Cathy offered their

Welsh counterparts tea, coffee and cellophane-wrapped twin packs of biscuits. Disappointingly, no one questioned the two officers' presence, even though they were unconnected to the original case; not even Cathy, who, like Lucas, always had a tiresome supply of questions in her armoury, but who was currently shyly nibbling the corner of a ginger biscuit and patting down flyaway strands of hair with saliva, not saying a word. She must have been so dazzled by Lucas Granger that she'd been rendered speechless. He had that effect on the opposite sex. They were like moths to a flame, never afraid to get burned. It was probably the fake tan. And the non-regulation rhinestone cowboy boots that at first glance gave him a slightly reckless and rebellious edge. A second glance and you saw a man fully embracing a midlife crisis.

Superintendent Forrester clinked a teaspoon against his coffee mug to attract everyone's attention.

'I'd like to extend a warm welcome to DI Sheena Kendrick and DS Lucas Granger, who'll be sharing their expertise with us on this case.'

He continued, 'We're working together on this one, so no office politics or petty squabbles. We all need to be on the same page. I'm looking at you, Perry Mason.'

He'd recently started calling Perry Saunders Perry Mason. None of the younger officers understood the reference.

Everyone laughed – everyone except Sheena and Lucas, of course, who were already on a different page. An in-joke by definition was always a leave-another-person-out-joke.

After the briefing the Superintendent assigned Cathy the task of giving their guests a guided tour of the station. As they were leaving, Rex heard Lucas tell Cathy that back in

Holyhead the station's refurbished reception area had cost more than his holiday home in Aberystwyth. She should come and take a look some time, he told her. Whether it was an invitation to see the police station or his holiday home, Rex wasn't sure, although he suspected the latter. He didn't hear Cathy's reply.

Rex remained in his car while the Family Liaison Officer, someone whom Rex had never met before and who was quietly humming, greeted Maureen and Malcolm Collins outside the mortuary.

A woman descended the entrance steps while he was waiting – black curls, petite stature. It could have been his mother. So many times it could have been his mother, but when they glanced up or turned round it was somebody else's mother or daughter, a stranger. One day, he thought, it might really be his mother, her features thawed and reanimated, and he won't recognise her. You think you'll remember a person no matter how changed they might be, but when you've spent years memorising the last glimpse of their face that you ever saw, no age-progression software can broaden your perspective.

He was fourteen when he last saw the face he remembered, May 24th, Tuesday. At breakfast his mother had been there. When he arrived home from school she was gone. She was always there when he arrived home from school, always desperate to hear about his day, but not that day, when he'd won a trophy in gymnastics and Lorraine Henry had deposited an orange-scented lipglossed kiss on his left cheek. And it seemed such a strange thing to happen on a Tuesday, he remembered thinking, on a weekday, when there were timetables to adhere to and routines to follow. It was the weekend that was subject to change, when anything could happen, and plans and arrangements were less rigid.

His father hadn't been unduly concerned when he'd asked, 'Where's Mum?' (*I've no idea*) or more accurately 'Where's tea?' (*You'll have to make your own tea*). He didn't even call the police. Rex had to call them.

Later, he overheard his father telling one of the neighbours that she'd been having an affair, spreading gossip about her when she wasn't there to defend herself. But she wouldn't have left without saying goodbye. *Would she?* The more Rex considered the possibility, the more plausible it seemed. He had no idea what she did or who she spoke to when he was at school, which amounted to approximately seven hours a day (more if he was attending after-school extracurricular activities), five days a week of not knowing. Anything could have happened during that time.

His father's words preyed on his mind, intensified the unease he was already feeling, until he too came to share his father's view that she was living a different life. He felt far less distraught hating her than believing her dead.

The police were as unconcerned as his father. She was an adult. She could come and go as she pleased. How many times had Rex heard those words over the years? Too many times. As if no one was supposed to miss you or worry that something terrible had happened to you if you were over eighteen, as if you should be able to defeat any balaclava-masked, knife-wielding assailant and not get yourself murdered now that you were no longer a minor.

And he wasn't the type of teenager who locked himself

away in his room, having no idea what kind of life his parents were living. He had conversations with them. He asked his mother questions and was genuinely interested in the answers to those questions. He knew the name of her childhood best friend (Joy Hargreaves). He knew she'd once stolen two oranges from Barrett's, the local greengrocers. He knew that she owned every Billy Joel album ever released on vinyl. When he'd asked his father where the albums were his father had shrugged and said what did it matter, she wasn't coming back. How did he know she wasn't coming back? Had she been in touch? Did he know where she was? How could he be so sure?

The only thing Rex didn't know was where his mother was.

A few months later Anita Montgomery, a theatre actress, moved in. Hideous Toby jugs and macabre porcelain dolls appeared like ceramic armies on shelves that had once belonged to Billy Joel, and photographs of Anita on stage looking similarly ghoulish hung on the walls that had previously held his mother's smile – Blanche Dubois in *A Streetcar Named Desire*, Vera Elizabeth Claythorne in Agatha Christie's *And Then There Were None*. There were so many different versions of Anita (he'd have been grateful for any version of his mother) and each one was more disturbing than the last.

He'd recently seen Anita on an episode of *Celebrity Antiques Road Trip*, her painted eyebrows arched in surprise, a blonde synthetic wig over her thinning hair. Denise had said, 'Isn't that Anita? I think she was on *Celebrity Come Dine with Me* last month.' He'd seen more of Anita over the years than he had his father.

He still drove past the house occasionally, wondered what

it would be like to step inside and revisit his childhood. No matter what renovations had been made, there'd be something, no matter how microscopic, that would remind him of his mother, that might belong to his mother, a nicotine stain on the bathroom ceiling, the Mexican marigolds she'd planted beneath the kitchen window, her handwriting on a box of Christmas decorations in the loft, something. He would have liked to have seen his mother hemming curtains on her sewing machine or laying the dining table again, even if it was only in his imagination.

He often searched for evidence of her in charity shops, hoping to see a copy of *Glass Houses* with her name written in pencil on the cover, or *52nd Street* with the inner sleeve missing and a lemon sticker on the record label, or one of her skirts or a favourite blouse unexpectedly fall from a hanger as he passed by, but he never did. He supposed it was a blessing really because he wouldn't have wanted to see somebody else walking around in his mother's clothes, somebody else listening to Billy Joel. He wouldn't have wanted to glimpse his mother on every street corner, in unusual settings, only to watch her disappear over and over again.

Sometimes he wondered if she'd ever actually left, if his father wouldn't let her leave, and she'd never thread a sewing machine or lay a dining table ever again, trapped for ever behind the anaglypta wallpaper on the living room walls that would have now been papered over.

Naturally, he hadn't been invited to the wedding. The first that he'd learned of it was when Denise had shown him the photographs of Anita and his father outside Wrenbury Hall in Cheshire in *Hello!* magazine. It shouldn't have mattered, but of course it did. His mother had been officially replaced, her smiling face no longer in family photographs.

A few years later Rex joined the police force. He'd wanted to see firsthand the steps that had been taken to find his mother. Very few, it transpired. Barely any steps had been climbed at all. But at least he now understands why. There are too many loose threads to untangle, frayed edges to unravel, laces that need tying that can't be knotted, full stops that need inserting that can't be added. You can spend years trying to piece together the last few weeks and months of a person's life like the broken shards of a Wedgwood vase and still never find them. Only the cracks that they've fallen through remain.

Some mysteries will always be mysteries.

A loud thud on the car window jolted him back to the present, his heart galloping like a racehorse. Jesus, was it the woman whom he'd just seen, walking down the mortuary steps? Was it his mother, back from the dead? No, it was a rosy-cheeked man in blue overalls.

Rex wound down the window.

'Sorry, mate. Can you move your car? We need access to that tree.'

Rex nodded and reversed into another parking spot further back.

That night Rex dreamt of his mother. She was washing something in the kitchen sink. He could see the soap suds, but he couldn't see what it was she was washing. She turned round and smiled at him and asked him if he wanted to see what she was washing. He shook his head. He sensed it wasn't dinner dishes.

Don't be scared, she told him, smiling sweetly. *I'm right here.*

Not wanting to disappoint her, he reluctantly approached the sink, his fingers tightly crossed behind his back.

When he finally looked down, three deep breaths later, he saw his mother's head rolling around in the washing up bowl. *Where's the rest of me?* the head shrieked.

Horrified, Rex turned to his mother, but it wasn't his mother. It was something grotesque with metal fangs and blood-red eyes.

Chapter Twenty-Eight

THINGS TO NOTE WHEN CONTACTING A MEDIUM

Jolene forced herself to look at the two dead rats, at the delicate soft pink fur inside their ears, at their wiry whiskers and blackcurrant eyes. The appalled part of her wanted to bury the rats and pretend she'd never received them, but the other more fearless part of her wanted to know who'd sent them, and for that she'd need Crosby's help. She wondered why they'd been sent. Was someone planning to abduct her? Did this mean Dolly was dead and she was next? Was it someone's idea of a cruel joke rather than a warning or a threat? Or was it a gift from Dolly herself? Did she want to stay hidden? A stream of increasingly more outlandish possibilities ran through Jolene's mind.

Hearing the jangle of door keys Jolene quickly hid the cake box beneath the sink behind the Ariel and Domestos and began ladling soup into two bowls. The only telltale sign that anything was wrong was the slight tremor in her right hand, but her mother didn't appear to have noticed, her hazel eyes sparkling like wine, her words tumbling like falling rocks, like circus acrobats. Apparently, she'd seen Joanne Collins's parents at the police station. She'd been waiting to speak to a detective to determine whether they still had Dolly's DNA on file because if they didn't (God forbid!) then she had Dolly's hairbrush with her.

Jolene glanced at the strands of hair in the plastic bag that her mother had placed on the kitchen table. It looked like Dolly would be joining them for supper.

'I never got to speak to anyone, of course. I might as well be invisible. Sometimes, I think they've forgotten who Dolly is.'

How could they forget? Jolene wondered. How could anyone forget?

'Anyway, who should walk in but Maureen and Malcolm Collins? We kept in touch for a while. Do you remember? I'm meeting them later at their hotel.'

Jolene hoped her mother hadn't caused a scene. She'd lost count of the number of times her mother had been gripped by the elbow and escorted towards a waiting police car, charged with disorderly conduct and inciting violence.

Although she'd forgotten Maureen Collins' name, Jolene remembered her handwriting, the letters identically sized and the words evenly spaced as if they'd been typewritten. The letters were still in her mother's dressing table drawer, secured with a rubber band. Lists of helpline telephone numbers and voluntary organisations that Maureen had found most useful, practical advice on the logistics of navigating police force bureaucracy, things to note when contacting a medium. She'd recommended someone called Lincoln Page. *He has dreams, and although he hasn't found her yet, I'm certain that he will. He has his own business cards.* Only parents of other missing children know what it's like, she'd written. Nobody else understands. They don't realise how many mountains you're expected to scale, how loudly you have to shout to be heard.

As if it was an exclusive club that nobody would willingly want to join, but if you were unfortunate enough to be offered membership then you should at least have access to all the relevant information.

They continued to write to each other over the following summer like pen pals with the saddest news, trapped in a torment that there was no escaping. And then the letters stopped, the tragedy that had cemented their friendship inevitably tearing it apart because it was like looking in a mirror at a reflection that you didn't want to keep seeing, participating in a sports tournament that you didn't want to keep competing in. Whose daughter would be found first? And would she be found alive?

And now that the Collins family were nearing the finish line, their experiences were no longer similar, their united front fragile and susceptible to collapse, their relationship potentially dissolving into bitterness and jealousy because Joanne had been found and Dolly hadn't, because Joanne was dead and Dolly might still be alive.

'I'm not convinced that it is Joanne,' her mother was saying. 'Why would she be buried here? They live in Anglesey. Of course I didn't say that to Maureen. And I'm pleased if it is her, that they've finally found her. Of course I am.'

The only thing her mother was truly pleased about was that it wasn't Dolly.

She'd recently returned home with flakes of dirt beneath her fingernails and police cordon tape in her hair. Jolene had pictured her frantically clawing at the earth where Joanne had been found, searching for a second set of remains, as if all missing girls were buried in one place.

As much as her mother believed that Dolly was still alive, that the absence of a body implied the absence of a death, an unbridled part of her still entertained the possibility that she might be dead, still searched for her beneath hedgerows just in case.

'They wouldn't have told them it was Joanne if it wasn't,' Jolene said quietly.

'They'd do anything if it meant closing a case,' her mother replied, dipping a limp finger of bread into her soup.

Her mother seemed to think she lived in small-town America, where everyone was related to the local sheriff and everything got swept under the carpet.

Jolene suspected that her mother's current objective was to ingratiate herself into the Joanne Collins case, possibly as a spokesperson, but ultimately to remind waiting journalists outside the Collinses' hotel that she was Dolly Edwards' mother. A microphone tended to bring out her more gregarious side. It was a means of reaching more people, of making herself heard, a legitimate excuse to mention Dolly's name. Her mother's motives, no matter how innocent they first appeared, were always about gaining maximum publicity for Dolly, ensuring that the Dolly on the flyers (Jolene often wondered exactly who it was that they were actually looking for. It certainly wasn't the fifteen-year-old Dolly on the missing posters) was regularly featured in national newspapers and on missing person websites and true crime podcasts.

Jolene lowered her spoon. The soup tasted like volcanic ash

on her tongue. She wished she'd opened a different one. Tomato soup looked too much like blood, too much like the two dead rats beneath the sink with their throats slit. She wondered whether they'd been killed deliberately or whether they were already dead. She hated the thought of someone killing them intentionally, solely for her benefit. Couldn't they have sent a threatening note instead, cut random letters from a newspaper and glued them onto an A4 sheet of paper?

Her thoughts turned to who 'they' might be. No one, except Crosby and his associates, knew she was looking into Dolly's disappearance. Could it be one of his contacts, an acquaintance? Was it something to do with her mother? Had she acquired some new, more violent, friends, people who treated prison cells like hotel rooms, people who would kill their own grandmother for a syringe of heroin?

She should have felt scared, agitated, panic-stricken, but now that the tremor in her right hand had stilled, she realised she wasn't any of those things. If anything, she was unexpectedly intrigued and noticeably incensed. She knew the more sensible response would have been to contact the police – there might be a fingerprint on the ribbon or the name tags – but she didn't know if she could trust the police to deal with it professionally and procedurally. She didn't share her mother's scathing generalised view of law enforcement, but she did accept the potential for human error. Once you handed over the only piece of evidence that existed, anything could happen to it. It could be lost due to carelessness, destroyed in a fire, a flood. Maybe it would be locked in a drawer and ignored.

When her mother went upstairs to change into 'something more suitable', Jolene retrieved the two dead rats from beneath the sink and transferred them to the outdoor storage shed alongside the remnants of Crosby's chicken curry. If someone was intending to abduct her or kill her, the rats seeming to suggest that she and Dolly would be reunited imminently, then this might be an ideal opportunity to find out who, to set a trap. She was willing to act as bait, if it meant discovering the truth. Maybe this was her destiny, her calling, the very least she could do. And Crosby would be there. He wouldn't let her die. He wouldn't let go of her. She trusted him.

And maybe Laura would be saved too.

She knocked on her mother's closed bedroom door to tell her she was leaving. She could hear the staccato hiss of hairspray or perfume, Whitney Houston being 'emotional' on the radio, as her mother readied herself for the waiting media.

Sunset House was eerily quiet and unusually deserted when Jolene arrived. She'd walked along two corridors and crossed the courtyard before she met another staff member – Val, the supervisor on duty, who always wore Ugg boots, even in summer.

Adam, who'd allegedly once cooked for royalty (he'd handed a PotNoodle to some distant fourteenth or fifteenth cousin of the Queen at a casino) and had a gambling addiction, was in the office, rattling locked desk drawers. Jolene had seen him numerous times playing online poker on his phone in the staffroom with a nervousness that you only ever saw in people who were gambling with money they didn't have.

Carlos, who'd lived in the UK for over ten years but who

always claimed not to understand what you were saying if he didn't want to do something, until you got tired of explaining and did the task yourself, was smoking in the designated smoking area. Jolene could hear him on the phone, '*Sí... entiendo!*' She suspected that as well as pretending to be linguistically challenged he was also drug dealing. He spent hours in the car park, passing brown paper packages through tinted car windows, his back to the CCTV camera.

The remaining three staff members on duty were in the staffroom.

Tina, who was married to John Paul, a long-distance lorry driver, and whose son, Noah, had learning difficulties, was wiping down surfaces with a homemade lemon-and-vinegar cleaning solution.

Michaela, a single mother to five-year-old Ebony June, who lived in a bedsit with no central heating and who always wore gloves, was flicking through a cookbook.

And Bridget, who was never without her knitting needles, was knitting.

Inside Jolene's uniform pocket her phone pinged. It was probably her mother telling her that a reporter wanted to cover Dolly's disappearance. Or that they didn't. She glanced at the text. It was from an unknown number.

Did you like my gift?

Chapter Twenty-Nine
TIMBER

'Angelina?'

It took Will a few seconds to realise that the young girl standing at the bottom of the stairs in pyjamas, her puzzled, pale face illuminated by torchlight, couldn't possibly be Angelina because Angelina was dead (*wasn't she?*). She was at the bottom of Sweetwater Lake, where Will had left her, although she still haunted his dreams even now and he'd wake up wondering if she'd been in his room, whispering in his ear, dripping water onto the carpet; their roles reversed, Angelina now following him.

Was this the girl in the photograph on the sideboard? Had she stepped off the swing and walked into the hallway? Will wondered why she was alone in the house. *Was* she alone in the house? Or was there someone else upstairs? Was she even real? The yellow and orange tropical fish swimming across her pyjamas seemed to suggest so. If she did exist, Will hoped she hadn't seen his face, but as he'd glimpsed hers it seemed unlikely.

Suddenly, the torch slipped from his grasp, plunging the hallway into darkness, and, startled into action, Will slammed the back door closed behind him and ran to the car. As he was unlocking the door he felt a sharp pain in his left arm. Had he been shot? Did the girl have a weapon? He checked his arm for blood, but his hand came away dry. He tried to open the car door, but he couldn't grip the door handle. His heart was beating so fast that it was like a timer inside his chest, counting down. The pain swelled. He staggered and swayed and then tumbled to the ground or, more accurately perhaps, 'timbered' to the ground like a felled tree. It felt like everything fell with him – the pale moon, the polka-dot sky.

Reaching for the car tyre closest to him, he attempted to raise himself into a sitting position, pressing a palm onto the pavement to hoist himself up, but he couldn't feel his palm and he couldn't raise his head to look at his palm. There was a pain in his chest, a swarm of pain, a familiar, recurrent pain. It stretched across his torso like a bandage, continued down his arms towards his toes. He tried to convince himself that it was just another bout of indigestion or heartburn, the solution a couple of spearmint Rennies. But the relentless ticking continued, as if he was running out of time.

He could hear voices beside him, but he couldn't speak, he couldn't tell the voices that he couldn't breathe, that the ticking was slowing down and that there was no more time. He wondered if he'd hear an alarm when everything finally stopped, a siren, a clap of thunder, a round of applause.

Scenes flashed through his mind in no particular order.

Click.

The administration offices of Vodafone:

He's making yet another unscheduled visit to the third floor to gaze at Kerry Fisher opening filing cabinet drawers and typing memos. He's never uttered a word to her, doesn't know what word he might utter if he ever did find the courage to speak to her.

Click.

Later that same day:

Rick, the accounts manager, Kerry's rumoured boyfriend, warns him that if he doesn't stop following Kerry he's contacting HR. It's starting to 'freak her out'.

Click.

It's winter and he's in the Sunset House kitchen, opening a tin of peaches and a tub of raspberry ripple ice cream.

Roger Draper, the new kitchen assistant, is paying a little too much attention to his nutritional intake.

'Leave some for the rest of us,' Roger says.

He doesn't say it vindictively, but you can tell he means it. He's like a wasp in Will's ear that can't be silenced with the sole of a slipper.

When Theo bites Will's hand at the Sunset House Summer Fête, thinking it's a sandwich, Roger half-jokingly warns him he 'might need a tetanus for that'. It's Roger's fault that he can often only eat chocolate on the toilet and it can't possibly be hygienic, but it's the only place that offers him any respite, any time alone with his purchases without fear of reprisal.

Click.

St. George's Hospital:

He's sitting beside his father's hospital bed with a polystyrene cup of lukewarm coffee and a Crunchie from the vending machine, the honeycomb filling coating his teeth, turning them orange.

Click.

It's his eighteenth birthday:

He's eating a packet of KP Salted Peanuts in his bedroom, trying to describe himself favourably in fifty words or less on an online dating website, bookmarking a guide on *How to Write the Perfect Dating Profile*.

Click.

Church Lane Cemetery, his mother's grave:

It's hailing. He wishes it would stop. The hailstones are cactus-sharp. And the wind chime is missing.

Click.

The front garden, aged six or seven:

He's lying on the lawn adding the finishing touches to his Paramedic Superhero ('ParaHero') – the aluminium cape that regulates temperature, the leggings made of bandages, the hands shaped like syringes, the force field of metal shields to repel diseased cells, and the Supersonic Ambulance with retractable wings to enable it to rise above rush-hour traffic and liquid headlights to dispense lifesaving medication.

'I'll be able to save everyone,' he tells his mother.

Janette's Office:

There's a cake box on Janette's desk with Jolene's name written on it. Two gift tags that read 'Dolly' and 'Jolene'. Has she bought Jolene a gift? Dolly is one of the names in Will's notebook, the missing sister whom Jolene never mentions, but whom everyone remembers.

And then he's back in the present, back in the grip of his pain.

An image of the chocolate wrappers and crisp packets littering the car, the empty box of Creme Eggs, a brief intermission. This is how he'll be remembered, he thinks, his car a Thornton's franchise. He won't be remembered as a dedicated care assistant who spent his brief life helping others.

And then the show reel darkens.

Skips forward.

He sees the trinkets in the shoebox beneath his bed, the notebooks containing detailed descriptions of the people he's followed, the eye in the telescope, his father emptying his room, the bin liners on the landing. He watches his father place the bin liners in the boot of the car and then deliver them to the local charity shop and later, when the telescope is being unpacked, he sees the eye roll along the floor towards one of the volunteers, who bends down to pick it up and then screams. The manager calls the police and the police mistakenly believe he's a serial killer, that he searched for people to murder through his telescope and then, having murdered them and collected souvenirs, he tried to implicate a frail and vulnerable seventy-nine-year-old care home resident.

Angelina's blood is still on the bracelet. He never wiped it away. That will only incriminate him further. It won't matter that some of these disappearances may have occurred decades earlier when he was just a child. Children can be killers too.

He tries to tell the person closest to him the first line of his address, so they'll take him home and he can hide the shoebox and the notebooks and the eye, but his words are slurred, his thoughts confused. And his coffin is already being carried towards an unmarked grave that will later be identified and vandalised. He wonders if he'll see Angelina and his mother again. Does he believe in an afterlife? He isn't sure. But perhaps it's best if he doesn't see them again. He's tried to make amends for the terrible things he's done, but he isn't sure it's enough. You can't let someone drown and not expect there to be consequences. You can't watch someone die and not be punished.

He thinks about all the things he doesn't know about the people he's followed, things he should know. He should know everything. But sometimes the worst and best things happen when you're looking the other way. And if *he* doesn't know these things then who does? There's a fluttering inside his chest like the flapping of wings. He wonders if they're angel wings.

He sees Sophie beneath the car. She's waving at him. And then she disappears.

He's thinking about food again, sugary, calorific food, but he can no longer imagine the smell or the taste of anything. The pain moves around his body like it's on a racetrack and the show reel keeps rolling and the angel wings keep fluttering.

It's like he's watching a film, except that it isn't a film. It's his life. It's really happening, unravelling before his eyes. And there's nothing he can do to stop it. He doesn't want to watch the screening of his funeral anymore. There seem to be ongoing continuity issues. He doesn't want to mourn his own death.

So he presses pause before the closing credits appear.

Chapter Thirty

RUSSIAN JANUARY

Jolene was gazing at the postcards on the noticeboard: Mauritian pink sands and turquoise oceans, a neon New York skyline, a bearded man in lederhosen on an Austrian mountaintop, the Leaning Tower of Pisa. The furthest Jolene had ever been was Brighton. Or maybe it was St Ives. Was St Ives further than Brighton? She wasn't sure, but neither destination was as far away as she would have liked. She'd always wanted to see the Egyptian pyramids. 'They're just stone structures,' Laura would say. 'And I bet they're really small in real life. Most things are.' But they weren't just stone structures. They were extraordinary, magnificent wonders. And it didn't matter how small they were. Jolene still wanted to see them.

There was a business card in the upper right-hand corner of the noticeboard advertising The Lost and Found – 'Available for Weddings, Birthdays and Anniversaries', it read. Everyone had to start somewhere, Jolene supposed, although pint glasses spinning across hotel function rooms and mascara running down brawling bridesmaids' cheeks probably wasn't what Luke had initially envisaged when he'd first formed the band. At least he'd stopped texting her. She already received too many texts that made her wish mobile phones had never been invented. She briefly wondered whether Luke would agree that the Egyptian pyramids were remarkable manmade monuments or, like Laura, consider them hugely overrated. Probably the latter. She removed the drawing pin, tore the card in half and dropped it into the wastebin.

Idly glancing around the staffroom she noticed Will's locker was unlocked, the door ajar. She wondered whether to mention it to someone. She wouldn't want anyone looking inside her locker, particularly as there was a shirtless Cliff Richard Blu-tacked to the inside of the locker door. It had belonged to the previous occupant and Jolene hadn't bothered to remove it because she hadn't expected to still be here eight months later.

She wondered if Adam or Carlos had broken into the locker looking for money. They'd have been disappointed if that was the case because it was only ever filled with cake boxes. She often caught a headless Will (his head obscured by his locker door) demolishing an Angel Slice or a French Fancy when he thought no one was looking, crumbs falling on the carpet for Iris the cleaner to tut at and ignore.

Unfortunately, Jolene couldn't resist the lure of an open door either. Not that she was prone to thieving. She was merely curious. As much as she liked to 'live and let live' she still liked to take a look around occasionally. She was only human.

After rinsing her 'Drag Me To Hell' mug under the tap she

walked over to the locker. As suspected, it was practically a mini bakery – four boxes of Mr Kipling Almond Slices, six boxes of Iceland Jam Tarts, one packet of Cadbury Mini Rolls and a Dutch apple cake that sounded delicious but looked dry and dense and was now past its sell-by date. Something catastrophic must have happened for Will to let a cake exceed its sell-by date.

As she was lifting up cake boxes searching for the locker key she noticed his notebook on the top shelf beneath the apple cake. Pausing to check that she couldn't hear footsteps along the corridor she quickly flicked through it. Her moral compass was now somewhere between unacceptable and disrespectful, but she was sure there were things Will wasn't telling her. Just as she'd started to show a vested interest in what Gilbert was saying, Will had stopped wanting to discuss it with her. She wished she'd shown more enthusiasm earlier, sat with Gilbert herself so she could hear these things firsthand and know how much weight to attach to them.

An assortment of girls' names and random sentences were repeated throughout the notebook. Most of it made little sense. It was like a transcript of the first thought that popped into your head, a written version of an inkblot test. She didn't realise at first that she was looking for a specific name. But she was. And almost as if she'd wished it there, it appeared. She saw it. Four pages from the back. One word. Five letters. Nothing but white space around it. *Dolly*. Such a distinctive name. Who else could it be? Jolene didn't know any other Dollys, just as she didn't know any other Jolenes. And was that a drawing of an ice skate at the bottom of the page? She'd never before realised how violently a heart could be clawed from its cavity. Blood drummed loudly through her veins.

Hearing the click of heels approaching, she quickly returned the notebook to Will's locker and picked up a tea towel. When no one came in she checked the notebook twice more just to be sure she hadn't imagined it, that she hadn't wanted to see Dolly's name so desperately that she'd plucked it out of the air and onto the page. But it was still there each time she looked. She traced the letters with a fingertip and then took a photograph of the page on her phone so she could check it again later when she'd gathered her thoughts. She wanted to be sure.

She left the staffroom and went back into the lounge to complete the rest of her duties, but she struggled to concentrate and Bridget had to ask her three times to check on Sheila, who'd been pressing her alarm continuously for the past fifteen minutes. Val had apparently gone home sick. She rarely completed a full shift.

Sheila was sitting on the bed crying when Jolene finally went to check on her, wisps of damp grey hair forming question marks on her forehead, her apple-red cheeks crusted with tears. 'Where am I?' she asked Jolene. 'You're in your room and you need to go back to sleep,' Jolene told her, gently wiping away her tears with a tissue, but this only made her cry more. 'I don't want to go to sleep,' she said. 'I want to know where I am.'

Jolene felt like crying too. She didn't know what she was supposed to do with what she'd just learned. She didn't know how she was supposed to feel. She wished she'd never looked inside Will's locker. Or that there'd only been cake and nothing more. Certainly not this.

Was it worse, only knowing part of the story, the 'who' but not the 'where' or the 'how' or the 'why', the end but not the beginning? It was unlikely that Gilbert could enlighten them further. Yesterday morning he'd been walking around the care home with no trousers on, accusing staff and residents of stealing his father's fishing rod. John Thorley had calmed him down in the end, leading him away and glaring at Jolene as if she'd been the one responsible for the outburst. Maybe John Thorley was the keeper of Gilbert's secrets. He was always squirrelling things away in his bedside cabinet. There'd been five dead tulips and an empty sachet of Whiskas cat food when she last looked. She'd ask him about Gilbert when she next saw him.

Although perhaps it was nothing to do with Gilbert and he'd seen Dolly's case in the newspapers like everyone else, watched a television documentary about her disappearance on the ID channel, read *Disappearing Acts*, the *Sunday Times* bestselling true crime book written by C. J. McKinnon in 2012 that included a chapter on Dolly entitled 'Thin Ice', which, according to her mother, was full of errors and inconsistencies and read like a Jacqueline Susann novel, Hollywood fiction.

Her mother had wanted to sue the author over their slanderous claims, portraying Dolly as someone who drank and smoked and had underage sex, and who would have climbed into a stranger's car without a moment's hesitation. Nobody else had ever mentioned her drinking and smoking and having sex. Nobody else had ever made it sound like she deserved what happened to her. And what did it matter if she *was* doing all of those things? She was no less of a person because of it.

As a gesture of goodwill the author later donated an undisclosed sum to the *Missing Dolly* Facebook page and issued a two-sentence public apology for any undue distress that may have been caused, which at least discouraged her mother from hiring a solicitor she couldn't afford, to protect Dolly's now sullied reputation. People will never look for her now, her mother had wailed. They weren't looking for her before, Jolene had wanted to say.

Perhaps Gilbert hadn't killed anyone and Dolly was still alive, and Will was trying to squeeze square pegs into round holes. But what if he had and Dolly wasn't still alive? What if the past was now greeting the present, Gilbert's secrets not only entrusted to John for safekeeping, but now ready to be shared with an audience? Was he responsible for the two dead rats? Did he know who she was and where she lived? Did he pay someone to deliver them? Was he pretending to be senile? It sounded ridiculous and yet at the same time entirely plausible. Undercover journalists did whatever they deemed necessary to expose system failings.

And was Laura's disappearance connected to Joanne and Dolly, Gilbert having had an accomplice who was now working alone? There'd been no new developments in Laura's case, although Crosby was following a number of leads.

She wandered around Sunset House in a daze, deliberately avoiding Gilbert's room. She expected to be accosted by John. He had a habit of walking around the home like a battery-operated child's toy, getting under everybody's feet, but the corridors were quiet. She'd never felt so tired. At midnight she sought refuge in the laundry room, in the citrus scent of washing powder and detergent, the wind howling like a pack of wolves outside the window. Twice she thought she heard tapping on the glass, expected to see the masked face of an intruder staring back at her, but each time she looked up there was no one there.

Only bad things happen at night, she remembered thinking.

As she was closing the laundry room blind, something hit the windowpane, startling her. The string cord that she was holding slipped through her fingers and the blind fluttered back towards the ceiling. She waited for the masked face that she'd been imagining to bleed into focus – her heart pounding, the cord of the blind swinging to and fro like a pendulum. But there was only a terrified Jolene staring back at her.

When she couldn't stand to be in the same building as Gilbert a minute longer she sat in her car. It was where she liked to think. Or not think. During the fourth stint of sitting in her car with the wipers on, Carlos tapped on the car window, causing her to gasp, and asked her if she was intending to stay there all night. She told him he'd be the first to know should she decide to spend the rest of her shift in her car. He frowned at her. He seemed to have understood that.

During the fifth stint in her car she received a distraught text from her mother telling her that nobody was interested in hearing about Dolly, not even the female journalist with no eyebrows who always wanted an exclusive. And why wasn't she home yet? Jolene didn't reply. She was furious and seething and a thousand other emotions all at once and no amount of balm could alleviate the inflammation.

Mostly, however, she felt deceived. She couldn't believe she'd been dressing and undressing Dolly's murderer all these months, ensuring his tea was sweetened with two and a half spoonfuls of sugar (yes, two and a half! Most days he couldn't tell you his name, but he always knew if you'd omitted the half), dabbing ointment on his eczema and pulling a comb through the flyaway strands of his hair that came away in her hands.

Slamming the car door shut with a decisive thud for Carlos's benefit she pulled on her hood and completed several brisk circuits of the garden to clear her head, hoping that might inform any subsequent decisions she might make. There was a dead blackbird beneath the laundry room window, blood clotted around its beak. Another dead thing. She remembered Glen Taylor burying a dead bird in the woods.

Only bad things happen at night.

Her mobile beeped during the twelfth circuit. It was Crosby. *Gilbert Williams' wife committed suicide.* Why would Gilbert's wife commit suicide? Could she not live with the terrible things her husband had done? She should take her concerns to the police, show them Will's notebook. But then they'd want to keep it. And the notebook was all they had. And hadn't Will already voiced his concerns to the police? Besides, it was too late for justice now. Gilbert would be dead soon, his devastating secrets buried with him, unless he'd confessed his criminal past to a third party. Often, the only comfort left was the hope that someone somewhere knew something.

Carlos was on his phone by the entrance, undeterred by the pouring rain. Jolene marched over and told him she was heading back inside, the car park was all his. He signalled to a black BMW that was parked on the road as she was entering the door code.

Michaela was in the staffroom, the orange glow of an electric heater by her feet. She glanced up when the staffroom door opened, hoping to engage a passing colleague in a conversation about how cold it was, but when she saw it was Just Jolene, she returned to the *Simply Nigella* cookbook on her lap.

Bridget was knitting in the activity room, although she was unravelling more than she was knitting, in both senses of the word, cursing at her inability to follow a *simple!* pattern. She often spoke to herself. Sometimes, you'd think she was scolding someone, but when you entered the room there'd be no one else there. She'd also sometimes refer to herself in the third person. *For goodness' sake, Bridget, how many more times?* But at least she didn't adopt a different voice when responding to her own questions. Keith Stone, a boy who'd been in the same year as Jolene at school, would answer himself in a voice far deeper than his own, which was even more disconcerting.

After establishing the whereabouts of the two remaining staff members (Adam was checking the residents on the east wing and Tina was in Janette's office talking to her husband on the landline – *'Have you tried arranging his toys alphabetically? Why did you touch him? You know he doesn't like being touched. This isn't about me'*), Jolene slipped into Gilbert's room.

She noticed she was wearing latex gloves, although she couldn't remember pulling them on.

She watched him for a while, his hollow chest rising and falling, his breathing shallow, lingering, and she thought about his dead wife and Dolly's name in Will's notebook and the drawing of an ice skate and Joanne Collins. She suddenly wanted to shake him awake, shake the truth out of him, but, worried that someone might hear her, she instead reached for the spare pillow on top of the wardrobe and when no one walked in to stop her, she placed it over his face. It was as if someone else was holding the pillow and she was on the other side of the room, watching. It didn't feel real. He barely struggled. She could hear a strange gurgling sound, a spluttering. She pressed harder.

This was for her mother, she told herself, for the pain and the suffering and the endless texts, and how different her own life might have been had Dolly not disappeared, how her parents might have still been together, how she wouldn't have had to live with the weight of being all that was left.

His last breath left his body like a surrendering sigh and when she finally removed the pillow his open mouth was rigid with shock and his dull eyes stared back at her accusingly. She searched his room while he watched her, looking for evidence, something of Dolly's that would condone what she'd done, but there was nothing and it was too late anyway. The horrifying realisation that she might never now discover what had happened to Dolly and Laura coiled itself around her neck like a python. She shook the pillow, returned it to the top of the wardrobe, and left the room, concealing Will's notebook in her locker on her way back to the lounge. She didn't want anyone to see Dolly's name. She didn't want to be connected to Gilbert's death.

Cora was wandering along the corridor in a pink cotton nightgown decorated with red cherries. Jolene shepherded her into the lounge and sat her in front of the television, draping a blanket of colourful crocheted squares across her knees and resting a cushion embroidered with a sequinned giraffe behind her head. She made her a cup of cocoa and then sat down beside her.

Tina came in and tried to take Cora back to her room, but Jolene wanted her to stay, needed her to stay.

'I'll take her back after she's finished her cocoa,' Jolene told her.

'Well, if anyone needs me I'll be in the staffroom. There's a Moroccan lamb and apricot tagine in the fridge with my name on it, literally, although it didn't stop someone eating my chickpea and red pepper falafels last week.'

Jolene wondered what kind of person would open a Tupperware box with someone else's name written on the lid and consume the contents, until she realised she'd just looked in a notebook containing another person's notes and used that information to murder someone. She remembered that Tina liked to cook specific cuisines at certain times of the year – Russian January, Swedish December – and she'd once told Jolene that Noah would only eat food beginning with the letter 'B', so they ate a lot of beetroot and broccoli for a while. When he moved onto the 'O's, onions and okra and oranges, it required Tina to be particularly imaginative.

When Tina's footsteps had faded Cora began to quietly murmur beside her, something about still loving your children no matter what they do. Jolene wasn't listening. She was staring at the *Switchblade Romance* DVD cover on the empty chair to the right of her, at the blood dripping from the words 'unspeakably bloodthirsty'. She pressed play on the remote.

Cora closed her eyes and Jolene reached for Cora's hand, silent tears rolling down both their cheeks.

What had she done?

Murdered someone, she heard a voice whisper, but when she turned to look at Cora, her eyes were closed.

Jolene realised she was trembling. Her pulse was racing.

She decided to check the notebook again. She needed to confirm that it didn't say Polly, that the sketch wasn't of a wellington boot or a slipper or something unrecognisable. Switching off the DVD she took Cora back to her room. When she checked the notebook, it was definitely a 'D', but she was no longer sure that it was a drawing of an ice skate. She couldn't breathe. She needed to be somewhere else. She made a coffee and, helping herself to one of Will's Almond Slices (it appeared that she was now a thief as well as a murderer), she sat on the bench in the courtyard as if nothing had happened and she hadn't just killed someone.

It was no longer raining, but a whistling wind threaded a path through the trees. She zipped up her jacket. When Gilbert was discovered in the morning she'd have to behave normally, appear saddened by his passing.

How did people do that?

Kill a person and then move on with their lives.

Perhaps they'd know that it was her and she'd spend the rest of her life in prison. Would it be so different from how she lived now?

Suddenly, there was a crackle, like static, a sharp intake of breath, and then a pressure around her neck, a feeling of weightlessness, and as the coffee mug she'd been holding rolled into Luke's snapdragon flowerbeds, her world spun with it.

The Girls In Between

By the age of seventy-seven my health had declined drastically, penance perhaps for the life that I'd led and the things that I'd done. My left hip crunched like church gravel beneath me each morning and my ankles were permanently inflamed and swollen. I tried not to examine them too closely when I placed them gingerly on the floor, which was much easier now that my cataracts had become such loyal allies. Having once been able to hear the slightest vibration and identify the distant speck of a seagull on the horizon, my ears now muffled all but the closest and loudest sounds and my eyes had glazed over, intent on hiding the world from me. I didn't much like it, this new me (or, rather, this old me).

I despised my weak eyes, my decrepit bones and flaccid skin. I despised what I'd now become. I couldn't do any of the things I still dreamed of doing, any of the things I'd honed and planed into shape over the years like a much-loved china cabinet. I was rapidly becoming disposable and dispensable, an encumbrance, the lengthening years seeming to signal less of a presence rather than more of one. I couldn't even engage in the daily elderly rituals that

I'd once reluctantly embraced, an occasional pint of lager at the Rose and Crown, a fried breakfast at Jill's Kitchen. And the allotment that I'd regularly tended where teenage boys liked to spray-paint graffiti on walls was now too far to walk to.

I'd threatened to call the police numerous times. 'Keep your fucking fur on, granddad,' they'd yell at me. I'd wish I was younger so I could slit their throats instead of merely scowling at them, especially when the paint wouldn't wash off. Instead of 'piss-pots' it read 'issots'.

'Is it French?' Kenny Rogers (not the country singer) from a neighbouring allotment once asked.

I missed sitting in that worn leather armchair at the end of the day, a mug of sugary tea in my hand and a hot flannel on each knee, the sun a watery, milky opal in the sky, like one of my own eyes staring back at me, marvelling at the things I'd grown, the forests of broccoli, the four types of lettuce, and the things I'd seen.

Jill's Kitchen was where I met Vera. She'd sat down opposite me, noisily buttering her toasted teacake and slurping her tea. She'd smelled of hairspray and furniture polish, her lilac hair freshly blow-dried, deep wrinkles edging her face like creased fabric and milkshake-pink lipstick across her lips that had bled into her skin, her lips too thin and too dry to hold it firm. The look of her repulsed me.

When she later invited me into her home, however, I felt like a vampire being offered a blood sacrifice and I realised that being elderly might not signal the end of everything after all. A person of pensionable age was both trusted and ignored. They could do anything they chose to, health permitting.

Remember Where You've Buried The Bodies

While she was in the kitchen I studied the silver-framed photographs on the mantelpiece: a boy with severe acne and protruding teeth on his graduation day, a man with sleekly parted black hair and arctic-blue eyes in an army uniform, a woman I presumed to be Vera when she was much younger kneeling beside a picnic hamper, her short-sleeved, avocado-green checked shirt knotted at the waist. She'd been attractive once. Pink lipstick would have suited her then.

I was examining the bottom of one of the Royal Doulton figurines on the windowsill when she returned. She was carrying a plate of biscuits and my earlier feelings of despising her came flooding back like a wave. I sat down on one of the armchairs where there was no danger of her sitting next to me and noticed she'd applied another layer of lipstick while she'd been in the kitchen.

And was that a child's hairclip in her hair? It was making me furious just being there. But she'd dropped into my lap and that was something that I couldn't easily ignore, not at my age. So I sat in Vera's lounge, while outside white cotton sheets billowed in the breeze on the washing line like a row of ghosts, some of which I recognised, some of which were new.

Afterwards, I often saw Vera's cloud of lilac hair and her smiling wafer-pink lips behind The Balloon Man figurine I'd stolen that now sat on my windowsill, although it wasn't her, of course.

I hadn't had a serious relationship since the death of my wife, mostly visiting prostitutes or indulging in one-night stands, and my children rarely visited, even at Christmas. To escape the loneliness I sometimes felt, I took refuge in the past, in anything that reminded me of happier times. Everything reminded me of something or someone. The sweet scent of pear blossom would remind me of Lydia, a schoolteacher, one of the girls in between. I remembered the freckle on her left eyelid, the orchard trees casting their long shadows, the cache of knives that I'd buried years earlier.

The floral wallpaper in the bedroom, peeling like sunburn, would remind me of Jayne with a 'y', another of the girls in between. Her skin once the colour of a South Sea pearl, now slowly decomposing beneath the floorboards of an abandoned chapel, where vases of plastic flowers gathered dust by the pulpit. I remembered Lisa and the Perspex sandals, Charlotte and the vandalised telephone box, Mary and the Scottish heather.

Sometimes, I'd think of my mother – the sun setting over the quarry as she peeled tangerines.

Occasionally, regrets resurfaced – regrets that I'd not left England when I'd had the chance. I would like to have seen the churches of Malta or gone horseback riding with Argentinian ranch owners. I recalled one of the lorry drivers at the depot where I'd briefly worked telling me that they were always looking for drivers in Alaska, but because I could do everything that I wanted to do right here, Alaska became another missed opportunity. I'd still be the same person thousands of miles away, I told myself. I'd just be swapping rain-soaked gridlocked motorways for arctic Alaskan highways. Flying to another country would never change that, and everything I'd been and everything I'd done would travel there with me. I'd just be killing people in colder conditions.

And then the memories I'd meticulously constructed over the years began to crumble like house bricks, the shape of them jagged and imprecise. Unfamiliar faces, incomprehensible household *appliances, sentences that were as mystifying as a foreign language. Like trying to catch a ball that my hands couldn't grasp.*

A care worker called twice a day. She reminded me of Martha, another of the girls in between and one of the last to slip away, and I'd try to engage her in conversation so she'd stay a little longer, but once she'd made me a sandwich and given me my medication, she'd leave. She never even removed her coat.

Occasionally, a stray tear would fall from the corner of my left eye and I'd wipe it away. I could find no reason for it. But I did wonder what anguish lay ahead without the solace and companionship of my memories. When they were gone, like the first and the last and the girls in between, what would be left? What would replace them? What type of person would I be then?

I'd be a serial killer who doesn't even know he's a serial killer.

I'd be a man with thousands of memories he has no way of accessing.

A few weeks later I was watching a television documentary about a girl named Melanie Gray. The name seemed strangely familiar, but just out of reach. I glanced at the clouds outside my bedroom window, tried to find the name there, but the clouds were being unusually still and secretive.

Melanie Gray's tearful mother was staring at me. I wondered if I'd ever been to Tenby.

Melanie was fourteen when she disappeared, her mother told the camera. 'My husband and my son were building sandcastles on the beach and Melanie wanted to go to the toilet. The toilets were on the promenade walkway, not far at all, but I decided to go with her and wait outside, even though she begged me not to. Five minutes passed, ten minutes. The turrets were added, the moat. She seemed to be taking an unusually long time, but I didn't want to hurry her and upset her further, so I leaned against the promenade railings and waited a little while longer.

'The entrance to the ladies' toilets was on the other side of the building opposite the Lifeboat Station and I couldn't see it from where I was standing. Growing increasingly impatient I eventually went inside. She wasn't there. All six cubicles were empty. I ran back outside and scanned the promenade and the beach, but I couldn't see her.

'There were some steps behind the toilet block that led onto a busy road and I ran along the road, running into shops and hotels along the seafront, asking shop assistants and hotel receptionists if they'd seen her, stopping people on the street, Tenby was teeming with tourists that day, and there were hundreds of people lining the beach road watching a 'Miss Teen Tenby' parade, but nobody had seen her. Nobody ever sees anything. Because these people know what they're doing. They know how to blend in. They know how to abduct a person in broad daylight.

'I told myself there was a simple explanation and when I returned to the beach, she'd be filling buckets with sand and flicking water at her younger brother and grinning at me because she'd outsmarted me, but she wasn't there and that's when I knew someone had taken her, that someone had been waiting for a child to become separated from their family or perhaps they'd specifically targeted our child, our family. The thought of someone watching Melanie all afternoon made me shudder. I tried to remember who she'd spoken to or if anyone had spoken to her, but I couldn't remember anyone acting suspiciously, although they don't always act suspiciously, do they? Often they're just like you and me.

'We searched for her for hours, wondering if she'd been driven away in a car, in which case she could have been anywhere. That was *the worst thought, that she could be anywhere. My husband tried to remain hopeful but even he was starting to become concerned. We enlisted the help of fellow holidaymakers, searching the beach and the promenade and even the sea. We'd called the police by then, of course, but they were delayed because there'd been a bomb scare at the Clarence House Hotel so when they did finally arrive four hours had passed. Four hours is a long time when you've lost someone. She could have been in Europe by then. I often wonder if it wasn't a coincidence that the Clarence House Hotel received an anonymous phone call around that time.*

'The police did eventually manage to obtain CCTV footage from a camera that faced the toilets but, devastatingly, the steps to the toilets were obscured for fifty-two minutes by sixteen parade floats. And then a ray of hope; as the last float passed, a puppeteer could be seen standing beside the steps. I hadn't noticed him when I was running along the road. He was wearing an embroidered silk waistcoat and pulling the strings of four wooden puppets, dogs I think. When the police did manage to locate him they discovered that he was blind. I couldn't breathe. I couldn't understand how a person could just vanish like that, when they'd been no more than a few footsteps away. It made absolutely no sense.'

'Have I ever been to Tenby, Martha?' I asked the care worker.

'I've no idea. And it's Sarah, not Martha.'

Two weeks later I was transferred to Sunset House and I never saw Martha again.

Chapter Thirty-One

UNUSUALLY SMALL HANDS

The sound of digging woke Rex from a restless night's sleep and it was several seconds before he realised the noise he could hear wasn't the thud of a garden spade and a desperate rescue mission to exhume Denise before she ran out of oxygen, but his mobile phone.

Superintendent Forrester chirped cheerily in his ear.

'As expected, no cause of death can be determined from Joanne Collins' remains, so they'll be released for burial as soon as the paperwork's been signed.'

Rex failed to appreciate the urgency of this information, his clammy palm moisturising his phone, black spots flitting back and forth in front of his eyes like an arcade game in the lamplight.

Was this an aperitif, the bad news before the *actual* bad news?

Superintendent Forrester continued.

'Arrangements are being made to bring Gilbert Williams into the station later today for a formal interview in the presence of a social worker and a solicitor. DI Kendrick and DS Granger have been working through the night to make it happen.'

Of course they have.

'In the meantime I'd like you to pay Jacob Lyons a visit. I've scheduled a meeting for eleven-thirty this morning. He claims to have information regarding Laura Sykes' disappearance.'

Of course he does.

The band of pain around Rex's forehead was getting tighter.

'Is that really necessary, sir? Jacob Lyons isn't the most reliable of sources.'

'I'm afraid so. The information that he purports to have may be important, it would be remiss of us to ignore it, and, quite frankly, *any* information at this present time would be welcome. Take Cathy with you. She'll enjoy being thrown to the Lyons.'

Very droll.

Rex had lost count of the number of statements he'd collected from Jacob Lyons over the years, the hours of police time he'd wasted, the amount of paperwork he'd created.

It only served to remind Rex how mundane police work often was, administrative rather than pioneering, pedestrian rather than thrilling, a duplicitous cast list and a script punctuated with misdirection. Rarely were you chasing criminals in skyscraper elevators or engaging in shoot-outs. Mostly, you relied on a careless fingerprint or a deathbed confession. Cases weren't neatly concluded like they were in the movies. Sometimes cases were never solved at all. They lay festering and forgotten on police databases, people like Jacob Lyons muddying the waters further.

Rex could hear Lucas in the background.

'And one more thing,' the Superintendent said, imitating his favourite television detective, Columbo. 'We've been unable to reach Martin Williams. Can you call at the Williams home on your way to the prison? Gilbert's daughter is currently in California, according to the care home, and her phone appears to be switched off, but it would be a courtesy to apprise at least one of Mr Williams' next-of-kin of the situation.'

Lucas, it appeared, was now giving the orders.

'Very well, sir.'

The Superintendent failed to register the weary sense of resignation in Rex's tone.

'That's the spirit. No stone left unturned.'

It seemed to Rex that it was the same stone being turned. Over and over again.

Unless Martin Williams invited them inside the property voluntarily and they could take a look around without having to obtain a police warrant. Cathy hadn't flexed her meerkat muscles recently. Maybe they'd discover a body buried beneath the patio. That would take the shine off Lucas Granger's rhinestones.

Not that he wanted to find a dead body under the patio, of course. He didn't want to find any more dead girls.

Cathy was panting when she answered the phone. Mercifully, she'd just finished an online Zumba class and wasn't, as Rex had initially feared, in the middle of something more intimate.

'Sorry about the wheezing, sir,' she'd gasped, breathlessly.

Sensing Rex's discomfort, she'd provided further clarification, 'Early morning Zumba. Don't worry, if it was anything to do with Matt I'd be barely breaking a sweat.'

Rex was relieved there was no one to witness his cheeks flushing crimson. He suspected Cathy was spending far too much time around male police officers, trying to be 'one of the boys'.

'The number of times I wished my mother lived closer so I could go and stay with her for a while,' Cathy was saying, as Rex was attempting to parallel-park the car in the smallest of spaces outside the Williams family home. 'Sometimes you just need a break from married life.'

Rex nodded, although he'd never felt like that. He'd never wanted to be where Denise wasn't. And he wasn't sure why Cathy was telling him this. She shouldn't be telling him this. He wasn't a marriage guidance counsellor.

There was no answer when Rex knocked on the front door. Cathy stood peering through a downstairs window, a hand placed in salute above her eyes to deflect the sun's rays. It was barely eight o'clock and the sun was like a furnace. Rex didn't function well in extreme heat. While other people drifted around like they'd been born on a Spanish beach in a heatwave, Rex just felt lethargic and dehydrated.

'Nice fireplace,' cooed Cathy. 'They've got a wood-burning stove. It looks new. Shame about the exterior.'

She paced the perimeter of the property, looking for a way in.

Rex knocked again. Why he thought a second knock might rouse the occupant when the first one had so obviously failed, he didn't know. Cathy returned, hovering behind him impatiently, providing a welcome barrier between Rex and the sun, his plasma-sphered nemesis. She then began lifting up terracotta plant pots.

'You know we can't let ourselves in, even if you do find a key.'

'I know that, sir, but maybe we heard a gunshot or a scream.'

'And maybe we didn't.'

'Just joking, sir. Besides, my nan's the only person who leaves her front door key beneath a plant pot. I've told her time and time again that it isn't safe, but she won't listen. When I removed the plant pots, she attached the key to a piece of string behind the letterbox for even easier access. She has absolutely no concept of home security. I'm surprised she bothers locking the door at all.'

'Let's speak to the neighbours.'

When they reconvened, they had little to report. An elderly couple who lived next door hadn't seen Martin Williams recently and were 'about to begin battle with a Sudoku and a Copenhagen Slice, if that's everything', and the man living opposite, who wouldn't give his name and refused to take the chain off the door, concealing three quarters of his face and all of his hallway, said he didn't know a Martin Williams. 'He was definitely behaving suspiciously,' Cathy confided. 'But I need more than a solitary blue eye behind a glass lens and a cross section of cheekbone to read a person.

'I'll check the electoral register when I'm back in the office. Do we know where he works?' she asked.

'Who, the neighbour?'

'No, sir, Martin Williams.'

'No idea. I'll check with Superintendent Forrester after we've spoken to Jacob Lyons. We'll hopefully know the outcome of Gilbert Williams' interview by then and, if there's sufficient evidence to arrest him or he confesses, obtaining a warrant should be a formality and we'll be able to conduct a thorough search of the premises without Martin Williams' permission. Bring the dogs in.'

'If it's not too late,' Cathy cautioned, solemnly, as they were walking back to the car. 'Whole crime scenes can be disinfected and bodies incinerated in the time it takes to get a warrant. There's no element of surprise in policing anymore.'

She cast an embittered glance at the one-eyed neighbour's house. She disliked unfinished business. The downstairs curtains were closed.

'I wouldn't mind being a police dog handler myself at some point,' she told Rex. 'To be perfectly honest, I prefer animals to people, although it could be argued that most of the people we deal with are animals. I've always quite fancied having a partner that can rip a person to shreds. No offence, sir.'

'None taken. My teeth aren't what they used to be.'

'The police dog we usually use, Titan, reminds me of a rescue German Shepherd we had when I was a child, Bella. She scared the life out of me when we first had her, blocking out the sun like a solar eclipse and slobbering all over my legs, but God, did I love her. I told her everything. It broke my heart when she died. I temporarily damaged one of my eyes with all the crying I did and had to wear a patch for a while. I looked like a tiny pirate.'

She paused by the car. A small child dressed in a fairy costume was pushing her own pushchair along the pavement, while a stooped woman wearing a tartan beret trailed behind her. The little girl kept telling the woman to hurry up. They hadn't got all day.

'So many secrets in so many neighbourhoods. They're like breeding grounds for skeletons in closets, battlefields for the criminally insane. I dread to think what goes on behind most closed doors.'

She climbed into the passenger seat of the car and reached for the seatbelt.

'How mortifying must it be to discover your sweet and frail elderly grandparent was once a monster? I can't imagine my granddad ever parking on double yellows, but you just don't know, do you? He could have been getting up to all sorts when he was more mobile. Sorry, sir, I seem to be getting more introspective in my old age.'

She was thirty-two.

'But don't worry,' she assured him, flipping down the sun visor. 'It's nothing that a *Jersey Boys* matinee won't remedy.'

Featherstone prison was twenty miles south. It always caught you unawares, like a gasp, a mirage of olive-green lichen clawing at limestone walls that rose like a rocket from a launch pad as soon as you'd left the motorway. The windows ran along the limestone like coin slots and an electric diamond-wire fence crowned with barbed wire surrounded the prison grounds. The interior was more generic. It was what Rex suspected nineteenth-century asylums had looked like: plain white wall tiles, stainless steel sinks, and a solid grey door at the end of each corridor.

They were left waiting for thirty minutes – deliberately, Rex suspected. There was a history of mistrust between police officers and prison officers which, considering their mutual objective was one of justice and rehabilitation, was somewhat paradoxical. They couldn't even scroll through their phones because their phones were currently sitting in a plastic tray behind a glass partition.

Finally, the prison officer who'd asked them to wait reappeared.

Apparently, Jacob no longer wished to see them. He didn't want police officers visiting him in prison. Rex wished he'd mentioned it sooner. 'He's worked hard to rise through the prison hierarchy. He's respected in here,' the prison officer was saying. 'He doesn't want any trouble.' It didn't sound like Jacob speaking. It sounded like a heavily censored version of what had actually been said, namely, tell them to fuck off, I've changed my mind.

'Why did he contact us then?' Rex asked. The prison officer shrugged. Rex asked him to try again. They'd come a long way.

Twenty minutes later, success. Having been told that a

female police officer would be accompanying Rex ('that normally gets them interested'), Jacob had decided that he would now see them after all. The prison officer buzzed them through a number of identical doors as he recounted the exchange, verbatim. 'I don't suppose it would hurt,' Jacob had said. 'I'll say they're trying to pin some other shit on me, which they probably are.' This did sound like Jacob.

'We aren't trying to pin anything on him,' Rex sighed. '*He* called us.'

Rex was furious that Cathy had been offered as leverage and had been fully prepared to walk away. They weren't playthings. But Cathy had insisted it was fine. Rex told her that if she felt in any way uncomfortable then they'd terminate the visit immediately. 'I can handle myself, sir. It's nothing I haven't dealt with before.' Rex wondered if she'd experienced sexual harassment or discrimination in the workplace in the past or on a more personal level. He was aware of two senior police officers in their county currently under investigation for discriminatory behaviour.

Jacob Lyons was sitting at a table, smirking. Why did prison inmates always assume they had the upper hand? Probably because law enforcement were always pandering to their every whim, willing to travel miles for the pleasure of their lies. While Lucas was preparing to interview a murder suspect, Rex was humouring a habitual liar, who was starting to look more and more like his father, Walter (Walter was also detained at Featherstone, offending something of a Lyons family trait). In fact the likeness was so unsettling that on first entering the room Rex had mistakenly thought it *was* Walter smirking at him and that a meeting had been arranged with the wrong man.

Although we all turn into our parents eventually, Rex supposed. It was merely a matter of which one. Rex had often wished he looked more like his mother, his face a lasting reminder that she had actually existed.

It was only when Jacob spoke that Rex realised it wasn't Walter. Walter had developed a thick Scottish accent over the years, even though he wasn't Scottish, and he had a habit of repeatedly cracking his knuckles.

Jacob's attention remained solely on Cathy. She barely flinched under his leering gaze. If anything she looked a little bored.

Rex studied Jacob's straggly grey hair, the sleeves of old bruises on his arms, giving his skin a mottled, seafaring quality, the flexed fingers of his unusually small hands. His teeth were unnaturally white. He asked Cathy if she liked his new teeth. 'Not particularly,' Cathy sighed.

'I'll be sure to pass your comments onto the prison dentist when I next see him.'

'Please do.'

'So,' Rex asked. 'Aside from providing dental care feedback, why are we really here?'

'That girl who's recently gone missing, Laura Sykes – I've been hearing things.'

Hearing things rather than doing things was something of a departure.

'What things?'

'Don't suppose I could get a smoke.'

He looked at Cathy.

'You suppose right.'

'It isn't what you think.'

'And what do I think?'

'You think she's been abducted.'

Rex waited for him to expand, to lessen the lengthening silence. He didn't.

'So it's nothing to do with you?'

'Not everything's my fault.'

'It usually is.'

'Touché.'

'And if she hasn't been abducted?'

'Now that, I don't know. I'll need to give it some thought.'

Rex pushed back his chair. It squeaked loudly.

'You do that.'

'No need to be like that. You know I can't spill the beans without a little something in return.'

'I think we're done here,' Rex said, rapping his knuckles on the door to signal the end of the interview.

Jacob Lyons made a small room feel even smaller.

As Cathy was walking over to the door, Jacob relented.

'Okay, you win. A freebie it is. Have you ever heard of Derek Wilson, founder of the Halo Movement?'

Rex gestured to the prison officer to give them five more minutes.

'Hearts and Lives Opened?'

'That's the one. Derek's dead now, but his two sons, Elijah and Saul, now run things, a little controversially from what I hear. Anyway, wherever they settle they like to recruit new members. Sometimes these new members go with them voluntarily. Sometimes they're taken by force.'

'So you think she may have joined a cult?'

'They don't like the term cult. And I don't know how much say she had in the matter.'

Cathy was making notes. Rex hoped that this time they'd actually lead somewhere.

'Walter and Derek once shared a cell.'

Rex had always found it strange that Jacob called his father Walter, as if he was just another prison inmate, no relation at all. Rex was in no doubt that neither would hesitate in killing the other if provoked.

'He'd been convicted of sexually assaulting one of the Movement members after his daughter Naomi disappeared, considered himself a vessel of God.'

'Naomi?'

Rex glanced at Cathy, who'd underlined the name three times.

'I never forget a name, one of my many talents.'

Jacob glanced at Cathy, expecting a response. She yawned.

'They'd been searching for a place to build a commune, in Wales I think, when she disappeared. Derek was convinced that a teenage boy who they'd befriended was responsible. He'd been close to finding him a couple a times, he said. I don't know if he ever did. You'd have to ask Walter, although you won't find him as charitable as me.'

'He's got serious delusions of grandeur,' Cathy confided, as they were collecting their belongings. 'And was that an American accent? I thought he was from Wolverhampton.'

'The disappearance of Derek Wilson's daughter Naomi is

interesting though, if it's true, particularly as it's one of the names that Will Cavanagh mentioned,' Rex replied. 'Let's see if a missing person report for a Naomi Wilson was ever filed and whether Gilbert Williams can be placed in Wales around that time.'

Rex checked his phone. He'd received sixteen missed calls from Superintendent Forrester.

Chapter Thirty-Two
UNDERWATER

Will felt as if he was underwater.

As if Angelina was on the lakeshore, waving at him.

As if things might end differently this time…

Chapter Thirty-Three

MELTING LIKE SNOWFLAKES ON TONGUES

Superintendent Forrester's latest update had been delivered like fatal stab wounds, unexpectedly and escalating in magnitude. Jolene Edwards had never arrived home after an overnight shift at Sunset House, Will Cavanagh was in the hospital in a coma and Gilbert Williams had passed away during the night.

Having this morning been on the verge of a potential breakthrough, Rex and his colleagues had lost their footing and were now on the verge of a vertiginous precipice. It was unknown whether Will Cavanagh would regain consciousness and, if he did regain consciousness, whether there'd be brain damage, while Gilbert Williams had inconveniently taken any secrets that he might have had to his grave. And, although Jolene Edwards' car was still parked in the Sunset House staff car park, Jolene herself had mysteriously vanished. It seemed to Rex that all these incidents were in some way connected, but currently he could see no obvious link, apart from the adage that things often happened in threes, which was of little practical help.

Angela Edwards, Jolene's mother, had contacted the station earlier, demanding to speak to him. She wasn't going to lose another daughter, she'd said, bristling, as if he'd been solely responsible for the loss of the first. Police officers were frequently disparaged en masse. It was almost impossible to detach yourself from a colleague's ineptitude. But this time it felt personal. It felt as if the weight of this woman's sanity was on *his* shoulders alone.

He'd felt a sudden and intense admiration for the unwavering determination currently being exhibited by this grieving woman. He'd similarly mourned the loss of two loved ones, his wife and his mother, but instead of making him fearless and invincible as it had Angela Edwards (at least publicly), it had somehow diminished him, made him doubt himself, made him less able.

'Her mobile phone needs to be traced and her work colleagues interviewed,' Angela Edwards had instructed him sternly on the phone, 'and not in a week or a month, but today, this minute. Now! CCTV footage from the care home and neighbouring street cameras will also need to be reviewed before the footage is erased and a search of nearby bodies of water, secluded areas and construction sites should be prioritised. And don't even think about suggesting that Jolene's run away. She wouldn't do that.'

Rex had to concede that it would have been cruel of Jolene to have run away, but not impossible. Her mother was like a whirlwind, obliterating everything in her path. Perhaps her second daughter had been an unexpected casualty. He found himself blindsided by Angela Edwards' stipulations, the urgency with which she relayed her demands. She'd always been argumentative and brittle in public, maybe less so in private, but perhaps she'd had to be. Perhaps she'd had to be both a mother and an upholder of the law. When you were searching for a missing child you had to be whatever you were required to be, especially when all other avenues had been denied you and remained unexplored.

'And I expect to be kept informed. I won't be brushed aside as if I'm an inconvenience. This time I'm going to find my daughter,' Angela Edwards had asserted, entering Rex's office later that same day with the fieriness of a battling Boudicca, the militancy of a Joan of Arc. A phoenix rising from the ashes. There was no indulgent weeping or wallowing self-pity, much of what she'd specified earlier on the phone repeated for emphasis like bullets being fired.

Rex had nodded his obedient acceptance. 'I'm doing everything I can,' he'd replied, sounding disappointingly ineffectual and disengaged and media-trained. Fortunately, he'd had the foresight to lower the office blinds for more privacy. He hadn't wanted his hands-tied incompetence to be witnessed by the other officers.

Looping the worn strap of the brown leather handbag that had been resting on her lap across her shoulder, Angela Edwards stood up to leave. A button was missing on her grey jacket, the fabric of her trousers shiny in places from repeated ironing, a grief-stricken mother trying to look businesslike. 'I'll expect to hear from you this evening with an update, DI Spencer. I'll be at the care home if you need me.' Rex should have requested that she refrain from visiting Sunset House.

She might be tampering with crucial evidence, reaching inaccurate conclusions. But what would be the point? She'd go anyway. She was a civilian version of Cathy, to whom normal rules didn't apply.

And did it really matter? Previous approaches hadn't worked. People had melted like snowflakes on tongues, vanished like planes crossing oceans. This time they needed to 'bring their A-game', 'think outside the box', 'push the envelope' and any other Lucas-isms that might rally the troops. Failure was not an option. This time they were going to find Jolene Edwards. Alive. He was going to prove to his superiors and Angela Edwards and the watching media that a missing person could be found if you knew where to look.

Before then, however, Jolene's father, another person whose alibi would need to be verified, was waiting in reception. Suspicion followed Anthony Edwards like a Twitter account.

After lunch Rex scheduled an office meeting to ascertain what information had been gathered so far. Jolene's colleagues claimed she'd been her usual 'abrasive' self, if a little distracted, and images obtained from the care home's CCTV footage had captured Jolene sitting in her car on numerous occasions throughout the night, the final sighting of her at three a.m. when she'd exited a side door that led into a courtyard.

Her coffee mug had been found in one of the flowerbeds and was being dusted for fingerprints while a list of vehicle registrations captured by CCTV cameras at the care home and on adjacent streets between six p.m. and six a.m. was being cross-referenced.

Rex updated Angela Edwards, as directed. She was still at the care home conducting her own enquiries.

When he left the station to meet a private investigator named Crosby Knowles, who'd contacted him to discuss Jolene, Lucas and Sheena were in Superintendent Forrester's office 'strategising' (sipping malt whisky and drafting statements). Maybe they'd blame Gilbert Williams anyway. A dead man couldn't defend himself and his children didn't seem unduly concerned about his reputation. They'd been unreachable from the beginning.

According to Glenda, there were no plans to conduct a post-mortem. He was elderly and in ill-health. It wasn't exactly unexpected. And why would someone want to kill him? Rex had no idea, unless someone knew something that they didn't and his death was related to other deaths, a chain of consequence, but, given time, anyone could find someone who'd harboured a grudge, no matter how Good a Samaritan a person first appeared. There was always someone whose life would be vastly improved by your demise.

Chapter Thirty-Four

A MORRISSEY SONG

Cathy

Jolene Edwards had now been missing for four days, four days that would soon become five days, five days that would soon become six months, until a year had passed, seven years, seventeen years, twenty-seven years, missing for longer than they'd existed, and Jolene Edwards would be another forgotten missing person. Like her sister, Dolly. Rex wasn't wrong when he'd claimed that police work mostly consisted of repeated eyestrain from computer screens and the constructing of vague, incomplete timelines. Very little apprehending of criminals was actually being accomplished. Working at Vodafone would have provided the same level of job fulfilment.

And how were people still disappearing and falling into comas when the main suspect was dead? It was like a thousand ravens being released at once. It was like a Morrissey song.

Cathy enjoyed a mystery as much as the next person, but the lack of progress being made was scandalous. The perpetrators of crimes shouldn't have been outwitting the alleged experts, who had numerous password-protected resources at their disposal and should have already been several steps ahead.

While Jolene's digital footprint was being traced, Cathy had spent the last few days re-examining Dolly Edwards' disappearance and Derek and Naomi Wilson's possible link to the case, convinced that the three disappearances were somehow connected. Laura Sykes' disappearance she considered an anomaly, an outlier. There was currently no evidence to suggest otherwise.

This morning, she'd updated Rex on her findings so far.

'I don't think Naomi Wilson was ever reported missing – or if she was reported missing then no one was particularly interested in publicising it. Policing and investigative journalism weren't what they are today, of course. You were lucky to get a couple of sentences in the *Examiner*. And the fact that she led a mostly transitory lifestyle creates further complications. Transient people are by definition missing, so little is done to find them. As for Dolly Edwards, I'm cross-referencing the information that the private investigator you spoke to gave us with our own case files.'

'You should go home,' Rex had told her. 'Get some rest.'

'I *am* in desperate need of a hot bath, a glass of South African Shiraz and ten episodes of *Schitt's Creek* back-to-back,' she'd conceded. 'Maybe I will head home for a couple of hours.'

Before closing the office door behind her she'd reminded Rex, as if reassuring them both, 'It's a demoralising fact, but people do sometimes get away with murder. And it's not because they're unscrupulous masterminds who know how to commit the perfect crime or that we're a bunch of Keystone Cops who have no idea what we're doing. It's because they've been lucky – *this* time. It's because of somebody else's mistake. It's because there's too much that's out of our control.'

At the traffic lights, instead of driving straight on, Cathy impulsively spun the steering wheel left in the direction of Gilbert Williams' daughter's address. His son was never home but maybe his daughter would be, now she was apparently back in the UK. Maybe she'd be willing to discuss her deceased father and her elusive brother. Maybe there were things she'd been waiting decades to confess. She certainly couldn't run a relaxing bath and pour a glass of Shiraz when there were girls within their jurisdiction still missing.

Reversing into the first available parking space, Cathy was reminded how the flawless façades of detached new-builds only served to mask the commonality of the violent and addictive behaviour afflicting most households: husbands bruising wives, parents abusing children, class A drugs, alcoholism.

A woman dressed in sweatpants and a Stevie Nicks T-shirt was walking along the path, her hair pinned up loosely, lilac crescents beneath her green eyes.

'Ms Williams? I'm DS Daniels,' Cathy said, confronting the woman before she could disappear behind a closed door. 'I wonder if I could speak to you about your father.'

Cathy had been conducting background checks on Gilbert Williams' two children for no other reason than she liked to be thorough. She didn't just investigate the suspect. She investigated the suspect's family, their children, siblings, cousins, ex-spouses... A family member could lead them to a suspect or a suspect could implicate a family member. There were lifelong threads that needed to be unpicked.

Earlier, Juliet Crane, one of the PCs, had spotted Faye Williams' name on Cathy's computer as she was passing, her eyes glistening at the prospect of seeing something classified or confidential. Cathy had quickly minimised the screen, a second too late.

'I went to school with a Faye Williams, back in Inverness,' Juliet had said.

'I didn't know you knew the Williams family,' replied Cathy.

'I didn't, and I'm not entirely sure that it's *your* Faye Williams – she looked different then, glasses, permed hair. She was only there for a couple of terms and then she left. She lied a lot, I remember that, claimed her father was an eminent neurosurgeon and her mother died in a car crash when everyone knew her mother worked in the local pharmacy and her father was a taxi driver. I remember her threatening a friend of her brother's once, hissing and spitting at him. It felt like we were finally seeing the real Faye, like the glasses and the hair were a disguise. It was around the same time that five-year-old Natasha Jackson went missing. Faye had been volunteering at the primary school that Natasha Jackson attended. It was the Harvest Festival.'

'Thanks, Juliet. I'll request the case file.'

Cathy's Faye Williams was frowning.

'It won't take long, Ms Williams.'

Rex would be furious when he discovered she'd interviewed Faye Williams alone. 'Never enter a building without another colleague present' had been his only directive when she'd first joined the team, although there were now of course many more directives that she conveniently chose to ignore. A loose cannon, her father used to call her, as if she was a devastating influence on all those around her. Sometimes, it felt as if she was. Matt called her a liability. He used to call her his everything, but he hadn't called her that in a long time, presumably because he was sleeping with the babysitter of one of the neighbours and it was no longer strictly accurate. He didn't know she knew, seemed to have forgotten she was a police officer.

There was a delivery of post and a newspaper on the geometric-patterned hall carpet and Cathy could smell a cat litter tray, although she couldn't see any evidence of a cat.

Paula Sutton's house had always smelled like a cat litter tray.

Cathy remembered Mrs O'Connor telling them Paula wouldn't be coming in today and then, eight weeks later, that she wouldn't be coming in at all. Paula's body had been found on a stretch of wasteland barely a mile from her front door. Cathy had quietly inched her chair away from the vacant seat next to her. Everyone seemed to be holding their breath, especially Cathy, who'd been too afraid to exhale in case someone heard her, in case someone remembered where Paula had sat and thought that Cathy was somehow to blame for her absence.

Cathy had wondered who would fill the space now, who would sit where Paula had sat, who would be the one always to remind them. It was easier to pretend she'd moved back to Llandudno, while other Paulas occupied the empty seat beside her, taller, non-dead Paulas she didn't dare look at too closely in case they too disappeared to Llandudno one day without telling her.

She'd once seen evidence of Paula wrapped in cellophane and dated – a sherbet-lemon blood-stained sock and a neatly folded blue and white pinafore dress. She couldn't believe how small she'd been, how small she'd stay.

She'd been missing for eight weeks.

And then she was found – *Here I am!*

As if she'd been there all the time, nestled in a cool, dark hollow, one of her lemon socks missing and her pale limbs half-eaten.

That's why Cathy spends her life chasing murderers – maybe one day she'll catch the one that got away.

She wondered if the hallway was the furthest she'd be allowed to venture, but Faye Williams reluctantly opened the door behind her and motioned for Cathy to go through. It was the lounge and it was filled with an array of unusual memorabilia. There was a doll's house on a sideboard, the wallpaper on the doll's house lounge walls the same wallpaper that was in the lounge, and in the hallway of the doll's house miniature handmade envelopes and a newspaper were arranged on an identical geometric carpet in a similar manner to the ones she'd just stepped over. It was a Lilliputian replica of the house she was currently inside and it was somewhat dizzying imagining a smaller version of herself inside the doll's house, surrounded by pocket-sized versions of the same items: an Indian headdress, a collection of framed moths above the fireplace and a headless ragdoll beneath the television that looked as if it had been flung there in a rage.

The floral fabric sofa was stained with what Cathy hoped was ketchup or red wine, both the actual-sized one and the miniature one. She remained standing and offered her condolences.

'How was California?'

'California?'

'A business trip, I believe.'

She nodded.

Cathy immediately knew that there'd been no business trip, but chose not to pursue the lie further. She'd construct a more accurate timeline when she was back at the station.

'You're aware that certain allegations have been made against your father?'

'It's clearly nonsense,' Faye Williams replied, dismissively.

'Were you close?'

Before replying, she coiled a loose strand of hair around her index finger, glanced at the glass carriage clock on the mantelpiece.

'He didn't know who I was, so no, we weren't close.'

'Your mother committed suicide when you were a teenager, I believe. That must have been difficult.'

'It was.'

Cathy was frustrated. It was like listening to a string of infuriating 'no comments'.

'One of my colleagues, Juliet Crane, sends her condolences. You may remember her from your time in Inverness.'

Faye Williams' eyes narrowed.

'I've never been to Inverness. Is that everything? I'm due at the funeral home in an hour.'

'For now. Thank you for your time. I'll leave my details, should you think of anything else that may be useful.'

Cathy placed a card on the sofa, expecting her smaller self to place a similar card on a smaller sofa. It immediately attached itself to something sticky.

'Do you mind if I use the toilet?'

Cathy didn't particularly want to step any further inside the house. She imagined the rooms getting smaller and smaller until she was inside the doll's house and the smaller version of herself was in the actual house, the two of them having swapped places, but a home visit wasn't fully concluded until she'd taken a look upstairs. And she might not get another opportunity.

Perhaps the toilet was downstairs, although she couldn't see a downstairs toilet in the doll's house.

Faye Williams didn't respond. Cathy repeated the request.

'The toilet isn't flushing properly, but there's a public toilet a few streets away by the bowling green.'

'I don't think I can wait that long,' Cathy said.

Still somewhat hesitant, Faye Williams eventually relented and directed Cathy upstairs while she waited in the hallway. Cathy glanced back at her through the stair spindles.

'The door on the left?' she confirmed.

Faye Williams nodded impatiently.

An audit of the bathroom cabinet uncovered two boxes of

children's aspirin and a packet of Paddington Bear plasters, suggesting the presence of a child, even though Faye Williams wasn't known to have children.

Through the bathroom window she could see a corner of lawn, but nothing more.

She flushed the toilet, forgetting that it wasn't supposed to flush.

It flushed perfectly.

Faye Williams was still waiting at the bottom of the stairs.

'The toilet seems fine now,' Cathy told her, glancing to her left.

There were a series of bolts on the outside of one of the bedroom doors.

'I'm not sure whether I just heard someone in your back garden.'

What was she doing?

Faye Williams stared at her for a few seconds and then disappeared from her sentry post at the bottom of the stairs, presumably to check. There was the sound of a lock turning, the outside world drifting inside, distant traffic, birdsong, children squealing, and as quickly and as quietly as she could, which was difficult when opening bolts that were rusty and stiff, Cathy unbolted the bedroom door.

Before entering the room, she glanced back towards the stairs to check that Faye Williams hadn't returned, and then she slowly pushed open the door.

A child was sitting on a bed, staring at her. Or was it a doll? She couldn't be sure. It certainly wasn't Laura Sykes. Or Dolly or Jolene Edwards.

Suddenly, her mobile phone started ringing in her pocket. It seemed unusually loud.

'Shit,' she cursed, fumbling to silence it.

When she looked up there were three Faye Williamses staring back at her in the dressing table mirror, but before she could react one of them hit her on the back of the head with something heavy and she fell to the floor with a thud.

Chapter Thirty-Five
CONSTELLATIONS

Barclays deputy bank manager Nathan Sparks' first-floor apartment, located above Madeleine's, a French patisserie, was far more stylish than the postcode suggested. Rex was currently parked outside the apartment, watching a tall silhouette drift backwards and forwards behind one of the windows, dappled gold with afternoon sunlight. He wondered if Laura Sykes was restrained inside the apartment. Or Jolene Edwards. When he'd questioned Nathan Sparks' colleagues at the bank no one would look him in the eye, but they'd insisted that everything was fine in a way that implied that everything wasn't fine but it might be several years before anyone dared voice their concerns out loud.

When a traffic warden suddenly materialised in Rex's rear-view mirror he quickly fastened his seatbelt and sped away, his next stop the elusive Martin Williams, who he'd have assumed was imaginary had he not been a regular visitor at his father's care home. He recalled his conversation with Crosby Knowles beneath a constellation of lights shaped like throat lozenges in

The Coffee Parlour, Crosby's 'Del Boy' sheepskin coat and the festive orange Doc Martens. How he'd wished their investigation was like a constellation, one star neatly linking to the next like a Connect the Dots puzzle.

They'd discussed Dolly Edwards and Joanne Collins and Crosby's suspicions regarding a couple who'd lived opposite the Collins family at the time of Joanne's disappearance and whether it could have been Gilbert Williams, but Crosby hadn't recognised him when they'd been introduced at Sunset House by Jolene. Nor had he recognised his deceased wife Ruth from a stamp-sized black and white photograph of her published in a newspaper when she committed suicide.

Rex had shown him the photograph of the young Gilbert Williams on his phone, the one that he'd shown Maureen and Malcolm Collins, which he was now increasingly less certain *was* Gilbert Williams or at least *this* Gilbert Williams, but Crosby had shaken his head. Jolene had already shown him the photograph and it bore no resemblance to the man he'd met in Anglesey.

Crosby had then extended his search to include the couple's newborn daughter. The name of the child had been written in the margin of one of his notebooks, a testimony to his meticulousness in recording every detail, no matter how seemingly minor or innocuous. The child's name was Faye. A coincidence perhaps that Gilbert Williams' daughter was also called Faye.

He'd consulted Welsh birth records for that year, the year that Joanne Collins disappeared, but had found no Faye Williams. He'd then omitted the surname. Williams might have been adopted at a later date and although the couple might have changed their own first names (Patrick and Susan) they might have considered it unnecessary to change the child's. No one was looking for a child. This produced a birth record for a Faye Brennan and then no further reference to a Faye Brennan until nine years later, a school photograph, back row, third from the left. A class trip to the Jurassic Coast where a newsworthy fossil had been discovered. Children don't stay hidden for ever, Crosby had said. They want to be with other children.

When he next saw her she was fourteen and a member of a netball team that had won a national competition and was now Faye Williams, her hair darker, charcoal eyeliner smeared around her eyes beneath a blunt fringe, but the same Faye, a leaf-shaped birthmark on her right cheek. And when he'd seen Gilbert Williams' daughter at Sunset House the three images had bled into one, even though she'd looked different again. And there was no birthmark.

Of course none of this confirmed Gilbert Williams' guilt, Crosby had conceded, but an innate desire to procreate, to appear normal, ultimately proves to be a person's downfall in the end because children always lead you back to the beginning, to where it all began. They provide an alternative entry point into your life.

Rex was reminded of Cathy's philosophy.

'Have you interviewed Faye and Martin Williams?' Crosby had asked Rex and he'd had to admit that they hadn't, that they kept slipping through their grasp.

Standing on the doorstep of 12, Bedford Avenue, Rex wondered if it was Martin Williams who'd abducted Laura and Jolene. He was never home, they'd been unable to confirm a place of work, and when Rex had asked the care home to let him know when Martin was visiting his father, they'd said they were bound by data protection laws, but they'd pass on the message, and he still hadn't contacted them. Not that it was illegal to be unreachable and he wasn't obligated to speak to them, but it was possible that he was complicit in some way, maybe even responsible.

Rex recalled the last time he'd been here, the sun a blistering fireball in the sky, Cathy searching beneath the terracotta plant pots for the front door key. He knocked. Again there was no answer. Nothing had changed. And yet everything had changed. He walked along the side of the house towards the back door, knocked once and then tried the door handle. The door was unlocked.

'Mr Williams, it's DI Spencer,' Rex called through the open door, reluctant to step inside.

Protocol dictated that he couldn't enter a domestic dwelling, shouldn't even have opened the door, without first obtaining permission from the homeowner or from the Superintendent or on hearing suspicious activity and even then he certainly couldn't go in alone. He heard Cathy's voice in his ear, *crime scenes disinfected, bodies incinerated*, and desperately tried to quieten it, but it embedded itself in the corner of his brain reserved for more heroic imaginings that were sadly never realised.

As he was about to close the door and call the station for an update on Martin Williams' whereabouts, he noticed an unlocked padlock on what he presumed to be a cellar door, a dropped torch by an umbrella stand and a straightened paperclip beside a pair of muddy Wellington boots. Three more things that seemed somehow connected.

'Hello,' Rex called again. 'Mr Williams?'

Not hearing anyone and choosing, perhaps unwisely, to momentarily dispense with official etiquette, he hesitantly stepped inside. He heard the Cathy inside his head applaud.

When the success of a case was wholly dependent upon following the correct procedure, it made it practically impossible to do anything without first consulting a rulebook; it was paralysing. So this would either be the most irresponsible thing he'd ever done, or the most incisive. He thought about all the lives that might have been saved had the police relied on intuition and fearlessness, had they gone in 'all guns blazing'. Wasn't finding a victim still alive by whatever means necessary not more important than seeking posthumous justice for a deceased victim?

He paused outside the cellar door. He really should request that another officer attend the scene (he found disregarding official protocol extremely difficult, no matter how much logic he applied). There's no law against padlocking a cellar, Rex told himself. He should leave before touching anything else. Perhaps Martin Williams had mislaid the key and had resorted to using a paperclip. It didn't explain why the back door was open, but perhaps he was visiting a neighbour and didn't expect to be long, didn't expect a police officer to be crossing the threshold of his property illegally at that very moment. He hesitated. Surely it wouldn't hurt to take a look, just to be absolutely certain that nothing untoward had occurred.

He'd deal with the repercussions later. The Cathy inside his head high-fived him. An ashen-faced Denise looked on proudly.

Removing the padlock, he opened the cellar door and pulled the light cord. A single light bulb illuminated a set of steep steps. Without checking the rest of the house before proceeding, he placed the padlock in his pocket and propped the cellar door open with the umbrella stand. All rational thought appeared to have vanished. There was another door at the bottom of the steps, another open padlock and another light cord. Rex opened the second door that led into an extremely small cellar. It was empty. He wasn't sure whether he was relieved or disappointed. There was a faint smell of disinfectant as if it had been recently cleaned.

He switched off the light, climbed the cellar steps (fortunately no one had imprisoned him inside) and called the station. No amount of disinfectant erased everything. Maybe he could persuade the Superintendent to request a warrant, although an unusually clean cellar and a possible child placing Gilbert Williams in Wales at the time of Joanne Collins' disappearance hardly amounted to probable cause. They were merely hovering above ground, unable to land.

Craig transferred him to Perry Saunders for an update on what more they'd learned, which consisted of two gift-wrapped dead rats addressed to Jolene Edwards that had apparently been found in an outdoor storage shed, and a text from an unknown number she'd received the day before she disappeared, asking if she'd liked the gift. 'And Matt's trying to contact Cathy, but it keeps going straight to voicemail,'

Perry told him. 'That's odd,' Rex replied. 'She said that she was going home.'

According to Juliet, Cathy had been doing a background check on Faye Williams, Gilbert Williams' daughter, before she left, Perry continued, and when Juliet mentioned going to school with a Faye Williams and a five-year-old child going missing around the same time, Cathy requested the case file.

'Hold on a second, sir, Karen wants a word.'

Why was Cathy interested in Faye Williams and not her brother Martin? And what was the significance of the missing child?

'We've just had a call from Crosby Knowles, a private investigator, sir,' Karen said. 'He's currently parked outside Faye Williams' home and claims Faye Williams received a visitor over an hour ago who is yet to reappear. The car registration is Cathy's.'

'I'll head over there now.'

Was it a coincidence that both Cathy and Crosby Knowles' research had led them to Faye Williams? Had they been focusing on the wrong child, blinded by gender and stereotypes?

Chapter Thirty-Six

RUNNING OUT OF ALPHABET

At least she's finally stopped crying, but she isn't sure whether it's because there are no more tears left to cry or because there's little point. It doesn't change anything. She's still here, alone, in the dark. And it doesn't make her feel any less afraid. She tells herself not to eat the sandwiches or drink the juice that keep appearing, she'd rather starve to death or die of thirst than be sedated, or worse, poisoned, but she's so ravenous she can't help herself. Like Will, all she seems able to think about is food, listing vegetables and fruit alphabetically, listing everything alphabetically in fact – European cities, farmyard animals, Beyoncé songs.

When she hears the rattle of the stiff bolt, the scrape of the heavy door, the single cough, as if they're announcing themselves, she responds with an involuntary sharp intake of breath, a Pavlovian conditioned response. And hearing only the rattle and scrape of captivity has made her miss sounds that she wouldn't normally miss: a dentist's drill, roadworks, rush-hour traffic. She mostly thinks it's a man; she once saw their feet through the hatch that they slide the tray through, black boots. But it could just as easily be a woman. Women can be psychopaths too. When she'd seen the boots she'd wondered if they were building more walls around her and wished she hadn't seen them at all because a single thought in here can twist and turn and burrow so deep that she wants to reach inside her brain and tear it out before it becomes part of her, before it defines her. The person (in her head she's christened them 'Boots' because when you give something a name you lessen its power, its hold over you) now stands to the side, so she sees only floorboards, which she prefers. Her imagination fills in the rest.

She has no idea why she's even here. Boots fails to elaborate. Maybe it's because it's easy, because they can. Or maybe they haven't yet decided *what* they're going to do with her or to her. Maybe they haven't done this before. That seems more terrifying somehow, that she's been abducted by unpredictable amateurs, her future currently undecided, but when it is decided it will be far worse than this. But what could be worse than this? Death, she supposes, although quite frankly, death would be something of a blessing.

Of course it could all be because of Dolly.

And most likely is.

Was Dolly kept captive here? Is she still alive? Is she in the next room?

She's tried to engage Boots in conversation, tried to forge a relationship with her captor, create a bond that's difficult to sever – isn't that what psychologists recommend on true crime documentaries? – but when she asked them about Dolly the hatch whirred shut and she was left without water. No doubt her morose and uncommunicative captor is familiar with such tactics, although it's difficult to strike up a meaningful conversation with someone when you can't see their face. You think you can get used to anything if you have to, but she hopes she never has to get used to this. Sometimes the silence is deafening.

She obediently passes the bucket through the hatch in exchange for the tray and avoids any glimpse of Boots' feet as the hatch door closes, wondering if she should have named them something else, something light-hearted and frivolous. She'll go through the alphabet later. Think of a new name. It'll be something to do.

Her mother must have surely reported her missing by now, she thinks.

Unless she doesn't know she's missing because she's having a manic episode and hasn't been home yet. Or she's been injured in an accident, a warning voice cautions. Or she's dead.

If nobody reports you missing, are you actually missing?

The light bulb burns her eyes, as it always does when her sandwich arrives. The bread is curling up at the edges, the crusts stale. She watches a fly crawl along one of the crusts – an enormous fly with paper-blue wings that looks like it's eaten enough. How did it get in here? she thinks. Is the room not as airtight as it feels? She slowly re-examines the room with her hands, checking if she can squeeze the tip of a finger into a fly-sized space and if she can make that space bigger, but there's no space. Like before, there's no way in and no way out.

There's only her name scratched into the corner of one of

the walls with a rusty nail she found on the floor, the only evidence she was ever here.

Jolene.

The next time she opens her eyes something feels different. Has she been moved? She can hear breathing. Is there someone else in the room with her?

'Don't be scared,' a voice says.

A child's voice, she thinks.

If being locked in a room alone is terrifying, then having someone else locked inside the room with her feels even more terrifying. And because it's so dark Jolene has no idea what they look like. She imagines something wild and malnourished, blood dripping from a forked tongue, teeth as sharp as razors; something dangerous made to sound innocent.

'I'm not scared,' Jolene lies. 'I'm just a little surprised, that's all. I didn't expect anyone else to be here. What's your name?'

She waits for the darkness to respond, to explain itself, hopes it isn't about to sink its razor-sharp teeth into a carotid artery.

'I'm not supposed to tell you my name.'

'What if we choose another name then?'

Jolene recites possible options while the child repeatedly squeals 'No!', some of Jolene's suggestions making her giggle, Junebug, Pork Chop, until they eventually settle on Violet because it's also a colour and because they're running out of alphabet.

Just as she's about to question Violet further, the hatch opens and Violet slithers away from her. Jolene wishes she could follow her, but the hatch is too small.

'I've got to go now but I'll be back again soon. I promise.'

Not captive like her then, but free to come and go as she pleases. Perhaps if she's able to form a bond with the child, Jolene thinks, she'll help her escape. Children are more impressionable than adults, can be manipulated.

It's a while (hours? days?) before Violet reappears, by which time Jolene wonders if she imagined her. Please don't be imaginary, she silently mouths. You can't help me if you don't exist. But then she arrives with her sandwich in full Technicolor beneath the illuminated light bulb.

'I'm glad you came back,' Jolene tells her. 'I've missed you.'

Violet isn't at all what she expected. Her skin is pale and there are yellow ribbons threaded through her white hair. She's wearing a long black dress, no shoes, and is clutching a ragdoll without a head. Jolene hopes that the headless ragdoll isn't supposed to be her. She remembers the ribbon around the cake box.

'What's the weather like today?' Jolene asks her.

'It's twenty-three degrees with a slight westerly breeze and zero percent chance of rain.'

'That's a very comprehensive forecast. Have you been playing in the garden?'

Violet shakes her head, but doesn't deny that there's a garden.

'I'm not allowed outside.'

'Why?'

She doesn't answer.

'Do you live alone?'

Violet giggles.

'I'm too small to live alone, silly.'

'How old are you?' Jolene asks.

'I'm not supposed to say,' she replies shyly, staring at her bare feet.

'Would you like a sandwich?'

'No, thank you.'

Jolene doesn't want to eat it either. She's got stomach cramps.

'Have you ever met someone call Dolly?'

Violet holds out the headless ragdoll.

'This is a dolly.'

'It is,' Jolene agrees. 'Where's her head?'

'I got angry and ripped it off.'

'Why were you angry?'

She shrugs.

'I get angry sometimes.'

The hatch opens and Violet crawls through it. Jolene doesn't want her to leave. She's thinking about the rusty nail in her pocket and what would happen if she threatened to hurt Violet with it, did hurt Violet with it. They'd have to release her then, surely.

Could she do that, threaten a child, hurt them? She's done much worse.

'Bye, Jolene,' Violet calls as the hatch closes.

And the moment is gone.

Chapter Thirty-Seven
BLOODLINES

When Rex arrived at Faye Williams' address, Crosby was leaning against an oak tree smoking a cigarette. 'Herbal,' he told Rex, extinguishing it beneath his right foot. 'I haven't smoked a proper cigarette in years, but I do miss the feel of one in my hand. It helps me think.'

For Rex, it was the nicotine in his bloodstream that he most liked the feel of.

What do we have? Rex almost asked, before realising that it was what every police officer in a television crime drama asked, and, not wanting to be a police cliché, and Crosby not actually being a police officer, he instead enquired whether Crosby had learned anything new (which amounted to the same thing), wondering why Crosby knew this information and they didn't. Or perhaps they did. And that was why Cathy was here, both of them woven from the same suspicious piece of cloth.

'She lives alone, according to the neighbours.'

'What about the brother? Are they close?'

'It appears not. They were seen arguing a few months ago. He has a nine-year-old daughter with an ex-partner. Shared custody.'

Rex rang the doorbell, heard receding footsteps in the hallway.

When no one answered and, having acquired something of a taste for maverick policing, he pushed open the letterbox and demanded that the occupant 'Open the door!'

There was a loud thud, but still the door remained closed, the hallway empty.

'Police! Open the door now!' Rex repeated.

He contemplated gaining entry by force and dealing with the consequences later, something that wasn't as easy as it looked on TV and something that the man standing next to him shouldn't be privy to. But before he could take a steadying breath and a preparatory step back Crosby had produced a lock-picking kit from his coat pocket and gained entry in less than three minutes without causing any criminal damage whatsoever. Rex felt increasingly disappointed in his own crisis management skills, which seemed to consist mostly of shouting loudly through letterboxes.

Once inside, Crosby searched the ground floor while Rex took the stairs three at a time. Irresponsible and reckless in hindsight. The occupant(s) could have been armed, endangering both their lives.

Fortunately for Rex, there were no armed occupants, but he did find Cathy slumped against an open bedroom door massaging her scalp.

'What happened to the hot bath and the glass of wine?' Rex asked her.

'I decided to go for a knock on the head and concussion instead.'

Her brow furrowed.

'Am I big or am I small?'

Was she more seriously injured than it initially appeared?

'...because there are two of us and I don't know if I'm the normal-sized one.'

Two of her? Was she suffering from double vision? Hallucinations?

'Normal-sized,' Rex replied, unsure what it was that he was actually clarifying.

The bath taps were running, but there was no sign of Faye Williams.

'Where's Faye Williams?' Rex asked her, hoping for a sensible response.

Cathy shrugged, glancing towards the bathroom.

'I've no idea, but there are three of them,' she whispered, conspiratorially.

Three?

'Never mind, can you stand?'

She nodded, hesitantly.

'Being drowned in a stranger's bathtub wasn't the type of bath that I had in mind,' she slurred, as Rex held her upright.

'Let's get you seen by a paramedic,' said Rex, dialling ambulance services with his free hand.

'Where's the doll that was on the bed?' she asked suddenly, gesturing towards the bedroom door that she'd been slumped against.

'The doll on the bed?'

There was no doll on the bed. Was she referring to a child?

'She needs to come too.'

'Okay,' Rex said brightly, as if it was a perfectly ordinary request, 'but first I need to help you downstairs.'

Crosby joined them at the bottom of the stairs.

'There's no one else here.'

'Nice trainers,' Cathy observed, addressing the rainbow-coloured plimsolls on Crosby's feet, before suddenly sliding through Rex's fingers and dropping onto the hall carpet as if someone had cut her strings.

'Don't forget the doll,' she reminded Rex, resting her head against the wall and closing her eyes.

He should keep talking to her, encourage her to stay awake. He recalled his first-aid training. Was it worse when a head wound didn't bleed? He couldn't remember. In an effort to keep her engaged he googled the plot of *The Lion King* and began to recite the Wikipedia entry verbatim, hoping she'd interject if there were inaccuracies, but her eyelids barely flickered and she was still unusually fixated on the size of things. *Look how small my hands are!*

While waiting for the ambulance to arrive, Rex called the Superintendent to request that a search for Faye Williams, 'who may or may not be on foot', be coordinated. As it was currently unknown whether she had access to a vehicle, a detailed description of her would need to be circulated to local coach and train stations and taxi and car rental companies as soon as possible. He also requested that crime scene investigators be directed to Faye Williams' home to conduct a thorough search of the property.

'There's a false wall in one of the bedrooms,' Crosby called from the top of the stairs as Rex was returning his mobile phone to his jacket pocket.

The ambulance had arrived and a paramedic was shining a torch in Cathy's eyes. Rex assured Cathy that he wouldn't be long and went back upstairs.

'I don't like being small,' he heard her tell the paramedic.

'Help me move this chest of drawers away from the wall,' Crosby asked Rex when he walked into the bedroom. 'There might be a concealed entrance.'

Flattening their palms against the wall they ran their hands across the plasterboard, failing to notice the small hatch scored into the lower right-hand corner of the wall that blended perfectly with the paintwork. It was only when Crosby pressed one of the wall switches that the hatch revealed itself, slowly whirring open. Rex tentatively peered inside, expecting something feral and unwashed to charge towards him, but nothing stirred.

'Try the other switches. See if one of them is a light, while I search for a torch and a hammer.'

None of the other switches had illuminated the room when Rex returned with a torch and hammer, having first contacted Cathy's husband Matt to tell him that Cathy was being taken to hospital, purely as a precautionary measure.

'Any sign of a doll?' Rex asked.

'Take your pick. I've never seen so many children's toys.'

'What about photographs?'

'None that I've found, but there's a mountain of clutter to sift through. It's like unearthing a long-buried time capsule stepping into these rooms. Someone's either clinging onto the past or attempting to conceal what's really going on.'

Rex recalled Perry linking a missing child to a younger Faye Williams and, although it wouldn't be the same child, Rex decided to revise his initial instruction, open to the possibility that Faye Williams might not be travelling alone, that unlike her father she preyed upon younger, more compliant, victims, not killing them straightaway but toying with them (no pun intended), like a cat balletically tossing a terrified vole into the air as if it was a hot pan, which might actually prove advantageous if true, because a child made a person more noticeable. *And* slowed them down.

Tightly gripping the hammer he'd found in a toolbox in the utility room and wondering why there weren't more DIY tools at the property if Faye Williams had built the room, Rex concentrated on enlarging the area around the hatch, searching for a weakness, but the wall was surprisingly robust, possibly soundproofed with a layer of steel. The hammer barely made a dent. Nor did it rouse an occupant, which was both encouraging and demoralising. Either there was no one inside the room or they were too late.

'We need a power drill or a chainsaw,' Crosby said. 'I know a mechanic who lives nearby. I'll give him a call.'

Crosby left Rex circling the torch beam and talking to the open hatch. There was a faint grey outline in the furthest corner of the room that may have been a fleece blanket or, worst-case scenario, a person. Was it Jolene Edwards or Laura Sykes, or another missing person, someone who they didn't even know was missing? Sometimes you don't solve the cases that you'd hoped to solve, Rex thought. Sometimes you solve the cases you didn't know existed. And there was more than a kernel of truth in the belief that if you didn't find a missing person in the first few days then you might never find them at all.

He redialled emergency services, in case it was a person, wondering if finding only a blanket would actually be the worst-case scenario because that would mean that whoever *had* been there had been moved and they wouldn't know where.

Should they have taken a closer look at Gilbert Williams' children, examined the present more comprehensively, instead of focusing on the past?

While Rex was ruminating on what they might have done differently, Crosby reappeared with his friend Ray, a faceless man in a welding helmet dressed like a 'Ghostbuster', a chainsaw brandished like a weapon in his right hand. Rex stepped away from the wall.

Once the hatch was large enough to fit through, Rex crawled inside. The figure on the floor was Jolene Edwards, her pulse faint, but she was alive. Crosby followed the ambulance to the hospital, promising to call Jolene's mother on the way, while Rex waited for the crime scene investigators to arrive.

He surveyed the concealed room, the plastic bucket filled with faeces and urine, the name Jolene scratched onto one of the walls like an epitaph, sharp angles, crisp lines. He wondered why Jolene had been abducted if Faye Williams preferred younger victims, why she'd been kept captive and not killed. Perhaps it was the imprisonment of her victims that motivated her most, the control, the fear, the uncertainty. It was easy to kill something, far harder to keep it alive. Had Jolene discovered something that had placed her in danger, he wondered? Or was it a random kidnapping? Perhaps Gilbert

Williams had masterminded the abduction before he died in order to distract them, his daughter his accomplice, his apprentice. Or had Faye Williams been trying to falsely implicate her father in the disappearances? It made no sense, unless it was connected to Jolene's sister's disappearance in some way, the past and the present intertwined, like a tightly woven braid.

Suspicion had been cast on all three members of the same family, but which family member was responsible for which murder or disappearance?

And where was Laura Sykes?

His phone beeped. It was the Superintendent.

'We've finally located Martin Williams outside his daughter's school. He claims not to know where his sister is, says that they're not particularly close and he has no knowledge of a concealed room in her home.'

'Is there a child?'

'He doesn't know anything about a child.'

'Then we'll have to hope that Glenda and the team find something useful. I suspect the child, if there is one, isn't hers.'

Rex retrieved a pair of latex gloves from the car and returned to the house, a house like those featured on television programmes about compulsive hoarding where you couldn't see the carpet and were imprisoned by your own belongings. Children's items mostly; toys, clothes, books. It was like stepping into someone's childhood, some of the items new, the majority used: a tennis racket with a broken string, a glittery pink comb with four teeth missing, a white roller skate with a sprinkling of gold stars on the heel, a blade of grass wrapped around one of the wheels, coloured pencils with whiskers and ears, a plastic tiara, a magic wand…

Rex glanced around the master bedroom. Anything important would be here. He began with the wardrobes, the suitcases on top of the wardrobes, and then moved onto the three sets of drawers, the two bookcases and the storage boxes beneath the bed. The number of children's items in the house without any corresponding child to explain them was like a maths equation that he couldn't solve. Had he been a psychologist he would have deduced that the owner of the house had been deprived of a normal childhood.

He walked around the room checking behind picture frames (pressed flowers, abstracts), negotiating vibrantly illustrated picture books and boldly patterned fabrics spilling from carrier bags, tested the floorboards beneath him with his weight, until finally one creaked enough to make him wonder. He found a screwdriver in a kitchen drawer and eased the floorboard free. Inside, wrapped in cellophane, a silver jacket and a pair of blue gloves decorated with snowflakes.

His phone rang as he was replacing the floorboard. Could he secure the property before leaving? Glenda would be delayed. Human bones had been found on waste ground behind the multistorey car park, where a supermarket was being built. Rex studied the cellophane package in his hand, one snowflake fewer on the right glove.

Later, he'd learn that the rest of Dolly had been discovered too.

The Last Girl

Dolly

Then

The rage was rising, swelling into something uncontrollable, like the crashing of an ocean wave against the shore, and I couldn't stop it. I couldn't hold it back. Those who have never experienced genuine rage describe it as a red mist, but it isn't like that at all. It's much darker than that. It's as if the old you has evaporated and a new you has awoken.

    The first time it happened was the day after my eighth birthday. I'd been expecting a bicycle. I'd been talking about it for months, dropping unsubtle hints, pointing out the exact one that I wanted in Wesley's Wheels' shop window, the one with the ivory handlebars and the caramel leather seat. 'Isn'titbeautiful?' I'd slur, all one word, and my mother would say distractedly, 'Yes, sweetie,' barely even looking, but I still thought that I'd made my intentions clear.

When I saw a child's scooter in the kitchen, rockets and stars wrapped around it like a spacesuit, I realised that my wishes had been unheard or ignored. I didn't even unwrap it. There was no need. I knew exactly what it was.

'Don't you like it?' my mother asked.

Somehow I managed to nod and smile and tell her that I didn't want to ruin it by removing the wrapping paper and how much I liked the rockets and the stars, the latter part at least true.

The next day when my birthday smile had thawed into pursed spite I walked to the park and punctured the tyres of a child's canary-yellow bicycle that was lying on the grass with a knife from the kitchen drawer that I'd tucked inside the waistband of my trousers.

When the child whose bicycle it was eventually ran back to collect it, I went over to them and described in fictitious detail the person who'd done this. I said that I knew where they lived. I could show them. Mucus was running down the child's chin and their blue eyes were red-rimmed, and when I held out my hand, they took it and together we wheeled the bicycle into the shade of the trees.

I've often wondered since why I had to take both the child and the bicycle. If I'd only taken the bicycle then perhaps things would have been different, but there's no logic to rage. It doesn't behave as you'd expect, do as you ask. It's unpredictable. I expect I just wanted someone else to suffer too.

And that's how it started – the taking of things that weren't mine to take.

The safekeeping of those things, until they became too much of a burden, but even then they were still mine, would always be mine, because I was the only person who knew where they were.

I took the bicycle home, telling my mother that I'd found it abandoned.

'Look, it's got two flat tyres,' I told her, as if nobody could possibly want it now.

She stared at me for a while and then she said,

'I'll get your father to replace them tomorrow.'

I never rode it. I kept it in my bedroom where I could see it. It made my rage so pale and distant that I mistakenly believed it had disappeared for ever. Unfortunately, it was simply transforming itself into something much darker, something I couldn't possibly conquer. A darkness I'd seen in my father. And I didn't want to be like my father. I wanted my secrets to belong only to me, secrets I'd carried from one home to the next, small transportable secrets with wondrous expressions and tiny hands that had all the things I wanted, my untamed rage allowed to flourish because children are not taught to fear other children.

Children taken, sometimes cast aside and sometimes not, chosen because of something they had or something they'd said. For being loved and wanted and spoiled. Or not. For no other reason than a desperate need, an insatiable hunger, which soon became brazen and unfettered and ingrained.

Later, a small child wandering along the street unaccompanied. The child's hand taken, warm and sticky like chewed toffee. And then quickening footsteps. 'Jolene! Come back!' I wanted to keep walking, to scoop the child up and start running, but the child shook their hand free and ran towards their name. 'Dolly!' the child screamed.

I should have sprinted away – the person hadn't yet seen my face – but instead I turned round and smiled sweetly.

'I was taking her to the police station,' I lied.

The teenage girl standing in front of me didn't thank me. She didn't say anything at all, but she wasn't fooled. She knew exactly what I was doing, what I'd planned to do.

'Come on, Jolene, let's go,' she said brusquely, clasping the child's hand and walking away.

Just before they disappeared from view the older girl glanced over her shoulder, her narrowed eyes fixed on mine one last time, and I learnt two things that day. One, the rage inside me had been seen and two, I wouldn't be able to rest until the person who'd seen it was dead. I'd wanted that child so desperately, those soft brown curls and corduroy dungarees, and now I couldn't still the rage, couldn't silence the waves.

It wasn't difficult finding Dolly again, following her adolescent scent to youth clubs and amusement arcades and the ice rink, so that I could inflict my revenge. The squelch of winter boots on wet soil, carol singers, 'We Three Kings', 'Silent Night', Christmas fireworks lighting up the sky.

I never expected to see Jolene again. I suppose I have my father to thank for our lives colliding for a second time. I overheard her one afternoon talking to one of the residents (a private investigator according to Alison, one of the care assistants) about her sister Dolly. I hadn't been in contact with my father in years. In fact I'd hoped he was long dead, a fatal stab wound, a hail of bullets, a decapitation, something painful and violent, but when my brother got in touch regarding his residential care, as tempting as it was to leave the form-filling and superficial concern to my brother, who was far more forgiving than I was, I decided it was only fitting that I be there when my father died.

Nevertheless, it was still a shock to see him like that, his thoughts rolling away from him like coins, his face sallow and drawn, a reminder that we were all just skin and bone in the end perhaps, that even monsters get old, although I often caught glimpses of something more sinister beneath that papery exterior, something unsettling that was quickly blinked away. The fact that he seemingly had no idea who I was only added to my manipulation of him. My mother had died too quickly, too suddenly, but I could be there for every one of my father's failing organs and dying brain cells. I just hadn't anticipated the reappearance of Dolly. Or Joanne Collins.

I was born a few weeks after Joanne Collins' disappearance, materialising just as she vanished, and I've often wondered if my father was responsible for her disappearance, particularly as we left Wales soon after. I've also come to realise over the years that he may have killed other girls, girls who reminded him of me.

Killing me over and over again.

Not wanting Dolly's disappearance to be re-investigated I decided Jolene would have to disappear too.

I'd intended to place one of Dolly's gloves in my father's room before he unexpectedly died, but perhaps they'd blame my father anyway. Naming girls and making murderous claims, he was already giving them all the ammunition they needed.

And then I remembered Jolene's sticky hand in mine all those years ago, shaken free, and I realised this time there'd be no one to call her name, to lure her away.

Now

'Where will we go now?' Freya asks, as I strap her into the passenger seat of the car, both of us deeply suspicious of what the other might do next.

She's recently developed a 'tell' when she's wary, chewing the inside of her right cheek.

When I first saw her she was sitting on a swing in an empty

playground, there for the taking, the headless ragdoll on her lap, as if she'd been waiting for me, rather than vice versa. Never once mourning the loss of her family, never mentioning them at all in fact, the implication being there was no family and it was sorcery or witchcraft that had magicked her there that day.

Such stillness and composure, even now, that I sometimes wonder if she's older than she claims. You read of such things, an adult pretending to be a child. The structured way she plays, the pensive way she stares, her desperation in wanting to crawl through the hatch and be part of the 'game'. What would happen if I locked her in there too? I've asked myself. What chaos would I unleash? I've never been afraid of a child before, never had to keep them behind locked doors, like a caged animal, but it seems I've finally met my match.

'I know just the place.'

Epilogue

WEIGHTLESS

He's been dreaming about harbours and moonlight and burning girls. He can still taste the salt on his tongue, feel the heat of the flames. Most nights he's too restless to sleep. There seems to be a perpetual knot of anxiety inside his chest that requires his immediate attention, as if he's an overflowing in-tray on an office desk, and being surrounded by people who are always sleeping at odd times of the day doesn't help. But tonight he feels weightless, as if he's floating above canyons and oceans, deserts and plains.

He'd like a hot drink, but the room service is erratic and dependent upon other people's schedules. Where's the button that he needs to press? Where are his glasses? He should have asked the girl who was here earlier switching off his radio and his lamp without asking, the one who's always smiling and who shouts in his ear as if he's an imbecile. Sometimes he pretends he can't hear her so that she'll shout a little louder and lean in a little closer and he can smell peanut butter and toothpaste on her breath.

He prefers the other girl, the girl whose jagged contours scorch his eyelids, the girl who never smiles and tells him to zip up his trousers. Her eyes are cashmere grey, translucent, as if there's no colour in them at all, until you get closer and realise they're full of colour, full of all sorts of things, blood-red rivers and honeysuckle, shallow graves and meadow thistle.

Has he pressed the button yet? He can't remember. But even if he has they don't rush to his aid like they do the man he sometimes plays cards with, the man who always has soup stains on his cardigan sleeves and smells like milk. Everyone flocks around him as if he's Sean Connery. He can't remember his name. But neither can he remember his own name and the name stitched into his clothes never feels like it belongs to him. He can't remember who he was before or who he is now. Not that it matters, he supposes, he could be anyone. Names aren't important in here, although some names he remembers. Some names are always on his lips. But he doesn't know why.

He talks to Sean Connery about the past sometimes, releasing it piece by piece like the holes on a leather belt that's too tight. He's not sure of the exact sequence of events and some of the details are a little hazy, like looking through frosted glass, but some things need to be spoken and some things need to be heard. And it doesn't matter who's speaking, or who's listening. He needs to tell someone how fragile the earth feels beneath his feet, how the crucifix his mother used to wear glinted like a sunlit lake in the midday sun and how the gallery of faces on the corridor walls keeps changing.

Occasionally, he senses he should feel ashamed, guilty even, his heart carved from clay, his mind dark and depraved, although he isn't sure why, but it'll be over soon, so none of it really matters – at least not to him. Maybe that's when there's some kind of reckoning, when his heart finally stops beating, when he's pulled apart limb by limb, when he finally remembers what he's forgotten and who he was and who he is.

With difficulty, his swollen fingers curl around the keyring, *the letter J for Joanne in gold and a silver front door key.*

'She wasn't smiling when I killed her,' he whispers. 'She wasn't smiling then.'

Five Weeks Later

Sophie's sitting beside Will's hospital bed, wishing that he'd open his eyes, so that she can tell him how she rescued Laura Sykes. Well, not rescued exactly, but she did call the police to let them know where she was. He can hear you, Loretta, the nurse with the sad smile, insists. And although talking to someone who can't respond feels like confiding in a husk of sweetcorn or a priest during confession, Sophie tells Will what happened.

'When I saw Harrison in the shopping centre, my intention had been to "accidentally" run into him. That wasn't stepping too far into stalking territory, surely? I only wanted to say hello, perhaps orchestrate a third date, disappointed that I was *that* person, a person who prioritises a potential love interest over a friend, as I elbowed my way past that ridiculous hen party, ultimately losing him in the end. Karma, I suppose.

'When I next spoke to him online, there was no mention of

a third date and then he ghosted me, and I wondered if it was because I'd spilled the drink that he'd handed to me on our first date (intentionally, I never accept drinks from strangers) or insisted that I buy the drinks on the second date, with the ten-pound note that I'd stolen from his wallet *(she whispers the last part, in case Loretta's outside the room listening)*. I scrolled through his Twitter (I refuse to call it "X"), Facebook and Instagram accounts for places that he frequented, visited the fitness centre that had been printed on the card in the name of Lewis Sharp that I'd also stolen from his wallet, resigned to the fact that I was unlikely to ever see him again.

'The alias was the first indication that he might not have been who he said he was.

'It was purely by chance that I did see him again a few weeks later, in a car park on his phone, his aggressive tone surprising, which was when I decided to follow him, stalking him, like you, pulling on my hood and reaching for the plastic sunglasses in my pocket that I'd stolen from the hands of a sticky-fingered child in a pushchair only that morning *(this also whispered)*. Are there no limits to the depths that I'm prepared to sink to? His feet furiously slapped the pavement as he walked; evidently he was still angry. I wondered what had happened to the attentive, quietly spoken man I'd met in The Skylark, so unlike the men I usually date, who still live with their parents and are obsessed with computer games and "recreational" *(she mimes air quotes even though Will can't see them)* cocaine, although he clearly isn't Harrison Heath and probably not Lewis Sharp either. Married, I expect. Aren't they all? Although, in this case, not only fraudulent but dangerous too, as I soon discovered.

'I followed him to an isolated boarded-up property at the end of a row of derelict terraced houses that gave way to a gravel track and an assortment of abandoned household appliances that had been left to grow green with mould and fill with rainwater. And, concealing myself behind a refrigerator, I watched him prise a board from one of the lower floor windows and climb inside. When he reappeared, thirty minutes later, he carefully repositioned the wooden board, nailing it back in place with a hammer that he retrieved from the canvas holdall that he was carrying, and left. *Who walks around with a hammer?* I remember thinking.

'When he was safely out of sight, I walked over to the property and loosened the board with a house brick and the rest, as they say, is history. Laura Sykes was inside the property, chained to a radiator. No one knows why. A kidnap for ransom? Was she about to be trafficked? Was she being hidden until the news coverage died down? She was unable to describe her abductor, had been too heavily sedated and the ordeal had seemingly affected her ability to speak, although speech therapists later maintained that it was most likely selective and it was possible that she was being deliberately evasive.

'The police had to rely on my description, but Harrison/Lewis had had no unusual features so the police identikit was of a brown-eyed, brown-haired, ordinary-looking man with no discernible accent who could have been anyone. Or no one. And the only fingerprints discovered at the property belonged to the previous owners, a couple who'd been found deceased in one of the bedrooms years earlier.

'It was later reported that the deceased couple's daughter

had also disappeared in mysterious circumstances, her disappearance believed to be connected to the Halo Movement, who allegedly employ a variety of controversial experimental practices to recruit new members, one of the more disturbing claims being the massacre of a member's entire family to secure the continued dependence of the member, although the Movement strenuously deny this claim, of course, or indeed any involvement in Laura Sykes' disappearance.'

She recites the official statement that she's saved on her phone.

'We do not, and have never, used criminal or coercive practices when opening our doors and our hearts to new members. Members join us willingly in pursuit of a life without pain or suffering.

'Our thoughts are with Laura and her family at this time.'

'But they would say that, wouldn't they?'

Sophie falls silent when Loretta and her sad smile re-enter the room. She wonders if Loretta was listening, but Loretta busies herself with her duties, writes something on a clipboard and then leaves. Sophie then tells Will the best part, how she's being hailed a hero and has received a five-figure offer for her story. She squeezes the velvet pouch in her hoodie pocket as if it's a stress ball. Yesterday, when she'd offered to collect some toiletries and clean pyjamas for Will, she'd found herself on her hands and knees looking through the shoebox beneath Will's bed, tipping out the contents of the pouch and letting the cool metal of the bracelet pool in her palm.

Take me! Take me! the bracelet had screamed. So she had.

She tells herself that she'll give it back to Will when he wakes up. It might belong to his mother.

She's just keeping it safe.

But maybe she won't.

Even as a child, her mother would have to forcibly unpeel her fingers one by one in order to see what she was hiding in her hand.

Acknowledgments

Thank you so much for reading this novel.

Sunset House is loosely based on my late mum's care home – a place where I'd often find myself wondering about the lives of the other residents and the secrets that had been forgotten. Being a crime writer, those secrets inevitably turned into something much darker, but those visits always reminded me that the most interesting stories are often the ones that we never get to hear.

Special thanks to Jennie and the team at One More Chapter for their support and enthusiasm. I'm eternally grateful.

And love always to Mike, who read an early draft of the novel and genuinely seemed to enjoy it.

The author and One More Chapter would like to thank everyone who contributed to the publication of this story…

Analytics
Abigail Fryer

Audio
Fionnuala Barrett
Ciara Briggs

Contracts
Laura Amos
Inigo Vyvyan

Design
Lucy Bennett
Fiona Greenway
Liane Payne
Dean Russell

Digital Sales
Laura Daley
Lydia Grainge
Hannah Lismore

eCommerce
Laura Carpenter
Madeline ODonovan
Charlotte Stevens
Christina Storey
Jo Surman
Rachel Ward

Editorial
Kara Daniel
Linda Joyce
Charlotte Ledger
Jennie Rothwell
Tony Russell
Sofia Salazar Studer
Helen Williams

Harper360
Emily Gerbner
Ariana Juarez
Jean Marie Kelly
emma sullivan
Sophia Wilhelm

International Sales
Peter Borcsok
Ruth Burrow
Colleen Simpson
Ben Wright

Inventory
Sarah Callaghan
Kirsty Norman

Marketing & Publicity
Chloe Cummings
Grace Edwards

Operations
Melissa Okusanya
Hannah Stamp

Production
Denis Manson
Simon Moore
Francesca Tuzzeo

Rights
Ashton Mucha
Alisah Saghir
Zoe Shine
Aisling Smyth
Lucy Vanderbilt

Trade Marketing
Ben Hurd
Eleanor Slater

The HarperCollins Distribution Team

The HarperCollins Finance & Royalties Team

The HarperCollins Legal Team

The HarperCollins Technology Team

UK Sales
Isabel Coburn
Jay Cochrane
Sabina Lewis
Holly Martin
Harriet Williams
Leah Woods

And every other essential link in the chain from delivery drivers to booksellers to librarians and beyond!

One More Chapter is an award-winning global division of HarperCollins.

Subscribe to our newsletter to get our latest eBook deals and stay up to date with all our new releases!

signup.harpercollins.co.uk/join/signup-omc

Meet the team at
www.onemorechapter.com

Follow us!

@onemorechapterhc

Do you write unputdownable fiction?
We love to hear from new voices.
Find out how to submit your novel at
www.onemorechapter.com/submissions